SECOND KISS

THE
SPELL CROSSED
SERIES

The Paper Sword
Second Kiss

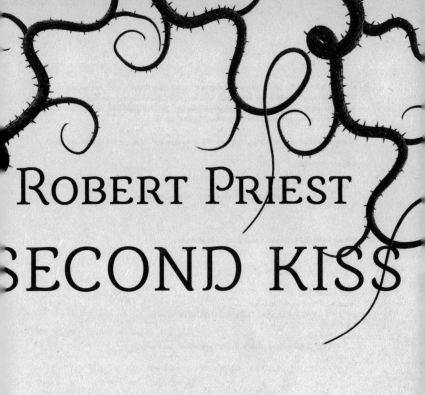

ROBERT PRIEST
SECOND KISS

BOOK TWO
SPELL CROSSED

To Trevor
My favorite WIERD
guy
— in friendship

DUNDURN
TORONTO

Editor: Allison Hirst
Interior and cover design: Courtney Horner
Map by Sherwin Tija
Cover images: bottle © img85h/shutterstock; vines © Deviney/Dreamstime
Printer: Webcom

Library and Archives Canada Cataloguing in Publication

Priest, Robert, 1951-, author
        Second kiss / Robert Priest.

(Spell crossed ; book 2)
Issued in print and electronic format.
ISBN 978-1-4597-3020-5 (pbk.).--ISBN 978-1-4597-3021-2 (pdf).--
ISBN 978-1-4597-3022-9 (epub)

        I. Title. II. Series: Priest, Robert, 1951- Spell crossed ; book 2

PS8581.R47S39 2015   jC813'.54   C2014-905052-6   C2014-905053-4

1   2   3   4   5   19   18   17   16   15

We acknowledge the support of the **Canada Council for the Arts** and the **Ontario Arts Council** for our publishing program. We also acknowledge the financial support of the **Government of Canada** through the **Canada Book Fund** and **Livres Canada Books**, and the **Government of Ontario** through the **Ontario Book Publishing Tax Credit** and the **Ontario Media Development Corporation.**

Care has been taken to trace the ownership of copyright material used in this book. The author and the publisher welcome any information enabling them to rectify any references or credits in subsequent editions.
                                                                    J. Kirk Howard, President

Printed and bound in Canada.

The publisher is not responsible for websites or their content unless they are owned by the publisher.

VISIT US AT
Dundurn.com | @dundurnpress | Facebook.com/dundurnpress | Pinterest.com/dundurnpress

Dundurn
3 Church Street, Suite 500
Toronto, Ontario, Canada
M5E 1M2

I am a parcel of vain strivings tied
By a chance bond together
— THOREAU

The river flowed both ways. The current moved from north to south, but the wind usually came from the south, rippling the bronze-green water in the opposite direction.
— MARGARET LAURENCE

For Marsha Kirzner, Ananda Lebo, Eli
and Daniel Kirzner-Priest,
my parents Betty and Ted Priest, Eitan and
Erez Lebo, and William Broome and Pearl Priest

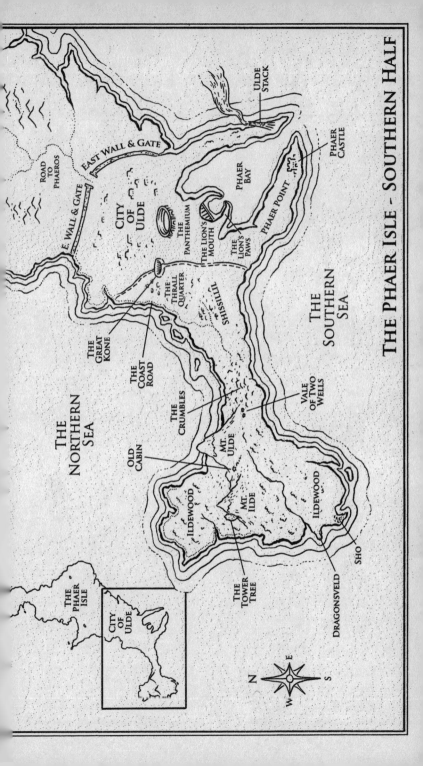

THE PHAER ISLE – SOUTHERN HALF

ULDE STACK

ROAD TO PHAEROS

EAST WALL & GATE

E. WALL & GATE

CITY OF ULDE

PHAER CASTLE

PHAER BAY

PHAER POINT

THE PANTHEMIUM

THE LION'S MOUTH

THE LION'S PAWS

THE THRALL QUARTER

SHISSILIL

THE SOUTHERN SEA

THE GREAT KONE

THE COAST ROAD

THE CRUMBLES

VALE OF TWO WELLS

OLD CABIN

MT. ULDE

THE NORTHERN SEA

ILDEWOOD

MT. ILDE

ILDEWOOD

SHO

THE TOWER TREE

DRAGONSVELD

THE PHAER ISLE

CITY OF ULDE

N E W S

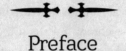

Preface

The following is a brief recap of Book 1 of the Spell Crossed series:

For fifty years the people of the Phaer Isle have been subjugated by the crystal-faced Pathans who live in the underearth. In order to prevent a resurgence of spell-craft, which they believe is rooted in text, the Pathans have destroyed all the literature of the Phaer people and executed all of the mages. Reading and writing and even singing are now forbidden and two generations have passed with the Phaer people living in slavery, hardly even aware of their great literary tradition and proud history.

Seventeen-year-old Xemion has been raised in an isolated, mountainous part of the island by a woman named Anya. Since he was young, she taught him to read from a collection of tiny books stored in a small locket. The collection contains, among other classics, the Phaer Tales

— epic stories from the island's legendary past. Reading these stories has given Xemion romantic ideals and convinced him that he will one day be a great warrior.

This desire only increases after he rescues a teenage girl named Saheli from a raging mountain river. There is a tradition in the Phaer Tales that two warriors who join forces in a fated love bond can gain even greater power together. Xemion is convinced that Saheli is his warrior beloved, but he keeps these thoughts to himself.

Saheli's physical wounds heal, leaving only a diagonal scar over her left eyebrow, but she still cannot remember anything about where she came from or what happened before she met Xemion. All she knows is that she has a deep fear of magic.

After the sudden death of Anya, Xemion begins to recite the stories to Saheli and to other children from Sho, the local fishing village. Two of these children are a boy named Torgee, who has feelings for Saheli, and his younger and very headstrong sister, Tharfen, whose feelings for Xemion are deep and troubled. Despite the Pathan strictures against the use of any kinds of weapons, the four also take to games of swordplay using sticks, though Tharfen uses a sling and stones, with which she has excellent aim.

Then one day Xemion discovers a stick that is so like the blade of a sword he can't resist putting a copper point on it and covering it in silver luminous paint to give it the look of a real sword. When he performs a sword dance with it, his performance is witnessed by a man named Vallaine who, strangely, has one red hand. He tells Xemion and Saheli that the Pathans are currently so embroiled in civil war that they've had to withdraw all their own troops from the Phaer Isle. Vallaine invites Xemion and Saheli to come with him on his ship to the city of Ulde where a rebellion against the kwislings — traitorous Phaer Islanders who the Pathans have chosen to rule in their absence — is about to begin. Xemion is tempted to go but Saheli is mistrustful of Vallaine. Besides, they are bound by previous vows and tell him they cannot go.

That evening when they return to the tower hidden inside a tree where they live, Xemion reads a new story from the collection in the library, but this time when he finishes it the locket poses a riddle: "Who'll be gouged and who'll be gored by the sword inside the sword. Will its power be ignored O who will wield the paper sword?"

Meanwhile, in Sho, a sadistic examiner — a Kwisling official in charge of weeding out children in the populace who may be spellbinders — shows up and catches Tharfen. He beats her until she provides him with information about the two teenagers who he has heard live alone in the forest. When he gets to the tower tree, he tries to kill their spell-crossed pet, Chiricoru, which is part swan, part rooster. Xemion thwarts him by using the painted sword, but in the aftermath of the fight their forest home burns to the ground and they are forced to flee. They decide to head toward Ulde and the rebellion.

The two are unexpectedly joined by Torgee and Tharfen, who warn them that the examiner is pursuing them with a pack of vicious Pathan dogs. Together the four stay overnight in the woods, close to an old hunting lodge. In the middle of the night, Saheli begins to be plagued by a strange melody that runs over and over in her mind. When the morning comes, they discover inside the lodge a large spell kone and, fastened to the ceiling, an old, long-haired, howling madman. They all flee in terror, but soon discover that the examiner and the dogs are closing in.

When the four travellers are trapped in a mountain pass haunted by ghouls, Xemion and Saheli are forced to drink water from one of the two magic wells in order to pass through the gates. Xemion drinks the water of memory and Saheli, despite the protests of a ghoul who turns out to be her mother, drinks the waters of forgetfulness. When the examiner arrives and attempts to follow them through the gate, Tharfen launches a stone with her sling that breaks the bottle he is drinking from. She has her revenge on him as he is attacked by a mob of ghouls, who take him into their fold.

As they continue on their journey, Xemion comes face-to-face with a dragon. Just as he fears it is about to kill him, it turns and kills the last of the Pathan dogs instead, and Xemion believes that the dragon deliberately saved him. Later, in the town of Shissilill (which due to spell crossing now has no friction), Xemion and Tharfen collide at great speed. Somehow they pass right through each other, but each retains a small piece of the other. Later Xemion is pained to discover that Saheli and Torgee have collided in the same way and now also share a piece of each other.

During their time in Shissilill, Xemion and Saheli get separated from Torgee and Tharfen. They continue on together into the deeply spell-crossed eastern side of the city of Ulde, where they again run into Vallaine, the mysterious man with the red hand. He warns Xemion to get rid of the painted sword as soon as possible and shakes hands with Xemion and Saheli before sending them on their way. Since, as he has implied to Xemion, he is a middle mage, the shaking of the hands activates the properties of the waters of memory and forgetfulness in the two. Xemion and Saheli take the path recommended by Vallaine, which passes right by the Great Kone, thought to be the origin of all textual magic on the Phaer Isle. To gain courage in this passage, Saheli, who has grown increasingly frightened of magic, for the first time takes Xemion's hand, and when they get safely by she kisses him on the lips, much to Xemion's surprise. Although Vallaine warned him not to read any of the exposed lettering on the Great Kone, as Saheli kisses him, Xemion's eyes alight on one letter — an *X*.

Xemion and Saheli cross over into the western side of the city, where youth from all over the island are gathering at an ancient stadium known as the Panthemium in order to join the rebellion and the new military academy. As they wait in line with the others, a young man named Brothlem Montither assaults someone. Saheli intervenes. Enraged, Montither turns on her with his weapon in hand, but Xemion uses the painted sword to subdue him. The incident ends with the arrival of the legendary Tiri Lighthammer, hero of the Battle of Phaer Bay, fought fifty years earlier.

Soon after, inside the Panthemium, the assembly is interrupted by a troop of kwisling soldiers led by the departing Pathan governor. In the uproar that follows, the governor is wounded and humiliated by Tiri Lighthammer and is forced to leave. But in all the confusion, Xemion and Saheli are separated.

Xemion searches frantically through the crowd, but just when he thinks he sees her, the leader of the rebellion, Veneetha Azucena, brings everything to a halt. She announces that all in attendance must immediately take the official vow of the rebellion's new military academy. This ritual involves all participants crossing their arms in front of them and grasping the hands of the two people on either side. When Xemion does this he finds himself wedged uncomfortably between a bitter and vengeful Tharfen, who has appeared out of nowhere, and the bully, Montither, whose hatred for Xemion is obvious. With these two contentious comrades he must take the vow of friendship and alliance.

1

Not Seeing Her Face

Xemion strained to see her face. But she remained turned away from him, seven rows ahead, her hair tied up in a topknot. *It had to be her. But it might not be.* He trembled at the thought that he may have lost her forever.

"Keep the grip!"

Veneetha Azucena's command reverberated off the ancient stones of the Panthemium. Xemion, along with all the others, stood with his arms crossed in front of him, his hands gripping the hands of those on each side. They had all just taken a vow of obedience. But he would break that vow, he thought. If he could, he'd let go right now and push his way forward to where the girl was standing. He had to see her face to make sure.

"See how you are all bound in and to one another," Azucena urged them. "This is how we will be bound in the endeavour before us. Not only each to all and all to each but to our ancestors, as well, who also made this grip. Feel it."

They stood silently; the only sound the rippling of the gorehorse flag flapping first one way and then the other in the crosswinds coming in off the sea.

"This one here," Veneetha Azucena said finally, pointing to a thin Phaerlander who stood at the front of the assembly, closest to her, "is directly connected to the one at the end." She gestured over their heads. "Each one sworn to each in alliance and friendship."

But Xemion felt only hostility from those on either side of him. In fact, he had just that morning publicly humiliated Brothlem Montither, the large, finely attired, slightly perfumed individual currently gripping his right hand. And Tharfen, the younger, shorter red-haired girl on the other side who kept yanking on his left arm trying to get his attention, was someone with whom he'd had nothing but quarrels ever since their first meeting. The fact that a recent collision in the spell-crossed borough of Shissilill had left a small fragment of her inside him only served to increase the amount of discomfort he felt in her company.

"Don't just look for Saheli. My brother may be up there. Look for Torgee, too," she hissed, jabbing her thumbnail into the back of his hand.

"Now, you will all soon be put to a test, but before we begin there is something I must stress very strongly." Veneetha Azucena paused and surveyed the crowd before her, the high red feather atop her black headdress bending back and forth in the strong wind. "There are still functioning spellworks to be found in these parts. Mostly these are devices retrieved from newly fallen houses by speculators. Certain Pathan scientists are very interested in acquiring such items. Nothing could be more danger-ous to our cause than these. We will not tolerate any kind of traffic in these items. They may not be owned. They may not be kept. And they certainly must not be used. Remember, they have held to their spells for fifty years and are now completely unstable. They must be destroyed. But not by you … by Mr. Glittervein here."

She pointed to a Nain standing to the side amongst the other faculty members. Like all Nains, he was short and broad of shoulder but well-proportioned. He had dressed neatly for the occasion in a red uniform and wore his long auburn hair so that it covered one side of his face, while the other side gazed handsomely out at the crowd. He gave a little nod.

"As our Provost, he will be in charge of our arma-ments and provisions. You've all seen the high chimney of Uldestack where he has his forge. Let me tell you, he can build such a fire there as will melt anything, spell crossed or not. So if you have found any spellworks since arriving here, or if any of you have somehow managed to acciden-tally bring any in with you, I will give you one last chance to surrender them to him today. After today, if anyone is caught with spellworks, they will be instantly expelled from the academy. We are firmly committed to this. And because here in Ulde we are once again in the presence of the Great Kone — the very root and source of the textual magic — do not think there is any intention to return to the easy ways of spell kones and conjuration. I bid you witness me: I will not have even so much as the rubbing

17

of some charm. I will not hear a wish, a prayer, or an incantation from any of you. Our actions are our wishes. Our will is our prayer. Our swords are our incantations. Now, have you got that?" Heads nodded. "Say aye."

A deep-voiced, solemn "aye" arose from the crowd.

"Many more of you than expected have shown up. But if you are hungry you will be fed, and all of you will be directed to lodgings after we finish here. Mr. Glittervein will have to make more swords, but you will all be given a sword and you will all be taught swordsmanship so that you may learn to ably defend us when these enslavers and book-burners return, as they surely will. In fact, given the treatment which their Prince has this morning so justly received at Mr. Lighthammer's hand, they may be back much sooner than we thought. That is why you are about to be tested. We need to find three dozen of the best fighters to take special intense and advanced training so that we may begin guarding our perimeters immediately. And to find such a number we must trust to the one true compass we know." She gestured elegantly. "Tiri Lighthammer."

Lighthammer had once had been a triplicant, but his heroic battle with the invaders fifty years earlier had left him with only two arms and two legs. This caused him to come forward now with a slightly asymmetrical gait. But as he stood before them in his red jacket, his broad shoulders decorated with golden epaulets, he looked powerful and impressive. He ordered that two broad doors leading into the stables under the stadium be opened. Slowly he drew his famous steel sword and held it up in the air. "The test is simple," he announced. "Can you hold onto a sword or not. First I will instruct you and then I will test you." These words calmed Xemion down a little. He knew how to hold a sword. And so did Saheli. He had learned the skill from the *Manual of Phaer Swordsmanship*, one of the tiny volumes he carried even now in the little locket library that hung on a chain about his neck. He had practised, and so had she. They would both be among the chosen. He knew it.

Lighthammer turned his blade into the light. "Do you see this hand here? This is the Phaer grip." Lighthammer stood with one leg forward and bent, the other back and straight, his sword held up before him at a forty-five-degree angle. Despite the slight sense of imbalance caused by the odd placement of his two arms and legs, he looked very forceful and elegant.

"A sword is not a bottle you grip by the neck to break over some drunkard's head," Lighthammer continued. "It is a deftly balanced scalpel you steer with deadly precision. Grip the hilt, not too tight, with the thumb up the haft resting on the guard. Do you see? Say aye."

There was a chorus of "ayes."

"Good then."

He touched the shoulder of a very large Thrall girl who had emerged from the chamber under the stadium. She wore a bulky grey cloak, but her head was bare. By the look of her bleached white eyes, she was blind. She carried a slightly rusty-looking sword.

"First, arrange yourselves in lines of twenty-four, but keep the grip within the lines. I will start with this fellow at the front. Step forward one by one, and when the first line is done, the line behind shall step forward. Do you understand? Say aye."

"Aye," they said in unison, and after a brief shuffle it was done. Seven rows back, Xemion's impatience gathered and his anxiety quickened. It would take so long before he had his turn and she was so far ahead of him. He thought about how she had drunk the water of forgetfulness at the Vale of Two Wells. What if it caused her to forget what had happened between them earlier that morning? To forget their kiss? What if somehow they were apart long enough for her to forget him altogether?

He strained to see her, but now that the crowd had shifted, a group of giant Thralls hid her from view. The same shuffle had, however, opened up a vista on the other part of the front line, and there, no more than a person or two away from where he believed Saheli stood, was Tharfen's brother, Torgee.

He leaned down and whispered, *"I see him."*

"Where? Where?" Tharfen, whose height prevented her from seeing much around her, actually jumped up and down trying to see over the shoulders in front of her. She succeeded only in annoying the burly girl on her right side.

"He's right up the front," Xemion whispered.

"Well, get his attention," she demanded, yanking on his arm.

"I can't," he told her, yanking back on her arm.

"You have to," she protested, digging her nail into his hand.

"No, I don't!"

Tharfen dug her nail in harder.

"Do it yourself."

Unfortunately for Xemion, he said these last words a

little too loudly. From the front, Tiri Lighthammer's iron-grey eyes found him. "Silence back there or you will be removed!"

On Xemion's other side, Montither turned just enough to sneer at him.

Back at the front, Lighthammer gestured to the first recruit, who stepped forward and laid down the staff he had brought with him. When the blind Thrall girl gave him the other sword, he did his best to grip it in the way they had been instructed. Lighthammer inspected his grip, corrected it, and when the recruit held the sword up before him, disarmed him so quickly there was a gasp from the crowd. "To the right," Lighthammer directed. The recruit proceeded through the great doors, to the end of the chamber, and then disappeared into a hallway on the right. And so it was with the next fifteen recruits, whether they were male, female, Thrall, or Phaerlander, the sword was stricken from their grip, usually with the smallest of movement on Lighthammer's behalf. After each, Tiri Lighthammer gestured with his sword into the chamber beneath the stadium. "To the right," he ordered.

Finally, as the front rank was fed into the lightning of Lighthammer's sword, the girl Xemion thought must be Saheli emerged from the shadow of the Thralls and stood unmoving before Lighthammer. Tharfen had by now resumed her pestering of Xemion. "What's happening?" But Xemion refused to acknowledge her in any way. "Tell me, you coward. If he leaves without me … you will be in such trouble!"

When the girl with the topknot took the blade and Lighthammer inspected the grip, he looked surprised and nodded with a pleased expression. He bowed his head courteously. "Are you ready?" he asked. The topknot nodded. "Fine then." Lighthammer flicked at her sword, but amazingly she held it firmly. Lighthammer was stunned. There was another swift swing but still she held her blade.

"Well, well, well." Lighthammer seemed truly impressed, almost flustered. He stared at her for a long time, until her head turned a little to the side — almost enough for Xemion to see her face, but not quite. Here, with a final ambush-like flick, he managed to disengage her. "Can you be ruthless?" he asked.

The girl shrugged.

"Well, you will need to be." Lighthammer raised his voice sternly. "You will all need to be ruthless. You saw the treachery of the Pathan prince this morning. They are not like us. They can only be met with complete ruthlessness. People, we have the first of our thirty-six. To the left," he said.

Xemion watched the back of her head drop from sight as the girl bent down and retrieved the weapon she had arrived with. Saheli's staff had been made from the hard, hollow stem of one of Xemion's giant sunflowers. It was very distinctive-looking, and if he could just catch a glimpse of it, he would know for sure if it was her. But she lifted the weapon horizontally in one hand only to waist height so that it remained below his line of sight. With that she proceeded straight on into the chamber under the stadium, until she stood in the shadow at the end where the two hallways diverged. If her hair had remained up in the topknot, Xemion would have been able to see her high cheekbones, her full lips as she turned, and he would have known for sure it was her, but all the effort of the contest with Lighthammer had dishevelled her hair enough that one side had released numerous tresses, which now hid her face.

And then she was gone.

In that instant, Xemion's fear that he would lose her increased markedly and his heart thumped double and then triple its pace. It had to be her!

"Tell me what's happening," Tharfen growled, jabbing her thumbnail into the crescent-shaped wound she had already left in the back of Xemion's hand.

"It's Torgee's turn now," he hissed. For the first time he squeezed her hand back angrily, using all his strength. With the effort, though, he unwittingly increased his pressure on the hand of Montither on the other side. Until now, Montither had seemed inert, almost unaware, of Xemion, but now with a quick, furious glance he squeezed back and maintained the pressure.

Xemion wasn't unduly surprised when Torgee also held onto his sword. Back in the mountains, Saheli had insisted on teaching him the Phaer grip, as well. Still, when Lighthammer called out "to the left," Xemion's stomach heaved with a painful emotion that he did not yet have a name for but which the world knows as jealousy.

The shortest of three Thrall sisters who had been blocking Xemion's view managed to hang on to her blade. Her taller sister was next, and Lighthammer found her even harder to disarm, which delighted him. "For you I will have to switch to my good arm," he said, with something close to a chortle. With this the blade flew from her mighty hand and she followed her sister down the hallway to the left, as did the massive third sister. Lighthammer now had six of his three dozen. At this point, the other faculty members, including Veneetha Azucena and Glittervein, with nods to Lighthammer, slowly filed into the chamber and were gone.

All this time Montither had been squeezing Xemion's hand harder and harder. Xemion was meeting him strength for strength, but Montither was clearly quite strong and it was beginning to get a little painful. By the time their rank came to the front of the stadium there was quite an intense struggle quietly going on between them. Then, in rapid succession, another three recruits passed Lighthammer's test, one of them a triplicant. Montither's thugs, Gnasher and Ring'o'pins, were next. Each of them stepped forward jauntily and both were quickly dispatched and sent to the right.

Finally, it was Montither's turn. Just before he released Xemion's hand, he gave his arm a quick twist and a yank that hurt so much he almost cried out. Xemion looked down at his hand, which was mottled white and bloodless, and gritted his teeth. Montither stepped forward and set down his own well-made blade. He grabbed the hilt of the rusty sword, expanding his chest wide and arcing his arms a little so as to look even more muscular than he was.

Before he could display his grip, though, Lighthammer lifted the point of his own blade so that it hovered in front of Montither's thick neck. He did it fast, but Montither did not start.

"Do you see this point?" Lighthammer asked him dryly.

Montither grunted in answer.

"If that was a yes, you say *yes, sir*. Do you understand?"

"Yes, sir." Montither answered.

"And are you sure that this is a real sword this time?" Lighthammer asked contemptuously.

"Yes, sir." Montither answered.

"You are sure that it is not some painted stick then?"

Xemion could not restrain a small smile at this. The man with the red hand, Vallaine, had warned him to never use his painted sword again, but Vallaine had been wrong. Without the sword, Xemion couldn't have prevented Montither from threatening Saheli earlier today. With it, he had backed him up against the outer wall of the stadium. He had executed this manoeuvre so quickly and so convincingly that he had briefly managed to terrify the bully. All who had witnessed it had seen his face turn white with fear. Who knows where the fracas would have ended had not Lighthammer himself intervened.

"I know how to tell a sword from a stick," Montither answered haughtily, "when it is bravely put before me in a manner befitting a member of the Phaer militia like yourself, sir. It is a little more difficult when one is ambushed in a cowardly way as I was."

"Well, what of the Pathans then?" Lighthammer asked sharply. "Do you think they announce themselves before they come up from underground in the dark of night and slit our throats as we sleep?"

Montither said nothing. He stood motionless.

"Will you ever be fooled by a painted stick again, do you think?"

"No, sir, I do not."

"So you have learned something."

Montither nodded and turned his hand to show Lighthammer his grip upon the sword. Quickly examining it, Lighthammer saw that it was strong and tight and correct. The two faced off. Lighthammer flicked at Montither and Montither flicked back at Lighthammer and almost disarmed him. There were gasps from the crowd. A look of livid rage crossed Lighthammer's face and he hacked back once, twice, three times, before, with the fourth quick flick, he disengaged Montither. Montither stood there proudly, his hands open at his sides, his head tipped aslant as though questioning.

"You've had training," Lighthammer stated, doing his best to restrain the anger in his voice.

"Not enough, sir."

Lighthammer said nothing, though his eyes squinted a little tighter as he took in the full measure of the beefy, well-dressed lad before him.

"And I know I have much to learn."

Lighthammer lowered his blade. "What is your name?"

"Brothlem Montither."

"Norud Montither's son?"

"In blood only, sir. I have repudiated him."

"But not the finely turned coat and the double-edged bronze blade?"

Lighthammer was clearly referring to the fact that Montither's father was the richest and most powerful of the turncoat traitors known as kwislings. Montither remained quiet.

"To the left," Terri Lighthammer said almost reluctantly.

"Tell Torgee to wait for me," Tharfen growled as

Xemion stepped forward to take his turn. Circulation still had not returned to his right hand and no amount of covert stretching of it had brought back the feeling. If anything, there was the slightest tingle of pins and needles in it as he grasped the still-warm hilt of the blade. It was heavier than he thought it would be; much heavier then the painted sword, which was currently reflecting sunlight back at him from the ground where he had laid it. Xemion took a deep breath and assumed the Phaer grip. Now the sword felt firm and right in his hand, and this gave him confidence. He held up the blade in a perfect stance. Lighthammer looked intently at him. "And you are the fellow who fooled that fool by pressing your little prop of a sword up to his neck."

Xemion nodded.

"But could you have pushed it through?"

Xemion actually smiled. "Quite willingly," he answered, perhaps a little arrogantly.

Lighthammer nodded inscrutably. "It is easy to be his enemy, but can you put that aside and trust him now and be his ally?"

Xemion hesitated only slightly. "I know that I can be trusted."

"I see. Do you feel you've got the sword held right?"

Xemion nodded.

"Show me."

Xemion turned the haft of the sword so that his fingers were clearly visible and a twinge ran right up his arm where Montither had yanked it.

"That is very good," said Lighthammer.

Xemion nodded.

"Do you think you are ready?"

Xemion nodded again. But he had a strange feeling as Lighthammer's blade zeroed in on his. Lighthammer struck quick as lightning right at the crook where the hilt met the blade. He hit hard and the sword rang like a bell and was knocked down so forcefully to the ground it bounced halfway back up again. Xemion let out a cry, shaking his hand, his shoulder in agony. People behind laughed. Loudest among them, Tharfen.

"No!" Xemion shouted. "No."

"Yes," said Lighthammer.

"No, I must have another chance."

"It would be no different."

"I must have another chance."

"One more word and you will be exiled from these precincts. Do you hear me?"

Xemion tried to be silent. "But the first one you chose, she is my—"

Lighthammer cut him off with an angry bellow. "The one thing you need to do right now is to obey my orders, and your vow. Do you understand?"

Xemion only barely managed to remain silent. Lighthammer turned to face the crowd.

"Listen to me. Some of you will be separated from your friends by this test. That is the way it is in the militia. But do not trouble me with it. We will all be meeting back here at noon tomorrow. Now, I don't want to hear any more about it."

Xemion said nothing.

"To the right," said Lighthammer.

2

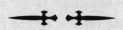

Tharfen's Piece

Xemion was riding the she-dragon he'd stood face to face with in Ilde, slashing with a paper sword at the sky, slicing away at the darkness of the night till he'd cut a brightly burning *X* into and through it. He was searching for Saheli. Slowly, the *X* opened at its centre and beyond it was the green luminous *X* he'd seen through broken brickwork on the side of the Great Kone. He cut through that *X*, too, and there was yet another dark one beyond it that shape-shifted. It became a whole alphabet of *X*'s and the different *X*'s were forming *X*-words, telling him an incredible *X* story. And at the end the *X* became the *X* of a kiss and it was that one kiss of Saheli's. The *X* of intersection where they crossed lives. The first kiss of his life. Everything else — the sword, the dragon, the sky — melted away like snowflakes in the simple heat, in just the thought of that first kiss, let alone any other conceivable kiss. Let alone a second kiss.

He opened his eyes. Saheli. Where was she? Somewhere in some other barracks. Nearby? Maybe even with Torgee. No one had been able to tell him anything about where she'd been sent after Lighthammer's test, and he'd waited all evening in an anxious fury. He clenched his fist in anger now as he felt again the pain in his wrist and shoulder where Montither had injured him. Noon. He would see her at noon. Then everything would be set straight. Then he would deal with Montither.

The door of the barracks opened and Lirodello, the quartermaster's assistant, peered in. "Everyone to the Panthemium. You'll get some vittles there." Xemion was up in a flash and out the door, jogging through the cobblestone streets of ancient Ulde toward the stadium. There was still a chance he might see her likewise jogging, likewise looking for him, and then noon wouldn't matter. But it was not Saheli, it was Tharfen who he saw. He rounded a corner and there she was, not too far ahead of him, her sling hanging from her right hand.

"Hey, Tharfen."

She spun round to look at him, her frizz of red hair aflame in the bright morning sunlight. She was clearly not in a good mood. She looked ragged and tired and angry. She scowled when she saw him, shaking her head with disgust and disappointment.

"What happened to you?" he asked, keeping pace with her. She answered in a great speedy flood of words one after the other without a pause, each one more bitterly spoken than the previous.

"Well, after that sword just slipped right out of your useless hands, the only way to get back to Torgee was to win myself, and the only way to do that was to beat that old man and the only way to do that was by using my sling. But the old geezer was too yellow. He couldn't admit it, so he pretended he couldn't fight me 'cause I'm not thirteen yet. So I argued with him, and he got mad. And he said the sling is a dishonourable weapon that no righteous Phaer soldier would ever—"

Xemion finally interrupted. "No, I actually meant what happened to you in Shissillil?"

Her expression changed to one of distaste. "We got spat out of some gate over that way by the castle. And thank you for caring."

"I knew you were safe."

"No. You just convinced yourself we were safe because you wanted to not care."

"No, I knew."

She felt his certainty. And he felt her feel it. He didn't want to acknowledge it, but it needed to be said. "Ever since we collided there …" She shuddered at the memory: him shooting toward her, dashing *through* her, and she through him, and out the other side. "It's like some little piece of you got caught in me and is still there and I can … *feel what it's feeling*."

She grimaced. "Well, I guess I might as well stop trying so hard to hide my hate for you, then, since you sense it anyway." She said this with a fair degree of venom and only a slight touch of humour.

"You only wish you hated me," Xemion shot back. She actually snarled at this, revealing her large incisors in the process. "Nevertheless, my brother and me took a great risk for you, didn't we?"

"For Saheli, maybe."

"Don't think you don't owe me, Xemion. And I'm telling you, if Torgee decides he's going to stay here and be some kind of special soldier, it's you, who can't even hold on to a sword anyway, who's gonna be getting me home. I—"

"I am definitely not going to be taking you home."

"So you're saying I risked my life on your behalf, faced ghouls and dragons … but you're too much of an arse—"

"I'm saying I came here …" He paused. "… I'm saying Saheli and I came here knowing we risked all. We didn't ask you to—"

"*Saheli and I came here,*" she mimicked nastily.

"And anyway, I'm sure someone else can take you."

Xemion had never succeeded in remaining so calm with Tharfen.

"You do know that my mother is in agony right now, afraid I'm dead?"

"She won't know you're safe any faster whether I take you home or someone else does. My duty is to be united with Saheli, as I have vowed."

"What do you mean, you vowed?"

"I swore to Anya I would stay with her till she was fully grown."

"She *is* fully grown, you idiot. And you still don't even know if that was Saheli up there or not."

Xemion's nostrils flared. This was the thought that hadn't stopped niggling away at him all night long. "She was the right height and she was wearing her hair up in a topknot like that when we got separated. So—"

"So what?" Tharfen interrupted. "I saw two other

girls, the same height as her, with their hair up. And one lad! You never did see her face, did you?"

Xemion didn't acknowledge the question, so she kept up her assault. "You know how long the gate was open after that crystal-faced Pathan coward marched in. People where I slept said they heard that some kids got dragged away."

"Nonsense," Xemion snapped.

"Ha ha!" She pointed at him. "Look at your silly love-sick face. You really think she's your warrior beloved, like in one of your stupid tales, don't you?"

This had now transgressed onto holy ground. "She told Vallaine she was my betrothed," he answered fiercely.

"Yes, because she was trying to get out of shaking his freakish red hand. Not because she actually—"

"I *know* she is my warrior beloved."

"How? Did she tell you?"

He tried not to say what he said next, but he couldn't stop himself. "She didn't need to. She kissed me."

Tharfen took a close look and she could see he wasn't jesting. "Where?"

"We had just come out of the shadow of the Great Kone and—"

"No, you fool. I mean whereabouts did she kiss you? On the cheek, I suppose."

He blushed and her lips lifted into a full on snarl of outrage. *"On the lips?"*

He didn't answer now, regretting what he'd said. But he couldn't hide it.

"Xemion! She was just some poor bedraggled thing that you dredged up out of the river—"

"How dare you!"

"How dare *you* take advantage of someone with amnesia?"

He failed the second time trying not to say something. "It was *she* who kissed *me*."

Tharfen saw that he wasn't lying, and the bushy redness of her hair and the brownish redness of her many freckles were suddenly accompanied by the blushing pinkness of her cheeks. She bared her teeth. "Well you let her, didn't you? In her state. All while recovering from a wound, I suppose, and drinking cursed waters from a well that wipes away your memory. She took a little bottle of that forgetting water with her, you know, aye? Seen her chugging on it lots of times. So even if such filth as you've just told me is true, she ought to be mercifully forgetting it right about now. Maybe with a little help from Torgee even."

Xemion was doing a much better job of ducking her many jibes and insinuations than he ever had when she had set out to annoy him back in Ilde, but this latest one was a challenge. He bit his lip. He didn't want anything to interrupt the steady flow of time toward noon, when he would see Saheli.

Tharfen could see she wasn't going to get him going so she stayed quiet a while as they traipsed through the misty grey streets of the ancient capital toward the Panthemium. Here the elaborately and minutely chiselled walls had been cleaned and were in good repair so that the intricate epic scenes that adorned them all along the way could be seen to good effect in the sea-scented morning sunlight.

"Well, I knew you was unfortunately safe, too," she

said at last as they drew closer to the crowd milling around outside of the Panthemium doors.

Xemion flinched. That strange feeling he'd had when he'd first been ejected from the high gate of Shissilill, the feeling that he'd lost some tiny part of himself in there, had quickly been subsumed in his feelings of losing Saheli. But now he felt it distinctly again and he glanced at Tharfen.

"Yes." She nodded with a slightly malicious smile. He looked away, not wanting her to see the shudder of his revulsion. She didn't have to see it, though; she felt it emanating strongly from the little piece of him that was in her. She'd never known it so clearly before — how strongly he detested her. She felt nothing about it. She picked up a stone, swung it around in her sling, and launched it at a gull perched atop a chimney pot on the building across the road. The bird sat there perfectly still as the little piece of fallen masonry sped toward it. Before Xemion could even shout to try and warn the bird, the missile shot by and continued on over the rooftop to the next street. Tharfen stopped in the street and stared at the bird, aghast.

"You missed," Xemion said softly, somewhat amazed.

"I wasn't trying to hit it, you fool," Tharfen snarled at him. "Oh, you want me to hit it? Sure, I'll hit it for ya." Before he could dissuade her, another piece of masonry had been launched, but it, too, missed its target, and the bird remained perched impassively on the pot. Xemion said nothing as Tharfen, enraged, took a third piece of masonry and proceeded to miss again by an even wider margin. The bird, finally alerted to the danger, flew off, and Tharfen, pretending to be satisfied, continued on her way without looking at Xemion.

After a while, he said, "Is this the first time you've used your sling since you knocked that bottle out of the examiner's hands?"

She gazed up at him red-faced. For a second she saw again the examiner's horrified eyes as the ghouls at the well yanked his head round backward. A second later, livid with anger, she was poking her index finger at Xemion so fast and hard and so close to his face he had to draw back defensively. "He got what he deserved. And so will you."

3

A Great Boon to Us

At the Panthemium, Xemion couldn't stop looking for Saheli, but neither she nor any of the others chosen by Lighthammer were present. After a breakfast of smoked haddock and some kind of crunchy grain that Xemion had never tasted before, Lirodello led him and a group of the others to the fairly intact remains of some majestic buildings that had once constituted the main body of the Phaer Academy.

The first thing Xemion noticed as he entered the white marble hall that housed his first class was the sunscope that had been mounted and assembled on a table. It was just like the one he had used in Ilde. Beside it, a group of Thralls had gathered over a book the size of a small window. Excited despite himself, Xemion quickly joined them, peering down over four sets of hunched shoulders to see a full-colour illustration of the hero Amphion, his sword held to the sky, a dragon exhaling steam at his side.

Xemion caught his breath. Until now he had only seen this picture as a projection from the miniature version in the locket library. The details and colours in this much-larger and richer version were astonishing. Tharfen, too, leaned in to look, doing her best to keep as far as possible from Xemion. She had never seen such a picture before, even as a projection.

"Yes, the picture is wonderful, isn't it?" said Captain Sarabin as he entered the room. Sarabin was very old. His face was lined and cracked like a dry riverbed, but his eyes sparkled. Xemion tried unsuccessfully not to stare at the two copper hooks that Sarabin now used skillfully to open the cover of the book. "But even more wonderful are the words written inside, which, I assure you, by the end of this season, you will all be able to read for yourselves. And not just this one volume. I am happy to tell you that we have been blessed with the full recovery of all the Phaer Tales."

"But how did these books survive?" Xemion asked, turning to face Sarabin.

Captain Sarabin closed the book and continued in a quiet voice. "Children always hide favoured things, and in the days after the Pathan betrayal they hid their favourite books. From a hundred pits and cupboards and buried boxes all over the land, one by one, every volume of the Phaer Tales has been recovered in the past two years, and we now have the complete collection several times over. It's a great shame that the old professors failed to bury just as many boxes of poetry and philosophy. But being Phaer, we always kept our books in public libraries, where the Pathans got at them rather quickly, I'm afraid."

It took a while for Captain Sarabin to get the recruits to close the book and sit in the wooden seats lining the room. Some of those who now filled the chamber had probably heard versions of the Phaer Tales told in secret by old men and women before, but few of them had ever seen a book of any kind, and that picture of Amphion clearly captivated them.

Sarabin was an enormously patient man and he asked repeatedly and in a quite calm voice for the class to come to order. Finally, when they had all taken their seats, he took the book of Amphion into his arms and, using his hooks with considerable skill, placed it open on his lectern. "You have all been forbidden to learn to read," he said in a burred voice. "You have been told that reading is mind-sickening and a pathway directly to the spellcraft. But that is wrong. You are the heirs of the greatest literary tradition in all the history of the Orb. And one of the greatest evils perpetrated by the Pathans, along with murder and slavery, is … was … stripping you of this ability. Reading is a great boon to us. There are great treasures to be had from reading … and writing. I am here to teach this. Now listen." Quietly he began to read.

Captain Sarabin was not a born orator. There was a reedy but wispy quality to his voice that was swallowed by any slight noise in the room. Everyone listened with ever-greater attention. Sarabin continued the story a long time, up to the point where Amphion is first separated from his warrior beloved, Queen Phaeton. There he stopped and closed the book. Looking up with a smile, he said, "And the rest, as soon as you learn to read, you can finish for yourselves."

This incited quite a lot of protest in the group, but Sarabin was unusually firm.

"Come, come, come. It will not take long. We begin with one letter and then we proceed to the next. Soon you will be reading for yourselves."

After that, he tried to teach them the first letter of the Elphaerean alphabet, *E*, but there was too much grumbling for him to continue. Eventually he had to make an agreement with them. If they would learn the first five letters of the alphabet he would read them the conclusion of the story tomorrow. "Any questions?" he asked.

Here, Xemion nearly spoke up. From the moment Anya had begun to teach him to read she had insisted on complete secrecy. Even when he'd told the tales to the children of Sho, he pretended that he'd learned them by hearing them, not by reading them. But was that pretense still necessary? Perhaps a little longer. He would wait till noon. Nothing must interrupt the slow, steady progress toward Saheli.

As Sarabin moved on tediously to the second letter of the Elphaerean alphabet, *D*, Xemion caught a glint of Tharfen's gaze, which she quickly turned away — but not so quickly that it did not reveal the intense malice she bore him at that moment.

"And what sound do you think this letter makes?" Sarabin asked, pointing to the letter *A*.

Along with everyone else, he spoke the sound of the *A*. Suddenly, on the other side of the room, Tharfen stood up. "Excuse me," she said loudly.

Sarabin was a little irritated to be interrupted. "What is it?"

"Is this teaching for those who already know how to read?"

Sarabin was taken aback. "You know how to read?"

"No," she answered, looking at Xemion, unable to keep the glint of vengeful glee out of her eyes. "But he does." With that, she pointed an accusing finger at Xemion.

Sarabin's head jolted back in surprise and a look of doubt crossed his features.

"Really?" he asked, frowning at Xemion.

Xemion was trembling. He couldn't lie. Not outright. "Yes, sir."

Sarabin's already pale features seemed to have found new recesses of pallor to draw upon. A slight tremble entered his voice. "All the letters?"

"Yes, I know them all." Xemion could feel the eyes of every member of the class upon him, and somehow he liked it.

"And do you know how to read them when they are put together in words?" Sarabin asked incredulously.

"Yes. In sentences, too," Xemion replied with a smile that included everyone but the still-gloating Tharfen. "Whole paragraphs even."

"I do hope you are not joking," Sarabin warned, giving him a severe look.

"Of course not," Xemion answered confidently.

"Well, here then, show us how you'd read this. It's something a little more recent than the Phaer Tales."

There was, at that time, only one volume of recent Phaer history available: *The History of the Battle of Phaer Bay*. It only existed because Sarabin, as a witness to the battle, had taken the risk of writing it himself, an act which he paid for with the loss of both hands. The Pathans then proceeded to burn not only his book, but his home and fields as well. Fortunately, they missed the second copy of the book, which he secretly buried in the forest. It was this hand-lettered scroll that he now passed to Xemion, who unrolled it carefully and took in the cramped letters neatly handwritten upon it. Anya had always insisted that he restrain the richer textures in his voice, but there would be no need to do that now. He held everyone's attention from the moment he began:

"And all the while the fool generals held back their precious gorehorses so that by the time they attempted to use them the battle was all but over. Only then did they send the poor beasts in where they hoped their horns might be good at least for goring. But though they galloped bravely into the ranks of the Kagars, they were turned away by the silvery, burnished shields made of some kind of metal unknown to us. And soon they had roped and corralled the gorehorses and we watched in horror as they rounded up the beasts and cut off their horns. There never was such screaming from a beast. And when they let them go, the poor animals were so unbalanced by the loss of their horns they could hardly stand. They kept staggering and stooping down to the ground as they tried to make their way away from the terrible carnage."

Xemion was completely caught up in the rhythm and emotion of the passage. His voice was soaring and swelling just as it had when he'd stood upon a stump in Ilde and held spellbound the children of Sho.

"And some of the gorehorses they slew there on the beach, and others they wrapped in reins and led off back toward the sea, for what purpose we dread to think. Only one escaped, and this poor beast now dying is the last of all the gorehorses on the Phaer Isle. And all for what? For the folly of Magick!"

When he finished, Xemion looked up to see many a rapt, sorrowful face among his fellows. Even Captain Sarabin was wiping away a tear.

"And there," said Captain Sarabin at last, "you have the beauty of the Elphaerean language. Superbly done, young man!"

Xemion shot a triumphant glance toward Tharfen, only managing to catch her eye long enough to see her disappointment and rage that her act had not hurt him more. For a while she fingered the thin leather sling she wore about her brow and Xemion watched warily, prepared to dodge should she choose to fire a stone his way. Meanwhile, the other members of the class had lapsed into animated chatter. Thrall and Nain, Nain and Freeman. Sarabin tapped on his lectern repeatedly but lightly and without much effect. The students were at too high a pitch of excitement. Not only because they had just heard Xemion's exalted recitation, but also because very soon they would be relieved from their uncomfortable perches on the wooden chairs and sent back to the stadium, where they would get to use real swords for the first time. Xemion's excitement was also at a pitch. Soon he would see Saheli.

"Please, please." Sarabin raised his voice, but just then there came the blowing of about ten whistles at once. The whole group cheered as one and began to evacuate their first literature class with great rapidity. Xemion finally looked at the sun outside the window and was relieved to see that it had notably edged up farther into the sky. Soon. Soon he would see her. Just then a cold piece of metal touched Xemion's shoulder — Sarabin's hook.

"Do you also write?" he asked Xemion very seriously.

"Yes, very well," Xemion answered, sounding only the slightest bit proud of himself.

"Well then, please, young man, I must ask you to come with me."

"But, sir," Xemion protested, alarmed. "I can't. I have to hurry." He made as if to leave, but his shirt was caught in one of Sarabin's hooks.

"I know, I know," Sarabin answered, his voice suddenly firm and authoritative, "but I have something far more important for you to do."

"But we are to be given swords today. And I have someone most important to meet at midday in the assembly."

"You will be back by then," Sarabin said, "but I have something of the utmost importance to reveal to you and I'm going to have to ask for your secrecy about it."

Xemion frowned but nodded. Tharfen, with one hand tangled in the red coils of her hair, had come up behind them, listening.

"What is it?" she asked.

"He says I have to wait behind," Xemion said angrily, turning around to face her.

"Do you also write?" Sarabin asked Tharfen.

"No, I don't."

"Then you can go," Sarabin stated. "But you, young man, you must come with me."

"But …"

"You will be happy you did," Sarabin insisted matter-of-factly. He seemed to be agitated and suddenly very determined. "And you, young lady, you can go along to the next instruction, and this fellow — what is your name?"

Xemion answered, a little sullenly.

"Xemion will come for his sword later," Sarabin told Tharfen.

"But—" Tharfen, sensing what she had set in motion, suddenly felt a sense of regret. But it was too late for that.

"Off you go now," Captain Sarabin said with impressive authority.

Xemion watched desperately as she walked away.

"I think you are going to be a great boon to … to our cause," Sarabin said with barely suppressed excitement.

4

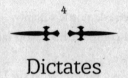

Dictates

Not far past the crossroads where the High Street intersected with the road that led up to the old castle on the tip of Phaer Point, Sarabin led Xemion down into the coolness of a deep stone stairwell. At the bottom was a doorway with the words *Song Is My Thrall* carved into the top of the frame. They entered a dimly lit stone chamber with a domed ceiling.

"Welcome to the underdome," Sarabin whispered.

Once Xemion's eyes adjusted to the low light, he could see that they were standing in an aisle between rows of seats. From the stage area in front of them, a periodic rattling whispery sound followed by a scratchy rustling could be heard. As he drew closer, Xemion made out three shadow beings gathered about a candlelit table on the stage. The one in the middle, the oldest person Xemion had ever seen, sat in a stone chair, withered and whispering. She was clearly a Thrall woman of some kind, her face set and hard, and she had large yellow eyes. Beside her, illuminated in the same sphere of light, an elderly grey scribe held the narrow end of a large moon-and-star-inscribed cone to the old woman's mouth. A second scribe sat across the table in front of the wide end of the cone, listening intently. The source of the scratching sound was the quill pen with which he was hurriedly writing her whispered words down onto a scroll of reed paper. And now that he was close enough, Xemion could hear the words that the cone was helping to amplify.

"And there shall be none and no one to know or *un*know the unknown ..."

Yes, the old Thrall was reciting what Xemion judged to be a book of philosophy. He knew only a little about philosophy. There had been one book entitled *Of Meaning* in the locket library, which, like all the books, due to some mechanism hidden in the locket, had to be fully read before access to any further volumes was allowed. Xemion had had to labour through page after page of long, complicated sentences, all aimed at finding out the true nature of the meaning of meaning. Not even Anya Kuzelnika had been able to follow the book's convoluted questions. It was an extremely long version of one of these kinds of questions that the scribe was now transcribing.

"As to what is and is not meaning — if one word is all words then are not all words linked in one meaning?"

Holding a finger up to his lips to signal continued silence, Sarabin handed Xemion a scroll of reed paper and a pencil. Xemion looked back at him, puzzled. Sarabin made a gesture to indicate that Xemion should listen to the old woman and write down what she was saying. Xemion had half a mind to resist, because even now he could see what was coming, but it was too late for that. The sooner this was over the sooner he would see Saheli again. He settled down flat on the stage and began to transcribe. After he'd written a page full of the old woman's rattling mumblings, they began to be interrupted by small, dry coughs. Xemion heard a deep voice say, "I beg. I beg. A nap now?" Xemion couldn't see where the voice was coming from, but the old woman obligingly stopped her recitation.

The scribe who was writing looked up, annoyed, but the old woman waved her hand to signal that a rest was indeed in order. She sank back just one small iota deeper into the tall stone chair and a second set of eyelids closed down over the glassy transparent ones she had been looking through till now.

In a whisper, Sarabin introduced the two scribes. The one who had been holding the cone was Ettinender. He had long, lank yellow hair. "It's hard for him to communicate. He was a singer once but the Pathans caught him and shredded his tongue." Ettinender nodded his head and tried to say something. But what came out was incomprehensible. This made him angry. Yarra, the other scribe, equally old, cocked his bulbous head jerkily in greeting.

"He can read! He can actually read," Sarabin whispered with great excitement. "Now let me see how he is at writing." He shuffled over to Xemion with the candle and used its light to peruse what Xemion had written. As he did so he read along in a muttering tone. His recitation began imperceptibly and slowly rose in volume, until by the end of the page he was almost speaking in his normal voice. Shaking his head, he looked at Xemion with long-ing. "How I envy you, young man. If I had but hands, I'd be down here every day, every moment. These hooks are good for much but not for that. I hope you realize how fortunate you are."

Xemion nodded uncertainly. How long had they been down here? It was hard to tell in the dark. Surely noon was almost upon them.

"This is a miracle," Yarra enthused, his full voice echo-ing off the stone overhead. "We have been so overworked for so long." Then, seeing that he'd awakened the old woman, he spoke more quietly. "I'm so sorry, Musea. I got so very excited here. You see, this young man has shown up and he can write!"

Musea's glassy grey eye turned toward Xemion and she lifted the hook of her nose and stared straight down over the big, bony curve and fixed him at the end of her gaze. Xemion saw something in her eyes shift and focus and shift again as though a thousand telescopes were looking through one another all at once, trying to view him. Finally, he felt the connection as she found him. She smiled, then instantly looked away. That such a smile came from such a seemingly stony face took Xemion by surprise, and he couldn't help but smile back.

"He is pretty," she croaked. She beckoned for Xemion to approach her. With the two scribes looking gleefully on, Xemion drew close to the old woman.

"Closer," Musea commanded in her scratchy voice. "Bring your face closer to me so I can feel it." Xemion did as requested and she placed her leathery old fingers on his cheeks and ran them over his brow, pausing there in the middle above his nose and then along his eyebrows and over his lips. As she did this she smiled and tears welled up in her eyes. "Yes, yes," she affirmed. "I do approve."

"I beseech a scrap of you," said that same deep voice that had spoken out before. Xemion started. The voice seemed to come from beneath the table.

"Shhh!" the old woman said. She looked down and Xemion saw her nudge a large black shadow with her foot.

"My dog," she said indulgently.

"He speaks?" Xemion asked, drawing even farther back.

"Only to beg." Sarabin spoke quietly from behind him. He lowered the candle a little. A massive triangle of black dogface was suddenly illuminated in the halo of light. The animal put out its large pink tongue and began to rapidly lick the old Thrall's unclad foot. She giggled. "Stop it! He's spell crossed," she croaked. "Aren't you, Bargest?"

Xemion could now see that the dog was oddly clad. A pink bow held a tuft of hair in place, where it hung down over one side of his head, while much of his torso was encased in a pink frilly coat with coloured buttons and tiny embroidered gorehorses. "Even, sir, if you have no scraps," the dog pleaded, having stopped licking, "I will lick your hand if you let me."

"Ignore him," whispered Sarabin.

"Bargest, be quiet," the old woman scolded. "Long ago two mages who were each other's beloveds were his first masters," she said directly to Xemion. "He was their retriever and he did such a good job they allowed him to live in their house. But Bargest kept on, let's say, 'retrieving' a lot of extra treats when his masters weren't looking. One mage decided that the way to correct this was to bind him with a spell to speak so that he could ask properly for the things he wanted. But you still didn't ask, did you Bargest? One day when her birthday cake was ruined the other mage bound a cross-spell against the first so he could only speak if he begged. That's why he always begs. But I love him anyway, don't I, Bargest?"

"I beseech you, do not stop," the animal rumbled back. He began to lick the woman's foot manically as though there were a soon-to-be exhausted sweetness there. This seemed to please her deeply. She closed her eyes and turned her face up toward the domed ceiling and soon dozed off, a look of rapture on her wizened features.

"She has magic recall," Sarabin whispered. "Early in her life she took thrall to the great classics of Elphaerean literature and read them over and over. And every day as she read, she drank from the wells of memory. As a result, she knows much of our lost Elphaerean literature by heart."

Xemion nodded, remembering the taste of those same waters on his own tongue. The memory of Saheli drinking the waters from the other well, the well of forgetfulness, flashed at him as though from the end of a long tunnel. *Soon. Soon.*

"She is the last remaining storehouse of Elphaerean literature. She has copied out fifty-seven books so far, but she is very old and no one knows how long she will last. When she first came here I am told she wrote till her wrists swelled. She wrote all day and didn't stop until she fell asleep, which, fortunately, she did with great difficulty, as she has insomnia, you see."

Xemion nodded.

"She is too weary now to scribe at all. That is why these two gentlemen are doing the scribing for her. But she has been so wakeful of late they have had no rest. She's dictating a classic of our literature that we thought we'd lost forever … and, well, we could use you, Xemion. One more scribe would be such a relief to all of us."

Ettinender nodded his bulbous head rapidly up and down to confirm this. "Ish dru," Ettinender said with some difficulty.

"So … so instead of going to the reading instruction, I would come here and write down what she says?"

"Well … yes, and perhaps during some of the other more superfluous classes, as well. You seem to be already such a well-educated fellow."

Xemion thought about it. "I will help, but right now I can almost sense the sun straight overhead. We must be very close to midday." He looked expectantly at Sarabin.

"Oh, yes, yes, yes, and I gave you my word, didn't I?"

Xemion nodded anxiously. Sarabin turned to Yarra and Ettinender. "I promised him I would get him back to the others for noon. But don't fret. I will return him to you as soon as possible."

"You must," Yarra said. "We are both ready to collapse with fatigue."

Ettinender also said something with great urgency and even a little anger. He seemed to be protesting Xemion's departure, but his speech was so garbled it was impossible for Xemion to tell for sure.

"As soon as possible, I assure you," Sarabin replied. "I have made him a promise and I must keep it."

This definitely angered Ettinender. He stood up to protest further, but when he reached his full height he let out a little cry, went limp, and dropped to the ground. There he curled into a fetal position and began to twitch and buck and let out choked staccato sounds.

"A fit!" Sarabin ran toward him. "Grab his hands," he shouted. "Restrain him. He'll push his own eyes out."

Yarra somehow managed to get hold of Ettinender's flailing hands while Sarabin did his best to restrain his feet. Ettinender was turning purple. The sinews in his neck were raised and vibrating like fishing line pulled taut, his mouth was opening and shutting, and his flaps of tongue were shuddering like convulsive ribbons in the wind of his creaking groans.

"I am going to have to go and get Mr. Stilpkin." Sarabin said, rising. "Xemion, come and hold his feet."

"But it must be midday by now, and you said—"

"I can't help that, can I? This is a matter of life and death. Surely you are here of your own will because you want to save a life!"

Right on cue, Ettinender began to buck anew. He jerked and wriggled like a worm on a hook, all the while creaking and shrieking.

"Yarra alone cannot keep him from hurting himself," Sarabin chided. "Your friend will come to no harm if you are late. But our oldest living scribe may lose his very life without your help."

"But—"

"And I will arrange a time and place for the two of

you to meet later," Sarabin cut in, "I promise it. What is her name?"

"Saheli," Xemion answered as he reluctantly took Sarabin's place holding on to Ettinender's hands. "She was one of the ones chosen by Tiri Lighthammer. I think."

"You think?"

"I couldn't see her face. She didn't turn. That's why I need—"

"Saheli, then," Sarabin cut him off impatiently. With that, he nodded to Yarra, said "as soon as possible," and hurried out. The old man's struggles continued for quite a long time as his laboured breathing turned into hoarse gasping. Yarra kept urging him "stay with us, my brother, stay with us," casting worried, tearful glances at Xemion. And for every moment of it, Xemion's feeling of panic that he would lose Saheli forever grew more and more desperate. Finally, a heavy, long-eared man arrived. He rushed forward and put a hand, which Xemion noticed was entirely green, gently on the middle of Ettinender's breast and stroked his brow. After a short while Ettinender's struggles ceased and his breathing became shallow and slow and almost imperceptible. The man with the green hand attempted to wake him, without success. He looked up sadly at Yarra and said, "I just hope he may wake one more time."

"Please wake up, Ettinender," Yarra beseeched, stroking back a lock of the man's yellow hair from his forehead.

"It won't be today, I fear," the man with the green hand lamented.

When Xemion finally emerged from underground, the sun was no longer in the sky. He was greeted by Sarabin, who was just returning. Sarabin's expression was unreadable. But his eyes didn't meet Xemion's. "I am sorry, young man. I have been unable to locate anyone at all by the name of Saheli among those who … remain."

This statement shook Xemion's whole being. Fear became cold panic in an instant and there were now goodly portions of anger accompanying it. "What do you mean those who remain?" he demanded, his voice raised.

"It has always been the strategy of the Phaer militia to spread its forces widely over the terrain. I'm afraid that the thirty-six have already been posted elsewhere."

"Take me to her then." Xemion's voice verged on outright anger.

"That is the problem. The elite forces train in a secret location, and I'm afraid they departed for it immediately after noon."

"No!"

"I'm afraid it is so."

"Where?"

"I'm afraid I am not told such things."

"But someone must know where they've gone."

"If anyone, only Veneetha Azucena herself."

5

Xemion Pleads

Veneetha Azucena crossed the ample floor space of her apartment on the top floor of an old tower at the foot of Phaerpoint and gazed out over the sea below. "But before you spoke the vow," she said, "we did ask all to declare if there were any reason of attachment or safety that should prevent them from committing at this time. We asked quite clearly and no one protested."

"But I didn't know we would be separated when I spoke that vow. I thought by speaking it I would be staying with her. My vow that I made to the woman who raised me to stay with her until she comes of age precedes my vow to you."

Veneetha was not as tall as she'd seemed upon the stage in the Panthemium conducting the vow yesterday morning. But she was still imposing. She had thrown a red robe embroidered with golden lions over her slight night garments and the contrast with her dark skin and the rich black coils of her hair seemed most becoming to Xemion even in his upset.

"Well, you *are* with her, are you not? In the sense that we are all with one another in one endeavour. In the sense that—"

"But I'm not even certain it *was* her. I have to make sure that it was her up there and that she's safe."

"How could you not be certain?" She turned from the window and walked to the middle of the room, where she stood in a beam of moonlight streaming in through a crystal dome in the ceiling. It was much like the dome that had illuminated the sunscope that Xemion used in Ilde to project the stories onto the wall.

"After we were separated, I only saw her from behind. I never saw her face."

"Surely, you recognized her in the way she moved, in the way she held herself." As if to illustrate this, she opened her arms in a lyrical gesture.

"I have to be certain. The gates to the stadium were left open when that Pathan and his kwislings came marching in. That's how we got separated in the first place. I didn't see her after that. I don't know if she might have been taken or if she forgot who she was. Maybe she got dragged out the gates—"

"How could she have forgotten who she was?" asked Sarabin, who had been waiting silently beside the doorway.

"On our journey here she had to drink from the well of forgetting."

A curious look came over Veneetha Azucena's features and she drew closer to him. "But the magic of those waters has had no real effect since before the spell fire — since Musea was a young woman."

"But it is supposed to have been bound by spoken spells by the old mages What if someone with a red hand were to initiate it?"

She looked up sharply. "Whatever can you mean?"

"Your man, Vallaine. He shook hands with us after—"

At this Azucena trilled with laughter. "Oh, surely you don't believe in those old superstitions?"

"He told me himself about middle magicians and how they are needed to initiate certain spells."

"But I'm sure he wouldn't have told you he *was* one," Sarabin said.

"He has a red hand. Isn't that supposed to mean he's a middle magician?"

"Xemion, of course not," Veneetha said. "That was never true. Some people are born with red hands, some with green hands. I assure you that Mr. Vallaine is not a so-called middle mage. That would be most unwelcome here."

"I just need to be sure that it was her."

She sighed and looked a little exasperated. "Well, can you describe her face to me? I saw the chosen ones as they left."

Xemion tried to picture Saheli's face. He'd never thought before of trying to put the magic of its facets, of its angles and elegance, into words. But her face kept turning and sliding away from him and the words that came were "she has eyes that switch from green to blue if you catch them when her mood is changing."

"Something … more immediate perhaps?"

He wanted to say that she was beautiful and that she had a look of great goodness in her eyes, but there was fear, too. But instead he said "her hair is long and black and it comes down to about here when she wears it down but she had it piled up on top for a while. She was wearing it like that yesterday. It came down but she might've put it back up again. She has high cheekbones and—"

"There were several like that."

"She was wearing a green cloak with a—"

"No, I'm afraid that won't help. When I saw them they were all dressed the same, in fatigues, for as soon as they were inducted they were quickly divested not only of their old names but of their old garments as well."

"She has a diagonal scar over her left eyebrow."

Azucena frowned, trying to remember. "I don't recall anything like that. But if her hair were down over her face, I might have missed it."

"Well then, just let me go where they are camped and—"

"Xemion, not even I may know that detail."

"No!"

"Yes, it was always that way in the Phaer Academies. They know where I am, but not I them. We keep our legions separate, so that we cannot all be caught in one trap."

Xemion persisted. "Then my friend Tharfen would know. If she met with her brother Torgee at noon she would also have seen Saheli."

"Well, there you have it then. Mr. Sarabin, please summon the quartermaster's assistant, Lirodello, and we'll find the girl and get her up here and relieve this poor fellow of his dreadful doubts." Sarabin nodded and quietly closed the door as he left.

As they awaited his return, Drathis, one of the pale, one-eyed youths whom Veneetha had rescued from the Pathans, came into the chamber through a door at the rear of the apartment and approached Xemion. He wore a black patch over his left eye, but what could be seen of the rest of his face was young and handsome. There was a delicacy to it that suggested great sensitivity. The only unusual thing was that one blue eye, which seemed never to be looking straight at anyone. Xemion kept trying to meet it as he approached but never quite felt any connection.

"Drathis," Veneetha said, frowning, "you were going to stay with the others until I returned."

Drathis shook his head. He walked straight up to Xemion, facing him.

"My, my," Veneetha said.

Drathis kept tilting and swaying his head as though he were trying to position that eye to look at Xemion directly. Finally he succeeded. And he and Xemion both smiled.

"My goodness!" Veneetha let out a burble of sandy laughter. "I don't know what's got into you, Drathis. I have never seen him greet anyone and I've certainly never seen him smile."

Drathis, still holding Xemion's gaze, reached his right hand across to Xemion's left hand. He took it and held it gently, nodding. Then, with Veneetha looking on and shaking her head with amazement, he turned and left the room as he had entered it.

"You look as stunned as I am," she said, half chortling

to Xemion, who was standing there gazing at his hand and looking troubled.

"I felt something strange when he touched my hand."

This clearly caught Veneetha Azucena's interest. "Really? Well, Xemion. You are one of the rare ones. Very few can feel that."

"What is it?"

She spoke quietly, solemnly, when she answered. "Many think that the magic our peoples once had stemmed from the Great Kone or from other lesser texts, or that all magic was originally blood magic such as that exercised across the western sea by the Necromancer of Arthenow. But some of us believe it is not the spell, it is the spellbinder, who has a natural magic. Spells just channel it. Even in the time of the spell kones, most of our people could spin a kone and get satisfactory results, but the Pathans could not at all. Drathis here has that tendency in rather larger amounts. He is, of course, innocent of any will to the spellcraft, but nevertheless the current runs in him. That is what you are sensing. That is why the Pathans took him from his home when he was four years old. Unfortunately for him, he had a full resonant voice, and that, alas, is one of their chief indicators." Xemion shook his head. "They took his eye and a piece of his brain from behind his eye and tried to keep him and it alive separately … so it could become a kind of living eye for a … living kone … of which I can hardly bare to speak this late at night."

"I'm so sorry," Xemion said, hiding the rich resonance of his own voice even more carefully than usual.

"We all are," Veneetha Azucena said. Just then Sarabin returned with Lirodello the Thrall. The last time

Xemion had seen Lirodello, his naturally comic features had seemed always on the verge of glee and humour. There was none of that in his face now. The news wasn't good. Indeed, there had been a Tharfen in the assembly at noon, but she was little more than a child. All those who were underage were taken down immediately to Vallaine's ship, the *Mammuth*, which had sailed into Phaer Bay just this morning. Vallaine was voyaging to the continent with a hold full of precious gems, in search of weaponry and supplies, and would drop the young ones off on the way. He is not due back for at least six weeks.

"But you saw my friend, Saheli, when we were standing in the crowd yesterday morning," Xemion said urgently to Lirodello. "She was the one with dark black hair and a diagonal scar over her left eyebrow?"

"I do wish I could confirm that for you," the lachrymose Lirodello said with a tip of his flat hat. "But I confess I had eyes for only one girl there: Vortasa." He looked at Azucena with large doleful eyes when he said this. "Alas, she held onto her sword harder than she held onto me and so she and her two sisters have been sent away. I found her and lost her all in the same day."

"Surely you would remember my friend," Xemion persisted. "She has such long, dark hair and—"

"Xemion," Sarabin interrupted "You obviously know nothing of what it's like when a Thrall finds his—"

"I see nothing else," Lirodello sighed, cupping his hands together in prayerful union.

"Well, the two of you have much in common," Veneetha said, gazing sympathetically at Xemion. "But as you see, Xemion, I can bring your slightly unreasonable dread no immediate relief. But I can tell you this — they will be sending a messenger from the camp in three weeks in order to summon me to the celebration of second skin. I will make you a deal. At that time, even if I have to breach protocol, provided of course you have done your service to us here, I will discover if there is one such as you describe with the scar over the left eye. And then you may at least proceed here with more ease about her safety to shore you up in your labours."

"I can't wait three weeks."

"You will need to, Xemion. In any case, you know it's her."

Xemion glared. "No, I don't. I hope it's her. I suspect it's her. But …" He couldn't say *but I have dreamed a thousand times that she would be taken from me*. He couldn't say *I feared from the very moment I saw her that I would lose her*. He could only say, "I need to know today that she is safe. And if she's not safe, then—"

"Then what?" Veneetha was beginning to get annoyed. "You will break your very solemn vow and attempt to leave us so that you can scour the wilderness to find her with your little practice sword and slay whatever dragon she may be captive to?"

Xemion looked down at the painted sword, which still hung in the leather scabbard at his side. But there was no time for embarrassment. "I believe she is my warrior beloved," he blurted out.

"Ha!" Veneetha Azucena's laughter trilled again. "Is this news to anyone?" She turned around and looked with amusement at Sarabin and Lirodello. "Well, Xemion, if you know about the tradition of warrior beloveds then you must know about the ordeal of not knowing."

"I know there are ordeals … in stories."

"Well, this is more than a story. This is the real thing. So don't take this impending ordeal as a sign against your feeling of being her beloved. Rejoice that it is more likely proof of it, for you have begun your ordeal of not knowing."

"But—"

"But what? It's classic. You can't get to her. Not tonight. Not tomorrow."

"But—"

"Feel in your heart and you know it's her. Who else would it be?"

"I need to see her face."

"You need faith."

"I need proof."

"Well, then … your sanest, not to mention most honourable, course is to stay here as you are called and pledged to do. With waiting here you will get your surety in three weeks."

"Three weeks of not knowing?"

"Yes. Just put aside your ideal of the standard form of knightliness. This service you give unto the Phaer people will far outlast the deeds any mere knight might ever unleash on fields of glory. By taking this hard course you gain your surety in three weeks, and in your ordeal, let's say you perform a great deed for the Phaer culture forever."

"I don't think I could stand it."

"I think you can and you will and you must." Veneetha Azucena did her best to hide her irritation, but she stared at him firmly. "That's without reminding you that you have made a vow to us and are bonded to us. I could, therefore, put you in chains and make you do it, but I would not have it that way. So instead I'll say that I promise you your long days of scribing will not go unrewarded. Someday if you come to me and you require some favour, if it is possibly within my power I will grant it."

"But if there are long days of scribing, when will I even receive instruction in the sword?"

Here she paused and looked at Sarabin questioningly. The old man nodded very slightly.

"The problem is this, Xemion," he said. "We don't know how it will fare with Ettinender. We do know that he will be doing no further scribing in the near future and that Yarra cannot possibly keep up with the dictation all by himself. And I'm sure you would not have us every day lose more and more of our literature."

"But she couldn't be dictating all day long, surely? Even if I just attended the instructions when she was resting—"

"Unfortunately, there is a problem with that approach," Sarabin said sorrowfully. "You see, there are those among the instructors here who might have no real objection to relics of the spellwork. But if any of them is likely to object to an old woman who recites from a memory enabled by the spell waters, or a dog who is enabled by some kind of spell to speak aloud, that person would be our most important instructor, Tiri Lighthammer."

"No one despises the spellcraft more than Lighthammer," Veneetha Azucena interjected.

"And rightly so," Sarabin continued. "But, when

it comes to a chance of recovering so much of our lost literature—"

"We can't be such purists as he," Veneetha Azucena finished. "We've made a compromise. We've let the old woman keep the dog, without which she says she might die of loneliness. And we can't take the chance that Lighthammer would intervene and stop it. And we certainly can't afford to lose him. So he simply cannot know about this. So, I'm afraid we cannot have you going in and out of his instructions because the old man is canny and he will know something is up."

"No!" Xemion's heart was beating terribly fast.

"We will have to say that you have an illness. That you are under quarantine," Veneetha Azucena said, eying him with great sympathy but firmness.

"No!"

"I'm afraid so," said Sarabin.

"I won't do it."

"You will," Azucena said firmly.

"It is wrong that it happened this way. No one would have chosen for us to be parted in this manner."

"It wouldn't be an ordeal if you chose it," Sarabin said, punctuating his remark with a little click of his hooks.

"If you really believe that she is your warrior beloved," Veneetha Azucena said, lifting a warm hand to Xemion's shoulder, "my advice to you is that you must love your ordeal as you bear it because ultimately it is part of what brings you back to her. You cannot get to her, except by going through this pain. So love it for that."

Lirodello lead Xemion through the darkening streets of Ulde to his new quarters. Xemion's disappointment and anger had him on the urge of hostility, but Lirodello was intent on comforting him.

"I want you to know, brother, that you are not alone in this. I only met my Vortasa a day ago. Our eyes only met briefly but in that instant she and I were bound together for all of time. Vortasa. Vortasa." He did a little spin on one foot. "Did you not see her? There were three sisters, huge like battle Thralls. With shoulders like oxen and arms like oak branches, but lovely; lovely, my friend, as life itself."

Along with everything else, Xemion was now feeling slightly embarrassed. "And now just as quickly she is gone and like you I know not when I will see her next," Lirodello continued, choking back a sob. "Have you not felt it, too, my brother?" Lirodello beseeched him, touching his arm gently. "Have you not felt it, that when the girl goes, she pulls the very heart thread with her, unravelling it over great distance till one's heart is thin, stretched empty but still utterly and forever attached?"

Xemion nodded, turning slightly to remove Lirodello's hand from his arm. Lirodello smiled up one side of his face. "We are brothers in this, my brother. Brothers in longing. Brothers in separation." It was getting darker. Seabirds were shrieking overhead and the salt breeze was drifting in steadily through the circuitous streets. Xemion sighed with despair as they approached his new residence. Most of those who were to remain in Ulde had been housed in the series of barracks near the stadium where Xemion had spent his first night. This new residence was on the third floor of an old marble tenement four streets over. "I want you to know that I already feel a strong bond with you," Lirodello said, "and though you may not have your beloved, you do at least have my friendship during this time." And with that he tipped his flat hat and swept it down in a bow. Standing back up, he stretched his hand out. Xemion reluctantly took the thin grey appendage and shook it, feeling a surprising strength there.

6

Quill and Blade, Blade and Quill

It was true: Xemion had an ordeal to go through. But not all of it would be faced alone. The whole colony had very difficult times ahead. But no one knew that yet. Xemion showed up obediently the next morning at the underdome, and with Yarra holding the cone up to the old woman's mouth, he scribed for twelve hours straight. When he emerged, it was nighttime already. He could hear from the next neighbourhood the sounds of carousing kitchen Thralls, celebrating the first day of their service. They sounded very jolly, and Xemion almost wished he could join them, but he was officially in quarantine, an almost secret resident of Ulde, and he had no choice but to make his way back to his solitary quarters alone. Later, Sarabin came by with his supper and thanked him and complimented him on the strength of his commitment to his vow. But Xemion knew the vow had nothing to do with it. He would break it in an instant if he knew where to look, how to find her.

The next day moved even more agonizingly slowly. And the next slower still. He felt like going down into the underdome and bellowing and cursing and kicking the papers and pens about. Once, while Musea napped, he actually did throw his quill pen. But it was a futile gesture. Being but a feather, it hardly flew any distance before twirling down to the floor. Suddenly there was a dark flash that caused Xemion to draw back instinctively. In an instant the dog, Bargest, had crossed the floor, scooped up the quill in his massive mouth, and brought it humbly to Xemion, setting it down at his feet and looking up at him expectantly, following every move of his hand.

Recovering from his surprise, Xemion picked up the feather, said a sullen "good boy," and gave the dog a biscuit he had brought with him for breakfast. The dog gobbled it down with one quick tilt of his head and waited at Xemion's feet.

Now that he could see him properly, Xemion realized the dog was much bigger than he had thought. The face was a long, wolfish triangle and the lips, when lifted in supplication, revealed long, full incisors. His jaws were massive and his paws huge — easily as big as Xemion's hands. When it became clear to the dog that no more biscuits would be offered, he slid through the shadows back to Musea's feet. Soon after that, Musea awoke and Xemion and Yarra went wearily back to work.

There was never any rest from his thoughts of Saheli and where she might be and whom she might be with. And when such thoughts inevitably brought him back to Tharfen and Montither, and particularly what Montither had done to him, he seethed with rage and a growing hatred that filled his head with homicidal visions. Still, Xemion laboured away, day after day, until his wrists were sore with the writing and his neck ached and his back hurt. He did his best to take Veneetha's advice and try to love this ordeal, but he couldn't help but despise it, and that only made it worse.

Musea would often have recited all night long had it not been for Bargest. The dog seemed to supervise the old Thrall. For when her voice grew so faint she could barely be heard at all, and yet she still continued trying to tell her tale, the dog would lick her toes and make her giggle, or start to beg for water or meat and so distract her long enough for her to get off the wheel of narration and realize she needed to rest.

"My lady, I beseech, cease before my heart bursts. I beg you." As always, the dog adopted the most miserable posture possible when he begged. He flattened his long pointed chin and cask-sized chest to the floor, kneeling down with his tail tucked between his back legs and whining pitifully in a high puppy voice that was disgraceful to hear. "Please, I beg you." Sometimes when Musea fell into a brief slumber the beast would transfer his fascination to Xemion, staring at him with infinite longing in his eyes, and no matter how Xemion glared back, he would not stop.

During the second week, Musea began to recite from the works of the great Elphaerean poet Huzzuh. Many of these poems left Xemion unmoved. They were complex, confusing, and far too full of rhymes. But when she got to his crowning achievement, the book wherein he made his breakthrough into the liberty and glory of free verse, there were piercing poems that so expressed the way Xemion felt that he almost wept. And when he lay sleeplessly in his bed that night he found that he remembered them perfectly. Indeed, having them play over and over in his head gave him some of the only moments of relief that he would experience, not only during this ordeal but in the many ordeals ahead.

The next week Musea moved on to a famous book about military strategy and then to an advanced manual on swordsmanship. Xemion took heart at this fortunate turn of events and began to practice secretly with his painted sword each night, glad once again that he had not discarded it as Vallaine had advised. Because he was living on the third floor of a house in an unpopulated neighbourhood of Ulde, and because he had no access to any outdoor space, he was forced to practise out on the remains of an extended balcony that jutted out dangerously from the side of the building. The floor was slanted and cracked and the railings had fallen off long ago, but it was the only place with enough room to perform some of the extended movements such as the star's thrust. Because he only ever had time to practise after dark, and because the silver paint he had used on the sword was made from the bodies of luminous sea urchins, the sword lit up, glowing brightly in the night. Unbeknownst to Xemion, the motions of his sword work — the diagonals, the circles, ellipses, waves, and points of it — shone like luminous green phantasms of an unknown alphabet to the excited eyes of the many runaway Thrall children who lived secretly nearby. They soon grew so fascinated by the light that they began to track him through the street as he walked to and from the underdome, and sometimes, especially when he returned home after dark, he would hear the little ones whispering, "Look! Look, the shining sword," as they scurried from shadow to shadow, following him along.

After a few nights of this, when it seemed their number might well be increasing, he decided to move his sword practice elsewhere. Hiding the painted sword under his cloak, Xemion made his way to Uldestack, the second of the two peninsulas that curved inward, enclosing Phaer Bay. This part of Ulde was usually dark and uninhabited at night. Uldestack, the towering volcano-shaped chimney at the end, was the very landmark that had helped Xemion and Saheli find their way into the city when they were lost. It had been built by a long-ago race of Nains when the city of Ulde had been one of the major centres for metallurgy in the known world. All around the wide diameter of the chimney's base were ventilation holes through which the sea winds roared in high season, capable of stoking so many kiln fires at once that the glow from them could be seen by ships miles out at sea.

Tonight, though, it was almost invisible in the dark and the fog. Xemion stopped in the pitch-blackness. He could hear the waves crashing on the cliffs below, and the call of a tern. Finally, he reached into his cloak and drew forth the practice sword. He had only executed the first few glowing sequences of his new regimen, however, when he heard a terrible screeching sound coming from the direction of the stack. There was a hideous supernatural quality to the sound, as though some demonic creature were crying up from underground in holy torment. Sheathing the sword, he ran closer. The fog was still dense but he could see, high above him, a barely flickering glow at the top of the stack. Then a faint echo of someone chanting reached his ears. He moved closer to distinguish the words:

> *Hard, hard*
> *As Earth is hard.*
> *Hard as luck,*
> *Seared and charred.*
> *Hard in death*
> *And hard in birth.*
> *Out of my mettle make this metal*
> *Hard, hard.*

The voice was unmistakably that of Glittervein, the Nain. And that flickering glow at the top of the stack was no doubt the kiln fire far below. And that hideous screeching, which now arose anew, was clearly the sound of Glittervein's machinery inside the smithy making swords for tomorrow. Still, the combination of the screeching and the chanting was deeply unnerving.

> *Hard, hard*
> *As my life is hard.*
> *Hard as rock*
> *As my heart is hard.*
> *Hard as my bones*
> *Make this shard.*
> *Of my mettle make this metal*
> *Hard, so hard.*

Finally, the sounds ended and there came a loud hiss as though a screaming jet of steam had burst from a vent in the Earth. That was Glittervein quenching the blade. Lirodello had told Xemion the stories about Glittervein — that he had learned to harness the crackling underearth fire to heat his forge. But the smithy must be below ground level because all was dark in the workshop. Xemion drew close to a window and peered in. He had to duck down quickly, for just then the sound of footsteps came up a stairway from underground, a door opened, ushering a rush of light inward, and Glittervein and the bulky, blind Thralleen stepped into the workshop.

"Well, wasn't that poetic?" he heard Glittervein say sarcastically in a slightly slurred voice. Xemion peered in as the Nain closed the great stone door at the top of the stairs. He inserted a big black key into the lock and turned it. Then, after scanning the shop for any observers, he pulled a brick from the side of his kiln, placed the key in a space inside it, and slid the brick back into place. "Very satisfying," he slurred. He took a wineskin, which he wore on a long string about his neck, and began to quaff deeply. After a few good gulps, Glittervein tapped the Thrall on her left shoulder to signal that her work was done. At first she didn't react, so he stood up on his chair and shoved her quite hard. "Go away!" he bellowed, teetering slightly on his perch. She nodded and groped her way toward a chamber on the other side of the smithy. Mumbling to himself bitterly, Glittervein made his way over to a small table only a few feet away from the glass through which Xemion covertly observed him.

Glittervein, like all Nains, was short and broad-shouldered, but he had particular thick arms and the sinews in them rippled with his every movement. One side of his long auburn hair flowed down over the side of his face while the other side was flung back over his shoulder, where it coiled down his back almost to his waist.

He removed a small pot of ink, a sheet of paper, and a quill pen from a drawer and set them on the table in front of him. For a second Xemion thought the Nain must be able to read, but when he did finally place the quill tip to the paper it was obvious that he was drawing something on it. Xemion strained to get a better look.

Just then Glittervein lifted his head and looked right at Xemion. Xemion felt the gaze lock into him and grab hold of him and then it seemed to go right *through* him. Frozen with fear, Xemion realized that Glittervein couldn't see him and was actually staring at his own reflection in the window glass. Xemion remained motionless, staring right into the unknowing right eye of the Nain. The right side of Glittervein's face had very delicate features, but as Xemion watched, the Nain, who was deep in thought, flung back his hair and turned the other side of his face toward the glass. Xemion had already heard from Lirodello that the Nain's face had been severely burnt in a kiln fire accident, but he was unprepared for how terribly damaged it was. It was as though someone had taken a wax image of a face, scorched it, and then smeared it over to one side. It was a scarry purple colour, its surface evenly pitted like rapidly boiling porridge.

Glittervein shook his head at his reflection and then proceeded to comb the long auburn hair back over his disfigurement, all the while gazing not only into his own eyes but also those of his silent observer.

Finally he returned to his picture. Xemion squinted to better see what the Nain was drawing. It appeared to be a crude representation of crossed swords. When Glittervein finished, he folded the note into a tiny square. After staggering to the back of the shop, he returned with a pigeon. Xemion watched as the Nain tied the note to the pigeon's leg, opened a south-facing window, and released it into the night. He stood, watching it as it flew out over the sea. Having done this, a smile of what looked to be satisfaction crossed his face. He sat down, took another long quaff from his wineskin, and rubbed his hands together so rapidly he might have been trying to start a little fire in his palms.

Just then Xemion heard a rustling sound behind him. Turning quickly, he saw through the thinning fog that he was surrounded by a ring of wide-open eyes, all low to the ground and at various heights, and all staring at him most intently. He didn't have time to think. He reached into his cloak and drew out the practice sword and held it high. It was at its full luminosity now; its glow was so strong it illuminated his hand, his arm, and the grimacing war mask of his face. Emitting his fiercest cry, Xemion ran between two of the sets of eyes, slashing the greenish shine of the blade to and fro. Once he was past, he dashed on as fast as his legs would carry him down the peninsula. As he ran, he could clearly hear the enchanted cry that rose up and followed him: "He is master, he is Lord. Hail, hail the shining sword."

7

A Lack of Appropriate Clothing

Often during his ordeal of waiting and not knowing, Xemion doubted so strongly that it had been Saheli he'd seen up at the front of the Panthemium that it was almost as though she had been confirmed missing. Other times, like now, as the third week ended, he was almost positive that it had been her. Either way, he wouldn't have to wait much longer for certainty. Soon, Veneetha Azucena would go to the camp, and when she returned she would bring word and he would finally know for sure.

Before she could depart, however, there was a sudden shift in the weather. It got quite cold as the wind came in off the northern sea, and Yarra began to mumble about a long and early winter to come. In the midst of this, the community was hit with an outbreak of influenza. It struck quick and hard, disabling many. Most began to recover toward the end of the week, but Ettinender and two others never recovered. These were the first casualties of the rebellion at Ulde.

Then, just a day before her planned departure, Veneetha caught the sickness, and it affected her so quickly and severely that she was unable to go. Xemion only learned after the fact that Tiri Lighthammer had gone instead. That next week was one of the most maddening and painful of Xemion's life, but somehow he managed to continue his scribing duties and his not-so-secret sword practice at night. Sarabin assured him that Vallaine and his ship, the *Mammuth*, were expected back in Ulde imminently and would likely be delivering not only a boatload of supplies for the kitchens but the returning Tiri Lighthammer. Veneetha promised Xemion from her sick bed she would personally ask him about a girl with a scar over one eye.

Days later there came a severe ice storm. When the denizens of Ulde arose the next morning, they looked up to see a conglomeration of floating spell-crossed houses frozen together above the city, all encased in and joined by a thick coat of glittering ice that extended from the houses on the ground to others quite high up, which were sparkling in the sky. The extreme cold quickly made it apparent to all that there was a lack of appropriate clothing in Ulde. Most of the recruits had fled their homes with little more than the clothing on their backs. Now, as winter came on, many of them would be in danger of freezing to death if appropriate measures were not taken. Veneetha Azucena generously donated numerous extra items from her wardrobe and insisted that even the old men's military garb carefully obtained by its owners for special ceremonial purposes be lent out to the shivering recruits. But there still wasn't enough warm clothing to go around, and while a team of finder Thralls scoured the uninhabited buildings of the city in search of anything that might be turned into clothing, many of the others were forced to remain indoors.

Fortunately, the weather warmed up again and there was a thaw. As a result, the houses, no longer held aloft by either the ice or the fifty-year-old spell cross that had lifted them, began to fall, some of the rubble landing on the isolated street where Xemion lodged. A crew of thick-chested Nains, including Tomtenisse Doombeard and his nonviolent brother Belphegor, came with wheelbarrows and picks and shovels and began carrying off the rubble. Such labours were always closely supervised by Glittervein. The houses had originated in the Era of Common Magic and often contained still-working spellcrafted devices. As Provost, he was responsible for making sure they were properly incinerated. He did his best to make sure not one of them missed his attention.

Xemion, as usual, did not participate in these labours, but one day when Musea fell into a deep sleep he went home early and was spotted by Glittervein. Ever since the night at Uldestack, he had done his best to avoid the Nain, but now that Glittervein had seen him and called out to him, he had no choice but to remain still as he stalked over. The wind was coming in cold again, whipping the long curls away from Glittervein's face. He turned the dis-figured side toward Xemion and spoke sharply: "Who are you? I don't remember seeing you at the gate on the first day. I personally inspected everyone who came in and I know a face forever. And I don't know yours."

"I came in from the eastern side of Ulde," Xemion

answered, a little nervously. Glittervein's pupils shrunk to pinpoints. "I knew nothing of this." His voice deepened by an octave. "You should have come in by the western gate and been screened and searched like everyone else."

"I couldn't get around the outside of the wall," Xemion answered.

"Well, how is anyone to know whether or not you brought in some spellworks?"

"I didn't," Xemion answered, a little offended.

"And how is anyone to know whether you are a spy, or a kwisling, or—"

Xemion's answer, tinged as it was with insolence, brought out the "high and mighty" quality of his voice. "I believe Mr. Sarabin would speak on my behalf."

Glittervein shook his head and just stood there for a long time staring at Xemion. "We'll see," he said finally, before stalking off.

A week later, a blizzard struck, burying the whole of the Phaer Isle in snow. The drifts were so deep in Ulde that the streets were impassable and there quickly began to be a shortage of firewood and coal. Vallaine still had not returned, and the food supply was definitely dwindling. It was so low, in fact, that as soon as there came a thaw several more of the newly formed brigades, many wearing rags on their feet for warmth, were sent to camps in the mountains that had been previously provisioned enough for there to be time to teach the recruits to forage and hunt. This would relieve pressure on the situation in Ulde.

And Lighthammer had still not returned — nor would he until spring. All the mountain passes were blocked by ice. For the rest of the winter travel on the Isle would be impossible. But no one knew that yet. Like Xemion, everyone waited moment-by-moment, hungry and cold, expecting imminent relief. They hoped for another thaw or a warm spell, but none ever came, only another outbreak of influenza. And because everybody was spending so much time indoors, quite a number more died. They might've all died had Lirodello not found in a secret cellar beneath the kitchen cellar vast storehouses of dried and pickled fish, which must have dated from half a century ago. There was also an assortment of old musical instruments and sacks containing multicoloured pellets, which, when thrown to the ground, could explode into small grey dinners. If Tiri Lighthammer had discovered this, he would have had them all destroyed, for they were surely the products of long-ago spellcraft. But Tiri Lighthammer was not here, and there was nothing else to eat, so the whole colony fell upon this food like locusts on a field. There was joy in the taste and eating of it, but in the end it had very little nutrition and some of those who ate a lot of it came down with a strange multi-coloured pox that left their faces pitted ever after.

Xemion wasn't alone in his longing and uncertainty. With the departure of almost all of the Thralleens to different base camps, there was hardly a kitchen Thrall who was not stricken with the absence of his true love. Lirodello was particularly affected. That same face that had seemed born and shaped for humour was now frozen in a sorrowful mask, and his wide, stricken eyes tended to fasten on inanimate objects as he stood, staring and tragic, shivering in the streets. Nevertheless, as one of the few people that Xemion had any contact with, he took care to deliver on his vow of eternal friendship, doing his best to rarely leave Xemion alone. For Xemion, he was one of the only sources of information, so he bore his chatter and yearnings, his lyric exclamations, and his long rolling laments for the love of Vortasa as best he could.

The winter solstice came and went, and all the while the severity of the weather increased. There was still very little warm clothing and what there was had to be traded back and forth among the outside workers while the rest huddled en masse in smoky rooms using whatever they could find for firewood, including the very desks and chairs intended for their studies.

In general, though, Xemion suffered less from the cold and hunger than most of the others. Because of its depth in the Earth, the underdome was much easier to heat than the surface rooms. He didn't know it, but often when even the kitchen Thralls went hungry, Sarabin saw to it that Xemion ate well. Sarabin needed to keep him healthy for the sake of literature.

In all those frigid days that became weeks and then months, the ache of not having her, the ache of not knowing if she was safe, was unrelenting. He kept telling himself that he wouldn't have wanted to dull the pain of it, because that would dishonour the full depth and intent of his devotion to her. So he bore it. The worst of it, though, came near the end of winter when the possibility of an actual spring was just beginning to fill the air and Xemion was allowing himself to hope. That was when

Musea began to dictate an old text detailing the day-to-day life of the ancient Elphaereans. She was reciting a passage about the ways of teaching in the ancient military academies, and when she got to a part about the practices used to integrate and harden those special ones chosen for the elite forces, she said this: "And it was always the practice then as now for both male and female to take part in all gymnastic events naked."

Nothing in life had ever so utterly undone Xemion's composure as did this piece of news. It sent a great jolt of cold alarm through every branch of his being right to his fingertips and the roots of his hair. "No!" he exclaimed.

It was one of those rare times when Musea actually stopped reciting and waited.

"Yes, yes, it is so," she said at last.

In truth he had never even thought of Saheli naked, but now that he had, that thought was accompanied by the next thought: *Torgee would see her naked.* This thought froze his blood in mid-pulse and he felt like vomiting. It was so huge a feeling that he had to struggle to push it back down inside. And then his only hope was that the scribing would continue as long as possible that day, thereby delaying his mind from veering back to the terrible cliffs of that thought.

He paid dearly for it when work was over. It rose up in him with a fury, and despite the cold he went out onto the balcony to practise his sword work. His luminous thrusts that night were especially savage — and therefore that much more thrilling to the wide-eyed Thrall children nearby who had by now learned to keep quiet. They watched the shining sword flash back and forth as

Xemion's mind brimmed over with jealousy, bitterness at the injustice, deaths he'd rather die than go on living, fights with Torgee he'd like to have, the torture and death of Montither, the burning of all Elphaerean literature, the disgrace of Tharfen, the dragging down of the sun into the abyss …

Later, when he put the sword aside and lay down on his straw pallet, the images kept coming at him like vultures darting about in the frailness of his remaining sanity, waiting for it to die. He couldn't sleep, not that night nor the next.

8

Second Skin

There was the sound of a shrill whistle. "Cut! Cut!" Ever since she'd arrived in the camp for special training, the one they called Zero had been spending many hours a day improving her accuracy by chopping off the heads of straw men. Sometimes her sword would find the narrow slit between their helmets and their body armour and sometimes it wouldn't. Sometimes she hesitated.

The whistle sounded again. "Cut."

Day after day Zero struck on command and with each successful blow one of the assistants would flip the straw head back into place and secure it for the next attack.

"Do not hesitate. Hesitation is defeat. Strike. Now."

The only alternative to the tedium of decapitating straw men was the monotony of exercise: trekking up the tall stairs of the turret two at a time and then trotting back down many times a day, all through winter. The weighted bags she lifted over and over reshaped her arms, made her shoulder muscles strong. The weird focusing routines, the complex sword patterns she was learning, knit new neural networks in her brain, and, once in place, it was as though they had been there a thousand years, deeply delved. She fell into them easily and fluently. Lighthammer, unperturbed by his long unintended stay in the camp, continued to be impressed with her. Aside from her martial abilities she possessed clear leadership potential. There was hardly a Thrall or Freeman among the recruits who did not look to her to set the standard in whatever challenge or task he put them to. He himself could not help but admire her, but knew she was as yet untested.

"Cut, cut, Zero."

For that reason he had her eating vast amounts of meat and drinking ale and slaying straw men. This often left her exhausted, but rarely miserable. She loved the rigorous physical training. She loved to climb, to slither through mud, to duck mock arrows, to make the same quick thrust a thousand times a day. She loved to practice the various kicks, the sudden lunges with the fist or the open hand designed to kill or maim. She grew skillful with a small hidden rapier. She knew how to slam the hilt of her sword against the side of a helmeted head so hard it could cause death or immediate unconsciousness. Such skills, as Lighthammer so approvingly put it, had the potential to "double or triple her casualty count." She loved the quickness of mind in sword work, the utter focus. It was like finding some extra missing piece of oneself.

Like most of those who had come to the camp as raw adolescent dreamers five months earlier, Zero was now much larger, stronger, and much more attuned to her fellow trainees. They were all "one scowl," "one muscle" as Lighthammer proclaimed, when he was not insulting them. But it was not just physical strength. Even when the competition amongst them was fierce and nasty she was courteous and kind in victory, always offering her opponents a hand up if she defeated them. Only the large one they called Stone despised her. His distaste was obvious in the expression on his face anytime he encountered her. And with every increase in the esteem with which others beheld her, he boiled and seethed more. Most days, as Lighthammer berated him for his anger, as the others avoided or even openly mocked him, and most of all as Zero advanced through the ranks, he hardly knew what to do with all his hate.

Lighthammer waited until spring was nearly upon them before he set Stone against Zero in a match. It wasn't long, though, before Stone lost his temper and began to hack at her wildly. She easily deflected his blows, but when Lighthammer blew his whistle and shouted at Stone to stop, he ignored the order and kept furiously hacking and hewing at her as though he wanted to kill her.

The whistle shrieked even louder. "You will stop immediately, or I will instruct her to do her worst to you," Lighthammer shouted. But to no avail. It only seemed to fuel Stone's frenzied onslaught. "Take him out then," he yelled to Zero. There were numerous gaps in Stone's defence and Lighthammer knew the girl was quite capable of finding an opening and ending the attack with one quick thrust, but she resisted. This time Lighthammer's whistle blowing was augmented by the furious stomping of one foot. "Take him out, now!" he bellowed, but she just

SECOND KISS

continued deflecting his blows. Suddenly Lighthammer
yanked his own sword out and, before Stone could even
gasp, his sword was struck from his hands. Lighthammer
backed him up against a wall, the point of his blade pressing into his thick neck at the exact point where Xemion's
painted sword had once rested.

"You are no longer with us. Take back your old name
and your old ways. The mountain passes are now clear of
snow. Just in time for you to leave us. Take your weapons and be out of this encampment before sundown," he
ordered in a quiet voice, his face livid with rage.

When he was gone, Lighthammer turned on Zero,
enraged. "Why did you disobey my direct order?" he
bellowed.

She hung her head. "I'm sorry, Tiri Lighthammer,"
she said, visibly chastened. "I ... I was waiting for the
right opportunity."

"I did not order you to wait for an opportunity."

"You ... you told me to take him out. But I would've
had to wound him severely to take him out in that
moment. And that seemed like it would be a waste."

"You are a waste. A waste of talent."

"I knew if I waited just a little longer he would leave
himself so open I could disarm him."

Lighthammer's only answer to this was to cough and
spit, quite voluminously, at her feet. After that, he set
out to test her. He instructed his assistant, Ingothelm, a
brawny youth from the northwest part of the island, to
begin stalking and ambushing her. Three times Ingothelm
managed to come in close and quick enough to rest the
edge of his cold blade upon her neck and say "You're

slain!" The fourth time he might have lost his own head if he hadn't been wearing a collar of mail, for Zero blocked, thrust, and slashed through his ambush with speed and precision that was startling.

As angry as the constant attacks made her, she could see they were working. Her response time was getting better and better, her attacks more and more automatic. Come the spring equinox when they would all return to Ulde to compete in the first Phaer Tourney in fifty years, there wouldn't be a shred of hesitation or mercy left in her. And that was good, because, just as in ancient times, the Tourney would be a fight "by all means." The vow of alliance would be suspended, the weapons would be real, and the combat would be intense and conceivably even deadly. *And then,* thought Zero, with increasing determination, *I will fight honourably but fiercely, and I will win.*

The only thing that made her question the degree of ruthlessness she would need to achieve this goal was her feeling for the three Thrall sisters — now known by their warrior names: Asnina, Atathu, and Imalgha — whose quarters she still shared. Not only did they each consistently maintain overall scores just as high as hers in the various challenges and bouts Lighthammer set for them, but they had become her best friends. If it came to it, she wondered, could she muster enough gall to defeat one or all of them?

They were, after all, her sisters in arms. Together, when they had any spare time, they did all the things that young Phaer women had always done. They sang the old songs, arm-wrestled, put war paint on, and, increasingly, traded tales of romantic gossip. The Thrall sisters thought themselves glamorous and did their best to bring out this quality in Zero. Their heads were full of rumour and speculation about whom Veneetha Azucena's beloved might be and who among the other recruits was smitten with whom. Sometimes, they would tease Zero that she was smitten with the recruit named Fargold. He had a long, elegant nose and his accent was a little like hers, and he seemed to always be staring at her. But Zero only shook her head and smiled. Once they asked her if she had ever kissed him, and she answered quickly, "No."

"Have you ever kissed anyone — on the lips?" Imalgha, the eldest sister, asked.

Zero thought about it a moment. "No" was the somewhat exasperated answer.

"But why not?" Imalgha persisted. "Kissing is delicious. When I get back to Ulde I'm going to kiss that little Lirodello's lips till I make him squeal."

Zero clearly found all this quite embarrassing, but she answered despite her red face. "I would only kiss the person I know for certain is my beloved."

This caused a strange pain in her heart. She felt it very rarely now. But when it came she knew what to do about it. She waited until she was alone and then she reached under the bed where she kept her staff and drew out the other thing she kept there — the little black bottle. There was only a little liquid left in the bottom. She no longer remembered where she had found it, but she certainly remembered its effect. Seeing how little was left, she hesitated. Maybe she should save it. She almost put it back under the bed but then she heard for the first time in a long time a fragment of a strange backward sounding melody running through her mind. She hated that melody. She removed the cork, tilted the bottle to her full lips, and took the last soothing sip.

9

Nonsense and Riddles

On the third day of his insomnia, when Yarra was absent due to a cold, Musea, who usually sat back in her stone chair with both eyes rolled back as she spoke, greeted him with a full-on stare and a big smile. Xemion was not in a very good mood but he returned the smile politely. He prepared a quill, and since Yarra wasn't there to hold the cone, he positioned himself as near as possible to the old Thrall so that he would not miss any of her words. But this particular afternoon she did not begin to speak. Instead she continued to stare at him, a small glint of mischief clearly visible in her huge Thrall eyes.

"When shall we begin to begin?" he asked somewhat tentatively, a little uncomfortable with that strange look.

"I don't know … when?" the crackly old voice asked.

Xemion didn't quite know what to make of this. His brow furrowed in confusion.

"Well?" she persisted.

"What do you mean, 'well'?" Xemion asked in return.

"Well, aren't you going to tell me the answer to your riddle?"

"My riddle?"

"You know, the one you just asked about when we'll begin to begin."

"Oh!" Xemion mustered a laugh. "That wasn't a riddle. That was a question. I was just asking you when you were going to begin dictating."

A look of disappointment crossed the old Thrall's face. "Oh, and I suddenly had such an appetite for a riddle."

"Sorry," Xemion offered respectfully.

"But now I *must* have a riddle. Do you know a good riddle?"

Xemion thought for a moment. "I can only think of one riddle," he said, "but I only know the question part of it … not the answer."

"Well ask me. Maybe I'll know."

Xemion hesitated before proceeding to recite the riddle that had been posed by the little locket library on the night he and Saheli had fled from Ilde:

> *Who'll be gouged,*
> *And who'll be gored*
> *By the sword*
> *Within the sword?*
> *Will its power*
> *Be ignored?*
> *O, who will wield*
> *The paper sword?*

Oh, that's so easy," the old woman chortled. But then she remained silent, teasingly.

"Well, what's the answer?" Xemion asked, though he wasn't sure now if he really wanted to know.

"Spell the word *sword*," she said eagerly, rubbing her ancient hands together. "You'll love this."

Xemion obliged. "S-W-O-R-D."

"Now just take off that first *s* and what's left?"

"W-O-R-D," Xemion replied.

"And what does that spell?" she asked, the glint of mirth threatening to explode at any moment in her eyes.

"Word," he confirmed. She laughed out loud and Xemion shuddered. An almost superstitious chill flickered through him and he remembered again that feeling of being mocked he'd experienced when he'd first heard the riddle.

"The word *word* is inside the word *sword*, you see? The word is the sword inside the sword." Xemion nodded, frowning. "Words can cut. Words can pierce," she added, raising her eyebrows.

"But what is the paper sword then?" he asked.

"I was just getting to that." She cackled again with true delight. "Spell it, too."

Frowning, Xemion began. "P-A-P-E-R-S—"

"Stop!" she ordered him. Xemion halted, and Bargest looked up from his mistress's feet, alarmed by the sharpness of her tone.

"Now, what have you spelled so far?" she asked, a knuckle at her nostrils as she tried hard to contain a laugh.

"What do you mean?"

"I mean what have you spelled so far? What does P-A-P-E-R-S spell?"

"Papers?"

"Yes, now go on. What's does the rest of it spell?"

"Word?"

"That's right. So what is the paper sword?" she asked with great relish.

"Paper's word," he answered quietly. And for a second time a superstitious chill flickered through him.

"And so what is the answer to the whole riddle?" Musea asked merrily.

"I don't know. Who *will* be gouged and gored?"

"You, Xemion." She was so taken by her mirth at this she had to slap her knee to help express it. "Who has been more gouged and gored by words than you, Xemion?" Xemion visibly flinched at this insight. She nodded and laughed out loud. "You see? You came to learn to swordfight but you've been having a word-fight ever since. And so the answer to the second part is also you. You, Xemion. Every day as you have scribed these old stories you have wielded the paper sword, paper's word — literature."

Xemion was looking less and less happy as she spoke. And then she said something that no one had said to him before but which several people would say to him later. She said it like it was just a last little teasing bit of gaiety. "Why, you must be severely spell crossed to have attracted a riddle like that."

"I don't think I attracted it," Xemion protested weakly. "It was just a coincidence that that riddle came up at that moment."

"Everything coincides. Everything is just a coincidence," Musea said knowingly.

"Time for dictation?" Xemion asked, as cheerily as possible. She nodded in reply. Xemion took a sip of water from the bottle that had been left on the table. It had a strangely familiar tang to it, but he couldn't at first place it. He took up his pen and said "Ready," but when she began to speak, strange syllables Xemion had never heard before emerged from her mouth.

"Musea, Musea, I apologize for interrupting, but I no longer understand you. I don't know what you are saying."

The ancient face cracked open in her broadest smile yet. "Listen."

"I can listen but I can't really write it out. I—"

"And remember."

"But how can I remember such a long thing?"

"You drank, didn't you, from the waters of memory?" She spoke so clearly. He felt a little shocked.

"I did, but how could you know?"

She nodded jovially at the bottle Xemion had just drunk from and he realized why the strange taste was so familiar.

"Show me your hand," she said.

Obediently but with some annoyance Xemion stuck out his hand. Then she did something that surprised him. He had always assumed that the whiteness of her hands was the result of old age. But all this time she had been wearing white gloves. She used her left hand now to peel off the glove on her right hand. Xemion saw only a moment of its bright red colour before it slipped into his hand, quick and warm. She shook it a while, gazing into his eyes, and then she released it and said, "So remember this."

Immediately Xemion's hand began to tingle and the strange words began again. Despite himself, Xemion listened attentively to the long, strange sentences that followed.

10

$$\blacktriangleright\!\!\leftarrow \blacktriangleright\!\!\leftarrow$$

An End of Stories

After that strange encounter with the old woman, there was barely a moment of the day when Xemion did not hear some fragment of Musea's strange words slipping through his mind. At night when he lay down to sleep they would go interminably round and round. Even if he forced other words over them, even if he recited poetry over them, or said "No No No" over them, the words would return and trouble him with their strange familiarity. They were like a long nonsense song always verging on becoming clear and making sense but never quite doing so. And, despite his fatigue, something in him wanted to know what they meant, so often he would find himself wide awake and intently listening. The combination of sleeplessness, aggravation, and outright anger resulting from this gnawed away at him and wore him down. *This dawn*, he thought, *I will stomp back to the underdome and demand that Musea explain*. And if she refused, he would refuse to do any more writing. Not even Veneetha Azucena could sway him any longer.

Lost in such thoughts, Xemion actually slipped into a badly needed minute or two of sleep, but he was soon startled by a sound outside, an awesome cry of some kind of animal, which echoed down Phaer Point and all along the moonlit High Street right to his room. And the cry did not stop. It was as though there were too much of it for this world. Xemion rose quickly, already dressed, and dashed in the direction of the underdome.

With the sorrowful echoes leading him on, Xemion made his way to the source of those cries, and it was indeed as he feared, reverberating up from the Thrall chamber. With the same quiet steps he had once executed along still forest pathways, he now made his way down the smooth, worn stone stairs to the underdome.

Sarabin and Yarra were both quietly weeping and wringing their hands as he entered, but the source of the terrible howling, as Xemion had suspected, was the dog, Bargest. Until tonight, the dog had only spoken in soft tones of supplication, but now, with his grief unleashed, his voice was gigantic. Musea had died in the night. Her still form lay slumped in the stone chair, the candle flame flickering eerily over her as the dog, between howls, urgently licked her feet. "Please, Mistress. Don't go now, my mage. Don't leave me like this," he whimpered.

Seeing Musea lying there, hearing the grief of Bargest fill the great stone bubble, Xemion couldn't help but be moved. But even as the first tear caught in his throat, the thought that her death might free him from his labours infected it with a tiny morsel of relief. Sarabin looked at

Xemion, distraught, and nodded. "She is gone," he managed to say.

"It is a great loss," Xemion said consolingly. "She was a remarkable woman."

A big bubble of grief arose so violently in Yarra's ancient throat that he could barely let it out. "Yes, yes," he blubbered. "And just as she was going to begin a recitation of *The Thaumatological Lexicon*."

"We'll never have it now," Sarabin lamented.

"Don't go. Don't go!" Bargest bellowed anew from the floor, filling the cold stone bubble to bursting with the ferocity of his anguish. The poor beast was so distraught he began to run back and forth in the chamber as though searching for her. "I beg of you. Retrieve her. Bring her back." He was like a large black lion stalking through the darkness, sniffing his way frantically along the aisles and all in between the rows of seats. "Please come back. I entreat you."

He only stopped when he heard the sound of approaching footsteps. The air was suddenly filled with a sweet orange blossom scent, and then a figure in a green, hooded cloak entered the underdome. Xemion could barely make out the face within the shadow of the hood as he stood just outside the flickering ring of candlelight. The woman with him leaned in toward Musea and cupped her hands over her mouth in disbelief. She approached the old Thrall woman and bent over her so that her mass of dark ringlets hung over the body like coils of shiny black smoke. Veneetha Azucena slowly took her hands away from her mouth and Xemion could see her lower lip trembling. As she looked up, the light from the flames fully illuminated her face and he could clearly make out the red threads woven into her hair. As she put her trembling hand on Musea's cold shoulder, a cry escaped her. This, in turn, set the dog off baying grievously again, and the sound of the two of them in the chamber was almost deafening.

After a time, Veneetha Azucena closed her eyes, took a long breath, and exhaled evenly as though to release the shock. Still weeping, she knelt down and put her hand on Bargest's back and said, soothingly, "Poor, poor thing." For a while she knelt between the dog and Musea's body and tears streamed down from her dark eyes. Her face remained still and composed except for occasional trembling at the corner of her mouth. Slowly her stillness seemed to spread to Yarra and Sarabin until they, too, grew quiet. Then she joined hands with the two of them, forming a circle, and they kept one another's gaze for so long that Xemion almost began to feel like a spy.

"So, it is done," Veneetha Azucena said at last, with a grave nod.

"We tried our hardest," Yarra whispered.

"There is so much we will never recover now," Sarabin added woefully, shaking his head.

"And … the book I mentioned to you?" Veneetha asked.

"I'm afraid not," Yarra squeaked, shrugging helplessly.

Sarabin emitted a sharp coughing sound, looked at her sharply, and cocked his head in the direction of Xemion, who still stood silently at the perimeter of the candlelight.

Veneetha Azucena squinted into the darkness and

noticed Xemion for the first time. "Ah, there you are," she said in her sweetest voice.

"I'm so sorry," Xemion managed to say.

She nodded.

"It is a great loss," Xemion added.

She nodded again and looked at him piercingly. "But every loss is tainted with some gain, I suppose." She flashed a wry smile at him.

Xemion looked puzzled.

"I mean, you cannot be entirely aggrieved with this."

Xemion almost blushed. It was true. With Musea gone there was no reason to keep him here in Ulde. He swallowed and nodded back at her. She saw the guilty look on his face.

"No need to feel ashamed," she advised in a soothing voice. "There are cross-spells and contrary currents in everything here, being so close to the Great Kone. There's no action that is not blighted by paradox. You have given good service. You can be proud of that."

Xemion blushed again, still feeling guilty.

"We will need to give Musea over to her people for a full Thrall burial ceremony, but you needn't feel you have to stay in Ulde for that. We have finally had word from Lighthammer. The mountain passes are now traversable and there is a supply caravan going to the camp in the morning from the crossroads at Brookside."

Xemion couldn't help it. He smiled.

"Yes. Tell them that Veneetha Azucena herself has sent you and they will take you. And take our gratitude with you."

Sarabin and Yarra tried to add their own remarks to

this but a new series of howling laments from Bargest thwarted their attempts. Veneetha knelt down again and put her hand on the back of the dog's neck, stroking it soothingly. "Poor thing. Poor thing."

It wasn't until he had almost reached his lodgings that Xemion realized why the title of the lost book kept tugging at his memory. There were a number of books in the library locket that had another text written crosswise to the regular text, utilizing the spaces between the letters and the lines. Normally due to the actions of what Anya had explained was a series of miniature tumblers and timers skillfully woven into the spines of the books by the Nains who had created them, you had to read a whole book before it could be inserted into its new slot on the opposite side of the locket. But this didn't seem to apply to the cross-written texts. Indeed, both Xemion and Anya had tried to read some of these cross-written texts but soon found the specialized language and the enormous length of the sentences impossible to understand. When they gave up on such readings they were still able to insert the book into its new slot on the other side of the locket. He dimly remembered now that *The Thaumatological Lexicon* had been among them. Xemion smiled. He didn't know for sure how they could extract it from the locket, but Sarabin had a sunscope and Veneetha Azucena had a crystal dome in her ceiling! This book could be saved! Xemion picked up the pace joyfully. Once he got back to his room he hurriedly retrieved his practice sword and took the locket from its place beneath his bed and set off with it back to the underdome.

11

Unexpected Meetings

An early cross-spell had left the roads and other surfaces of the borough of Shissillil without friction. Anything thrown through the various gateways into the borough simply slid away and disappeared. This made the portal on Castle Road halfway along Phaer Point perfect for waste disposal. On evenings like this when the dark was coming in off the sea like a damp, dead sky spirit, this aspect of the portal could also be a kind of blessing to some of the more criminally inclined youth of Ulde, for instance those drink or herb Thralls, who sometimes had to dispose of their forbidden potions and liqueurs at very short notice. During the fifty years since the spell fire, other things had been disposed of here, too: weapons, poisons, even bodies, some said — living and dead. But of all the terrible deeds done here, there were surely very few that were more cowardly than the one about to be committed.

The triplicant terrier, Jackinjo, whose three eyes were currently peering out of the net bag he was captive in, trembled as he awaited his turn. The squeals of the most recent victim still vibrated in his mind, echoing up under the cruel laughter of his captors.

"All right. Next!" a large, half-hidden figure in the shadow of the portal shouted. He wiped his lips and nodded at a fellow with a black tooth, who grabbed the mouth of the bag. Jackinjo began to whimper and whine in terror as the big man took up a thick black bat. Jackinjo's terror increased as the bag was raised.

"Are you ready?" one of the men asked. A ring of leering, laughing youths looked on, gathered about the portal, bottles hanging from their fists or tilted to their lips.

"Ready," the large one said with a strange drunken leer. "Go!"

The black-toothed fellow flung the yelping dog into the air, and as the bag came down the large man swung his thick black bat at it full force, connecting squarely with it and sending poor broken Jackinjo, with one last truncated yelp, soaring through the portal and away after his fellows, lost forever.

The one with the bat shouted "Yes!" and gleefully took a swig from his bottle. His colleagues likewise broke into fits of laughter and began to jump up and down and suck away at their many bottles and pipes.

Xemion did not at first notice the group as he made his way back to the underdome with the locket. He was distracted by the light of the setting sun, which shone brightly off the dark surface of a pond that stretched along the side of the road. He had to hold his hand up to his eyes to shade them from the brilliant flares of red that reflected off the water. It wasn't until he was nearly upon them that he noticed the group, and he was shocked when he realized that the hated Montither was among them. What was he doing back in Ulde? This jolt of fear and hatred was for a second mixed with a shred of hope. If Montither had come from the camp, he would surely know whether Saheli was there or not. He doubted that Montither would supply him with an easy answer to this question though, so, because he was on his way there anyways, and would find out for himself soon enough, he decided to give the group a wide berth.

He had almost slipped past unnoticed, when Gnasher, the black-toothed fellow who always accompanied Montither, suddenly looked up. He caught Xemion's eye and grinned menacingly. "Why, look. It's the great swordsman." He laughed, causing his jaw to vibrate up and down as though it were quickly gnashing at something.

Xemion nodded in greeting.

"And how are you today, my friend?" Gnasher asked with mock politeness as the others began to close in around him. Gnasher clapped Xemion forcefully on the back. Montither was standing back a bit, leaning against the portal, his eyes spilling sheer static black hatred.

"I'm in a hurry," Xemion replied angrily, yanking his shoulder away.

"Oh, no you're not." Gnasher had a hint of evil mischief in his eyes.

"Oh, yes I am," Xemion replied, trying to brush his way through them.

Suddenly, Montither let loose an insane-sounding

growl and dashed straight at Xemion, launching his fist into his right cheek, knocking him to the ground. Xemion leapt back to his feet as quickly as he could, but he was reeling and off-balance. Before he could raise his fists to defend himself, Montither struck again. Xemion hit the ground a second time and Montither began kicking him. He caught him on the hip where the painted sword hung. If he had been enraged before, the sight of the object that had so humiliated him was like oil on the fire. Montither flew into a frenzy of kicks and then he ripped the sword away from Xemion and tried to break it over his knee. But the sword was not the least bit brittle. It bent and easily absorbed the force.

"What of your oath?" Xemion managed to scream from the ground, where he was doubled over into a protective ball. Shrill laughter rose from the crowd.

"Who are you calling an Oath?" Gnasher mocked. He turned to the others, snickering. He went to kick Xemion in the head, but Montither stopped him.

"No, he's right." he growled suddenly withdrawing, holding his fists at his side, still clenched. There was complete silence. "I swore an oath of alliance." There was a sinister undertone in Montither's finely accented though somewhat slurred words. The thugs, knowing that look, knowing the changeability of his moods, looked on with anticipation. "Now get up!"

Xemion rose painfully to his feet, wary in case he had to defend against another flurry of kicks or punches.

"Hold out your hand and I will return your sword to you," Montither ordered with only the slightest suggestion of a sadistic smile. When Xemion refused, Montither nodded and someone grabbed Xemion from behind. He struggled with all the strength of his rage and indignation, but they were many more than he and all his strength could not tear him free. He jerked his face around toward Montither and sneered. "I'm not afraid of you."

"Hold out your hand," Montither demanded. Xemion could smell the stench of vomit and wine on Montither's breath. He tried to resist. He gritted his teeth and clenched his fist tight, but other fingers pried at it and opened it against his will and held it there, bare beneath Montither's vengeful glare.

"Now let me return your sword to you." Montither raised the painted sword and brought it down as hard as he could across Xemion's palm. Xemion's whole body bucked with the impact of the blow, but somehow he absorbed it silently and managed to glare back impassively into Montither's cruel eyes. Again Montither struck and again Xemion took the pain without a cry.

"Coward," he uttered, looking straight into Montither's eyes. He braced himself for a third onslaught, but Montither stopped and the painted sword hung for a moment at his side. The slight smile that twitched at the edges of his mouth could not hide the anger that was rising in him.

With a casual motion Montither threw Xemion's painted sword back over his head. It spun through the air high above the dark swampy water and then plummeted into the blackness with a gulping liquid sound and disappeared. Slowly, Montither drew his long iron sword from its scabbard, keeping his gaze focused almost hypnotically on its fine edge as he slid it in front of Xemion's eyes.

"I'm going to cut off his hand," he announced in a strange, overly controlled voice. Montither's gang laughed out loud at this and several of them began to applaud and whoop and jump up and down.

"Hold his hand over the stone," Montither ordered. His voice had become clipped and even more haughtily nasal than usual.

"No!" Xemion struggled but his captors were many and they once again had him in position, open-palmed, with his wrist on top of the large rock that Montither had indicated. Montither took the hilt of his sword in both hands and raised it over Xemion's wrist.

"Hold it tight," Montither instructed.

"No!" Xemion screamed again as he struggled against his captors.

"Ah, so you *can* scream," Montither sneered. "I thought so." His smile was pure bloodlust.

"No, Montither. Don't. It's my sword hand!" Xemion let loose a scream of terror so loud it echoed all along the roadway, causing the Nains and Thralls who were still at work busily renovating the castle, hundreds of yards away, to look up with concern.

Montither paused sadistically and adopted his most aristocratic tone. "Oh, don't worry, I won't kill you. I wouldn't want that. I'd much prefer you to be alive to see what I do to that she-dog of yours in the Phaer Tourney on the equinox."

The little mob cheered loudly, urging Montither on.

"He's going to cut her heart out," chortled Gnasher.

Montither looked into Xemion's eyes, raised his sword up over his head, and surely would have cut off Xemion's hand then and there but for the sudden blast of a whistle, a shout, and the sound of fast-approaching footsteps.

"Hey!" a man's voice yelled angrily. "Stop that!"

"The law!" Gnasher hissed.

Before he ran off, Montither caught Xemion off-guard with another punch to the face that sent him reeling back to the ground. Within seconds, they had all disappeared. Xemion looked up at the person who had rescued him. The man wore a tricorne admiral's hat and a long black cloak over a red uniform with gold brocade. His face was tanned as though he'd just returned from the tropics, but the hand that he reached out to Xemion was a deep red colour.

Vallaine!

12

Little Locket Library

"**X**emion!" Vallaine grabbed the young man's hand to help him to his feet, but Xemion let out such a howl of pain he immediately let go. Standing up on his own, Xemion gazed at his open palm and winced. Where Montither had struck him there were now two raised welts in the shape of an *X*.

"That looks rather painful," Vallaine sympathized.

"I can't hear you very well," Xemion answered quite loudly. "My ears are ringing. He struck me in the head."

"What … with the whole mob of them holding you down like that?"

"Yes. They were going to cut my hand off," Xemion said with barely suppressed rage.

Vallaine shook his head in disgust. "Well, lucky for you the winds chose this day of all days to allow my return."

"The cowards," Xemion seethed, his eyes narrowed to slits.

"Who were they? Did you know them?"

"Yes, I know them," Xemion growled.

"And?"

"You've heard of Norud Montither?"

"Not that damaged monster-child of his."

Xemion nodded, taking some satisfaction from the virulence of Vallaine's description. "His name is Brothlem Montither."

"Oh, I know his name, believe me. And worse than that, I know his reputation. In fact, I spoke out against him being here at all, but I was overruled."

"Well, I humiliated him on the first day we arrived here in Ulde, and ever since then he has hated me."

"He hates a lot of people — or at least their achievements. So I hardly need warn you, Xemion. Be wary. He is reputed to have killed a young man in Phaeros."

"He was really going to cut my hand off," Xemion repeated, as astonished as he was outraged. Vallaine laughed that big rich laugh of his.

"Well, let me tell you something that I learned the hard way. When thugs grab you like that, they do not deserve to be fought like gentlemen. The very best thing to do when someone grabs you from behind is to stamp your heel down as hard as you can on their foot."

Xemion nodded.

"I know it is not gallant. But, when necessary, it is quite effective."

Xemion tried to smile, but he was still too full of rage and that other, colder feeling: Fear.

"We've all been awaiting your arrival," he said at last.

"I'm sure you have. We've only just sailed into the

harbour this past hour," Vallaine said. "We have a cargo of fruits and vegetables from the southern islands, so I know the hungry, at least, will be very happy to see us."

"People feared you were lost," Xemion said, not meeting Vallaine's eyes.

"Not lost, but becalmed. On a heavenly isle, no less."

"And you delivered the one called Tharfen back to her village?"

Vallaine laughed. "Not before she made a thorough bother and nuisance of herself."

"Talk of stones and slings?"

"Constant."

"She was beaten by an examiner quite badly before we left. We didn't know it, but the man followed us and he almost caught up with us. He would have gotten away from the Vale of Two Wells, but just as he was going to drink the water that would have opened the gateway, Tharfen shot a stone at him with her sling and smashed the bottle right out of his hands."

"She does have amazing accuracy. I remember it from our day in Ilde."

"I don't know if she still does. I think what happened to the examiner after that might have done something to her aim. The ghouls there at the wells all had their heads twisted round backward, and when they caught him they did that same thing to him."

Vallaine grimaced and smiled at the same time. "It sounds like he got what he deserved. Is it true that her father is a pirate?"

"That is the story. Other than the red hair, which she got from her mother, she looks nothing like her seven brothers." Xemion shrugged. "Of course, none of them look like one another. Torgee says it's because they all had different fathers."

"I saw her mother when I delivered her brat back to her. She is a great beauty and a powerful woman."

"Did Tharfen give you any message for me?"

"No. Not one." Then he looked lightly at Xemion. "Why? What message do you await? Might it perhaps be about your betrothed?"

Xemion looked away. "We were side-by-side in the Panthemium when the Pathan Prince burst in, and in all the chaos we got separated. They promised me I would see her the day after we arrived, but something happened."

By now they had come to the crossroads leading up to the castle and the underdome. "Which way are you going, Xemion?"

Xemion pointed in the direction of the castle.

"At this time of night?" Vallaine asked. "Well, I'm going that way too. Why don't I join you?" He paused before continuing. "And why don't you tell me exactly what's been going on."

Something in Xemion wanted to hold back the truth, but as they proceeded he blurted it out anyway, the whole story about what had happened since he'd last seen Vallaine: the first kiss, the separation, the scribing, the riddle in the locket, and, finally, the missing classic. When he had finished, he saw that Vallaine was looking at him doubtfully.

"You are a noble fellow, Xemion," he said with a mixture of sympathy and merriment. "But I did tell you to destroy that painted sword of yours, did I not?

If Montither has done one good thing in his life, it is in finally ridding you of it."

Xemion shrugged as Vallaine continued. "Still, I thank you on behalf of the Phaer Literature. I'm sure the one you saw at the front *was* Saheli, but I know nothing will settle it for you until you have seen her face with your own eyes. And that chance, fortunately, will come soon enough by the sound of it. But in the meantime, I am wondering how anything as small as a locket could possibly contain as many books as you have described."

"They are as small as fish scales."

"But even if it were conceivable for someone to have scribed such tiny texts, how could you possibly have read them?"

"We had a device called a sunscope in the observatory where I lived, and at the right time of evening it could catch the setting sunlight and use it to project the texts onto the walls. I have read them with my own eyes."

"Yes, I am well aware of sunscopes. Marvellous devices. But they were invented for the examination and study of the microcosm. I don't imagine their inventors expected them to be used for such a purpose as reading tiny little books. Very clever of you," Vallaine said. Then he added, somewhat skeptically, "Perhaps you could show me this locket." Again Xemion had an urge to resist, but he couldn't. He pulled the locket out into the light, holding it in his uninjured palm so Vallaine could see it. Vallaine let his red hand hover over the locket.

"Xemion, have you ever wondered whether there might be some spellcraft involved with this locket?"

"Certainly *not*. It was crafted by tiny Numian Thralls."

Now Vallaine looked truly amused. "Xemion, surely you are jesting with me."

"I'm not." Xemion said indignantly closing his fist about the locket and quickly stuffing it back into his pocket.

Vallaine shook his head to clear away his mirth and then responded in as solemn a voice as possible. "Xemion, you have never seen a tiny Numian Thrall, have you?"

"Of course not. But—"

"That's because there is no such thing as a tiny Numian Thrall."

Xemion's jaw dropped a little and he turned red. "How do you know that?"

"Xemion, they are just the stuff of children's stories."

There was a long, silent pause. At last, in a much quieter voice, Xemion acknowledged "Anya Kuzelnika did often make up stories to teach me things."

"It's not uncommon," Vallaine said with a nod. "So, concerning how your locket came to be—"

A cold feeling crept into Xemion's skin as he remembered how close to her heart Saheli who was so terrified of magic had worn it. "You think it was spellcrafted?"

"Class C, I suspect. That means it wasn't created by a spell but it has been altered by a spell, or even two spells. I doubt the books themselves are spellworked. They've probably only been shrunk by a spell to protect them. That would have to have been at least fifty years ago. After the spell fire, the last of the mages, before the Pathans caught them and hung them, used their final energies to shrink as many things as they could to make them easier to hide. They might even revert to normal size one day. But you're going to have some explaining to do to Glittervein tomorrow."

Now Xemion was truly alarmed. "Tomorrow? But I'm leaving here early in the morning."

Vallaine's brow creased and his lips pursed. He pulled on one side of his long moustache. "But this is a real problem. If you give this to Sarabin he will be honour-bound to bring it to Glittervein and tell him where he got it. Glittervein, I assure you, will not be at all pleased. He will destroy it immediately and then he will definitely want to talk to you."

"I have been told to leave tomorrow by direct order of Veneetha Azucena," Xemion asserted angrily.

Vallaine continued to puzzle it over. "See now, I know there was no intention on your part to smuggle the locket in. You have acted honourably. It would be a shame to have your trip delayed over such a technicality. Why don't I take your locket. I will submit it to Mr. Glittervein and tell him I found it in my travels, and you will say nothing to anyone about it."

Xemion considered this for a moment. "I would have to tell Saheli when I see her," he said at last. "She will notice it's gone."

"Tell her, then, but only if she asks and not before. The less said the better. It's safest that way."

Xemion nodded uncertainly.

"That's the spirit, Xemion," Vallaine said. "Put it there." His red hand reached out to shake Xemion's, but noticing Xemion flinch, he switched in mid-course and shook the young man's left hand instead. Xemion felt the familiar jolt of energy as their palms met.

"But what will happen to the books when you turn the locket in?" Xemion asked.

"If he has even the slightest suspicion that a spell mage was involved in its creation, Glittervein will have no choice but to incinerate them."

"But what of the missing classic?" Xemion protested. "There must be a way to take it out and copy it? Captain Sarabin said it is a very significant book."

"Well," Vallaine let loose with that sonorous laugh of his, "Captain Sarabin thinks all books are very significant. And so do we all, but that would be up to Glittervein. He would probably burn it in his smithy."

"But it is a shame for us to destroy our own literature."

"You have a point. Here then, Xemion. This is what I'll do. I will take the locket first to my tower and quarantine it. I have a sunscope of my own — more powerful even than that ancient one you described. Let me tinker with the locket a while and see if I can extract the book in question, and if I can, I'll hold onto it until I can get it copied."

Xemion thought about it, then nodded. "Please."

"But you mustn't say a word. You mustn't acknowledge it in any way. I could get in a lot of trouble, not only with Glittervein, but with my lady Veneetha Azucena."

Xemion nodded.

"Do we swear then?" Vallaine asked.

"I swear," Xemion said, though he sounded a bit unsure. Vallaine shook Xemion's left hand for quite a long time, nodding his head and smiling as he did so. Xemion smiled back and held up his end of the shaking and nodding.

"So then ..." Vallaine let the hand go at last.

"So ... what?" asked Xemion, his heart beating fast.

"So ... are you going to give me the locket?"

Again, something in Xemion made him hesitate before reaching into his pocket and handing the locket over. Vallaine stashed the tiny library inside his chameleon cloak. "Well, Xemion, I've got a full cargo to get unloaded and a fair maid to see. You're a good man and you've done the right thing here. I've saved you from harm twice now, but I may not be around to save you a third time. Be wary of those cowards and don't be ashamed to do them harm if they would harm you." He reached out and once more shook Xemion's left hand exhaustively. "And one more little piece of advice. If I were you, I would hide that voice of yours. It has deepened since you and I first met and even here in Ulde it is likely to get you in trouble."

Xemion nodded woefully. Vallaine smiled, and in his most monotone manner said, "And so I bid you adieu." With that he tipped his tricorne hat, tossed a strand of his long black hair over his shoulder, wrapped the camouflage cloak about his body, and rapidly walked off into the gathering fog.

13

Pleas and Demands

For a few moments Xemion felt a pang of regret for having given up the locket, but the feeling soon passed. Nor did he miss for long the painted sword that Montither had flung into the swamp. Even the urge to track down Montither and have at him one-on-one quickly faded. In fact, despite the ringing in his ears and the pain in his palm, he felt liberated and lighter with each step he took toward his quarters.

Soon he would see Saheli.

He had even forgotten the jealousy he had felt toward Torgee — or anyone else. She was *his* warrior beloved. She had chosen *him* with a kiss. He had no doubt. His ordeal was almost over and soon he would see her.

The night was settling in cool and quite foggy, but Xemion made his way through the narrow streets with the first bit of spring he'd had in his steps in a long time.

Not far from his quarters, a guttural voice spoke right behind him.

"I beg."

Xemion turned around alarmed and saw that it was Musea's black dog, Bargest, who now began creeping along beside him. The dog had obviously encountered some mud on his journey, for his usual pink finery was wet, ragged, and filthy. He nudged Xemion's hand with his snout.

"Bargest. What are you doing out here? Shouldn't you be at the underdome?"

"I beg you, help me," the dog implored with a look of loss so intense that Xemion couldn't help but feel compassion for the poor creature. He almost knelt to pat him but stopped, repelled by something disjointed in the dog's spell-crossed gaze.

"What is it?" he asked.

"I beg you. Ease my pain."

"Bargest, I have nothing to ease your pain. I'm sorry. But, is it safe for an animal so affected by spellcraft like you to be loose out here?"

"I beg."

"You should go back to the underdome, Bargest. I'm sorry."

"I beg you to own me, Xemion. Even if just for—"

"I have no need of a dog. Especially not a spell-crossed dog. Besides, I'm leaving in the morning for a place where dogs may not go."

"I could go if I were your war dog. Please, let me be the one who finds you bread when you are hungry."

"Bargest, there are so many others here who would love to have a dog like you."

"I beg. Let me be the one who shouts when you are voiceless."

"No, I'm sorry, Bargest." Xemion was trying to harden his heart to the animal's pleading, but it wasn't easy. There was something about him that reminded Xemion of Chiricoru, the spell-crossed bird he had been raised with and who had died on their journey to Ulde. Taking pity, he knelt and undid the clasps and ribbons that bound the muddy pink outfit to the dog's body. Perhaps this was a mistake, for it seemed to energize the dog's hopes and he began to leap about a bit as he begged.

"I beg you, lord. You would never need for a friend ever, ever, ever again, my friend."

"No, sorry, Bargest."

"Please."

By now Xemion had reached his door. "I'm sorry, Bargest, but you cannot be my dog and you cannot come with me. I'll be leaving in the morning. I've made up my mind and nothing will change it."

The moon shone down through the thickening fog, and the grief and yearning in the dog's heart was released as he lifted up his snout and emitted a long, pitiful howl. But Xemion was not to be deterred. "Go home!" he said as severely as he could. Though it was a hard thing to do, he closed the door behind him. A high-pitched crying continued outside the door.

"Please," the dog whined, "I beg you."

Xemion found he could not be as hard-hearted as he wished to be. He pulled open the door and patted the poor dog's head. "I'm really sorry, Bargest," he said gently. "You are a wonderful dog, but I have to leave in the morning, and I can't take you with me."

"I beg you."

"Yes, but I am begging you, Bargest. Please return to the underdome."

"But—"

"I beseech you, Bargest. They will be worried about you. They will be searching for you."

"But—"

"I beg you, Bargest, go."

Stymied by this reversal, Bargest looked up into Xemion's eyes and licked his hand before turning away. Xemion watched him plod along the cobblestones until he reached the street that led to the castle, at which point the dog turned his head and glanced back. In a heart-rending voice he called out: "But please do not try to keep me from serving you, from calling you master."

Xemion waved him on.

"I will be calling you master anyway. I will be dreaming that you are master. I will be at your side even when I am not at your side."

It took Xemion a long time to fall asleep. Pain throbbed up his arm from his palm, where Montither had struck him. But it was more than the pain that kept him awake. He was remembering that small sliver of the terror he'd felt at that moment. And just when he thought he'd never shake that feeling, it suddenly changed. Instead, Saheli's smiling, welcoming face hovered before him, beckoning him onward. That painful tingling he felt was her hand in his hand — the way it had been as they passed the Great Kone. Two more breaths and the tingling became the sword. Criss and cross, it sang in his grip. His last thought before he slipped into slumber was of Vallaine and the look in his eyes when he had spoken to Xemion outside the Great Kone. *What had he said?* "You have a great destiny and those who have great destinies have the least choice in the matter."

Ha! he thought.

Xemion was awoken a few hours later by a loud knock on the door. When he opened it, thick fog, illumined by a tallow lamp, streamed in. Xemion didn't recognize the person who stood there, but he was huge — easily two feet taller than Xemion and twice as wide at the shoulders. The hood of a grey cloak hung over most of the upper portion of his face, but below it, a large jutting slab of stubbled chin and a tight mouth with crooked teeth remained in view. "Glittervein!" the figure growled, pointing with his thumb in the general direction of the castle.

"Who are you?" Xemion asked nervously.

The man reached into his cloak and showed Xemion a seal with a gorehorse embossed on it. "Glittervein," he said, with exactly the same tone and jerk of thumb as before.

"I have to leave here early in the morning," Xemion protested. He thought he'd encountered everyone in the colony but he had never met anyone as large as this man before. He was sure of it.

"Glittervein," the man repeated, adding, perhaps for variety, "now."

A chill of fear ran through Xemion as he threw on his clothes. Had Vallaine betrayed him? At first it hardly seemed possible, but then he remembered Saheli's mistrust of the man, and his suspicion began to deepen. On the way to the castle, the fog grew so dense that the hooded man sometimes had to find his way by running his hands along the walls or sweeping the way ahead with his staff.

When they arrived at the castle, a grumpy guard opened a broad wooden door to let them in. Xemion and his taciturn guide proceeded down a long hallway, which here and there was dimly lit with a candle or the red glow of embers in exhausted incense pots. Through foggy corridors they walked into a banquet hall, lavishly renovated by the Nains in the ancient Elphaerean style. Down the centre of the room ran a long marble table containing the remains of the previous night's supper. The floors were jewelled mosaics and great tapestries hung on the walls.

At the end of the hall, the man in the cloak, eyes still hidden behind his hood, pulled a small lever beside a closed door. Xemion heard the sound of a distant bell. Soon a little window in the door slid open and the prettier side of Glittervein's face peered out. He opened the door, and with the semblance of a friendly smile, his deep, booming voice rumbled, "Ah, yes, Xemion."

"Yes, sir. What is it, sir?" Xemion asked nervously.

"Nothing to worry about. I just wanted to clear up some questions that have arisen." Glittervein's words had a command hard to resist.

"Sir, I have to leave for Tiri Lighthammer's camp in the morning. I—"

"Yes, yes, I am aware. That is why I called you in tonight. This must be done before you go."

"But—"

"Come along now. This won't take long. Lethir, bring along a torch for light."

14

Examinations

Lethir had to hunch over as he lit their way through a low-ceilinged subterranean passage that led to an underground chamber hewn out of the solid rock of Phaer Point. Glittervein gestured to a stone chair and told Xemion to sit. It was shaped like any simple chair, all straight lines and right angles, unadorned except for the small crescent-shaped depression cut into the top of its high stone back. Xemion felt the bite of its coldness as he sat. Lethir placed the torch into a bracket on the wall and stood in front of Xemion with his arms folded across his chest. Beyond him, the light flickered against the darkness, causing shadows at its perimeter to dance and disappear. How far that darkness might extend was hinted at by the echo of each sound. Xemion had a strong sense that, somewhere in that darkness, someone was watching.

"Now don't be alarmed. This won't take long, I promise

you." Glittervein was clearly doing his best to subdue the more grating tones in his voice. "I have been hearing lately about your … voice." As he said this, Glittervein kept the undamaged side of his face toward Xemion and allowed his long hair to hang over that mess of scarred ridges on the other side.

"My voice?"

"Yes. To be specific, your reading. I am told that you read aloud in quite a compelling manner."

Xemion shrugged noncommittally.

"That is very unusual in our era. As you know, it is actually illegal."

"Yes, but since we're not observing the Pathan laws here, I thought it would be dishonest to hide it," Xemion answered curtly.

"I see. And who, may I ask, taught you?"

"My guardian. Her name was Anya Kuzelnika."

"Who were your real parents?"

"Sir, I don't know."

"How can you not know?"

"Anya said she found me living among the monkeys in the forest."

"That's ridiculous."

"That's the only story she would ever tell me. I used to ask her about it all the time, but she never gave me any other answer than that."

"And why do you think she taught you to read?"

"She was a very old woman and her eyesight had failed her, and one day we found an old copy of the *Phaer Tales*." Without even thinking about it, Xemion had nervously omitted any mention of the locket or the size of the books. "She said she wanted to hear them all one more time before she died, so she taught me to read."

"But she put you at such great risk."

"Sir, I knew that. But she was old and sick and not entirely in her right mind … and … I couldn't refuse her."

"How often did you read to her?"

"Every night."

"You must read very well."

Xemion shrugged. "She always complained about my enunciation."

"Well, I am a lover of poetry. Perhaps I can get you to read for me."

Xemion nodded and Glittervein produced a large, gilt-edged volume of the *Phaer Tales* and held it open before the light, pointing to a text. Despite his growing suspicion of Vallaine, Xemion did not disregard his advice. He began to recite in as toneless a voice as possible:

> *Their horses' hooves come hammering down*
> *On roads not of this Earth.*
> *Nor do they know the pain of love,*
> *Nor loss or savage birth.*
>
> *They ride the wind ten million strong,*
> *And longing is the spur*
> *That pricks their flesh — Ride on! Ride on!*
> *The Knights who never were.*

When he finished, Glittervein eyed him skeptically. "Really, Xemion. Is this the best you can do?"

"Did I enunciate poorly?"

"Your enunciation is perfect. But are you reading now exactly the way you read to Mr. Sarabin's class?"

"Yes, the way I always read."

"Perhaps you wouldn't mind reciting the poem again."

"Certainly."

"But this time I want you to take a big breath and speak louder and put some feeling into it. Gesture with your arms."

Xemion breathed in deeply and, in an appreciably louder and more baritone voice, repeated the poem in exactly the same clipped, deadpan manner as before.

"And you are suggesting to me that this is you at your most eloquent?"

"Sir," Xemion said with the same degree of earnestness he had often used when deliberately misinforming Anya about some of his more dangerous activities in the forest. "Sir, I think some of the Thralls who heard me read in Captain Sarabin's class may have attributed qualities to my voice that are actually qualities of the Phaer Tales themselves. They are so complete that I have never had any urge except to speak them clearly and without effect."

"I see. Well, please, indulge me one more time?"

Xemion shrugged.

"But this time, fight that urge. Be more like an actor, if you will."

"I will, but I warn you the story always ends the same way." He grinned, trying to look at ease. Joking. In an even louder tone he repeated the verses, this time with numerous stiff gestures and barely less of a monotone than before.

"I see. Well, I do hope you're not hiding the fullness of your voice from me."

"Of course not."

"Because there's nothing to fear here. No one is going to punish you if it turns out that you can recite much more eloquently than that."

"Sir, I've never really liked reading aloud. I only did it to please my guardian. I'm not hiding anything."

Just then a scraping sounded from somewhere at the back of the chamber. Xemion squinted into the darkness and felt a surge of fear.

"May I?" asked a voice like ground glass. The coldness in the room, heightened by the dampness of the fog, began to penetrate.

"Most assuredly," Glittervein answered. "I wish you would."

Whoever had uttered that cold question now slid slowly forward and stepped into the circle of light. He was of medium size, head and body covered in a hooded grey cloak, face hidden behind a shining black oval with two slits for eyes.

"Greetings, Vihata," Glittervein purred. For Xemion's benefit, he added, "a colleague of mine." Glittervein removed a sizable pipe from his cloak and clacked it against his lower teeth as he prepared to light it.

"Greetings," said Vihata, bending forward to look at Xemion more closely. Through the slits in the obsidian mask, Xemion caught the glint of two dark eyes and turned away.

"Look at me," the crystalline voice commanded.

Despite himself, Xemion obeyed. Vihata extracted

a large lens from his cloak, lifted his visor, and looked directly into Xemion's left eye. Xemion felt the magnified gaze go deep into him and became aware of a quaking feeling in his stomach. Vihata extended his index finger and lifted Xemion's eyelid a little higher. His finger was so cold it almost burned. He applied a little pressure on the orb of Xemion's eye. So much so that Xemion feared for a moment he might pop it out of his head.

"Hey!" he complained, lifting his arm to push Vihata's hand away.

At this Lethir rushed forward and grabbed his wrist in a grip of iron. In the process his hood was swept back onto his shoulders. For the first time Xemion saw the upper portion of his face and understood the source of his uncanny strength. At the centre of a thin band of brow, one large, round, aggressive eye looked back at him. He was a Cyclops. Xemion tried to twist his wrist out of Lethir's grip but the mighty hand just grasped it harder.

"Please remain still," Vihata said sternly.

"What is this Cyclops doing here in Ulde?" Xemion shouted angrily.

"All will be answered in good time." Glittervein said in his sweetest voice, pressing his own hands gently but firmly on Xemion's shoulders as he puffed on his pipe. "Now, may I ask you to please rest your arms with your palms down on the arms of the chair?"

Xemion tried to stand but Lethir pushed him roughly back down and pinned one wrist to the flat top of the armrest while Glittervein clicked a lever at the back of the chair. With that a metal loop slid into place over Xemion's wrist. Moving quickly, the Cyclops snagged Xemion's other flailing arm out of the air and likewise pinned it down so that soon both wrists were bound.

"What is this?" Xemion shouted, struggling against the bonds as Lethir's one big eye blinked impassively back at him.

"I'm sorry," Glittervein chuckled. "It's a necessary precaution during examinations."

"What do you mean examinations?" Xemion shouted.

"If you had come in by the western gate as you were told," Glittervein assured him, "you would have been examined then and we could have avoided this. Now please co-operate, and let's get this over with." Glittervein punctuated his exasperation by expelling a quick burst of smoke.

"Mr. Glittervein," Xemion protested. "If I am to be questioned like this, why is Veneetha Azucena not here?"

"It will be over soon, I promise you," Glittervein purred. He exhaled another long stream of grey smoke, which disappeared into the darkness.

"Show me your throat," Vihata demanded. When Xemion didn't respond, he moved the lens out of the way so that Xemion could at last see his naked, unmagnified features. Xemion gasped despite himself. The face was Pathan, almost lizard-like in shape and appearance, but instead of scales the flesh was a multiplicity of facets as though entirely made of tiny shattered green diamonds. The brightest were the thin flat-line stars in the centre of the lozenge-shaped eyes, which now held his. The Pathan managed a small, tight smile, revealing a row of pointed teeth.

"I said show me your throat," he ordered.

Xemion felt a surge of rage. "Glittervein," he insisted loudly, "I am not sworn to obey Pathan masters. I am under instruction from Veneetha Azucena herself, and she said to say so. Now let me go."

"Mr. Vihata may be a Pathan, but he's on our side and he is our expert when it comes to detecting spellbinders," Glittervein replied sweetly.

"I am not a spellbinder!"

"Well you may not know what you are or what you may be. It is more your capabilities — your tendencies — that we are trying to determine here. So let's not delay this any longer. I know you need to get away in the morning."

Thus persuaded, Xemion reluctantly opened his mouth. The Pathan brought the lens back into place and through it peered into Xemion's throat.

"He certainly has the vocal cords and palate of a spellbinder," Vihata said. "But I can't be sure."

"But it is obvious," Glittervein shot back at him, obviously frustrated. "I could see it from the moment I set eyes on him." He puffed furiously on his pipe, sending billows of grey smoke in Lethir's direction, causing his eye to blink with irritation.

"Of course you could," Vihata said testily, "but it's not your money that's being spent, is it?"

Glittervein nodded and sucked so hard at his pipe the embers glowed and sputtered. "Of course."

"I want to hear him read. Really read."

"I can't help it if he resists!"

"I did not resist!" Xemion shouted.

"Well, I have something to fix that," Vihata said, ignoring Xemion.

Glittervein shrugged. "By all means then."

"A little libation, shall we say, that lets out whatever is held in." Vihata's glass face shifted its facets into the Pathan version of a smile.

"Mr. Glittervein," Xemion bellowed, "I insist I be released."

"I will just need a little blood," Vihata said. In a flash he drew a small blade and brought it to the middle of Xemion's forehead, where he made an incision. Xemion screamed, more in rage than pain, and yanked at his bonds so fiercely that they cut into his wrists. Behind him, Lethir bore down on his shoulders while Glittervein stood before him, ready to intervene if necessary. Smiling, the Pathan held a tiny golden cube against Xemion's forehead and allowed several drops of blood to absorb into it.

"Why the blood?" Glittervein asked.

"It helps the action of the potion. Something we learned in Arthenow."

That chill that had bitten into Xemion's blood at the first sight of the Pathan's face was now burrowing down into his marrow as though desperately trying to hide. Blood and Arthenow meant only one thing — necromancy.

But necromancy should have no power on this side of the western ocean. Still, he couldn't help but fear it. He watched in horror as the Pathan produced a small corked bottle from his cloak and dropped the bloodied cube into it. There followed some hissing and a plume of dark red steam. The Pathan held the goblet under his nostrils and took a quick sniff. He nodded to Lethir and suddenly Xemion felt himself grabbed from behind by the hair and tugged back so that his neck was wedged into that crescent-shaped groove in the back of the chair.

"Now open your mouth," the Pathan roared. With all his will Xemion tried to weld his mouth shut, but Lethir pushed his thumbs into Xemion's jaw muscles and Glittervein tugged his chin down. Once this was done, Vihata began to pour whatever liquid was in the bottle into Xemion's mouth. He spat and choked but they held his nose closed and when his mouth was full Lethir pressed his jaw shut, preventing Xemion from breathing until he swallowed. A great gulp of something thick and fungal and bloody made its way down his throat and into his stomach. With a gagging groan he almost vomited it right back up, but Lethir clamped his mouth shut until he kept it down.

"I'm sorry," said Glittervein, trying not to laugh. "It had to be done."

Xemion spat at him and howled in rage. "You bastard!" In response, Glittervein opened his mouth in an oval shape and with three small pumps of his down-curled tongue, propelled smoke rings directly into Xemion's face.

"Now, listen to me," the Pathan said. "You will soon feel the effects of what I've given you. It is not unpleasant. Some people take it for their own enjoyment. I have given you quite a lot of it, but should it become necessary I have more — and you, of course, have lots more blood."

Even as he said this, a dark, tired feeling began to wash over Xemion. Everything was taking on a slow, red tinge. The Pathan pulled a book with a red cover from the pocket of his ragged robe. He opened it and held it before Xemion. "Look."

Xemion's gaze shifted down to the dark, blood-red text that was printed on a slightly less red page that appeared to have been woven from some kind of crystalline fibre. A strange warm crimson sensation began to wind its way into his bones.

"It's an invocation," Vihata said in a glass-splintering tone, perhaps meant to be reassuring.

"But—"

"Read."

Xemion felt one more surge of extreme rage but with his next breath it melted away. He began by reciting as tonelessly as his trembling voice would allow.

"Resist me not," he began. "With brittle thought. With bitter lot, scar or blot. Through tie and tangle, tear and knot. Resist me not."

"Now read it with feeling," the Pathan ordered.

"Resist me not. With magic mind. With twisted tongue, root or rind. Unvein me now, unskin my thought. Resist me not."

"You are resisting it. Stop resisting it. Again!"

Xemion began again but the Pathan shouted him down. "Do not resist it, I warn you. Again!"

Xemion gritted his teeth. His nostrils flared as he took a deep breath and started over.

"Resist me not. With brittle thought—"

"Louder!" the Pathan shrieked.

"With bitter lot, scar or blot. Through tie and tangle, tear and knot. Resist me not."

"Louder!" He poked a sharp, cold finger into Xemion's ribs and Xemion felt the blood welling again in his forehead. He was now yelling the words, still trying desperately to keep his voice expressionless. But the taste of blood was thick on his tongue and something was uncoiling deep in his cells.

"Resist me not."

"Sing it," the Pathan roared.

"Resist me not."

"Chant it!"

Something like a knot slipped out of itself in Xemion's stomach and suddenly the voice in his belly was unleashed and that tone he had used when reading to the class, that spellbinding tone Anya had tried to stifle in him all the days of his life, sprang free for a moment, ringing out with the full glory of the Elphaerean tongue.

"Resist me not."

"Go on!" the Pathan roared.

"With magic mind," Xemion sang. "With twisted tongue, root or rind. Unvein me now, unskin my thought. Resist me not."

That last loud *not* echoed in the dark space and then there was silence. The Pathan slammed the book shut resoundingly and nodded, smiling slightly. Glittervein grinned with pride and, after tapping his pipe upside down against the chair, put it away in his pocket.

"Glittervein, I love you," Vihata enthused, his voice like tiny, grating crystals. "You have given me so many precious gifts. But this — this means I love you forever."

"And he is full grown." Glittervein emitted a small, tight laugh of delight. "I've been watching him a long time. I was sure of it but I knew you would want to see for yourself."

"Let me go!" Xemion bellowed, straining at his bonds.

Glittervein turned toward Xemion, but his attempt at a smile did not quite reach his eyes. "I'm sorry, but I can't, Xemion. Unfortunately, you've failed the examination."

Xemion began to swear. Every foul imprecation he'd ever heard the drink Thralls hurl at one another in their drunken stupors bellowed out of him so loud he thought his throat might burst. But it wasn't just words that welled. All sorts of impulses and fractured visions were hurtling through his brain in a mad scramble to be known.

"Such lungs." The Pathan nodded with approval. "He's perfect."

"And he's yours. This very night if you like. If … if you have the funds of course."

"Of course I do," Vihata replied jovially, his voice taking on a glassy lilt. He reached into his robe and extracted a fat bag of coins, which he plumped into Glittervein's waiting hand. "As agreed."

So many words were competing at once to come screaming out of Xemion he began to stutter and shriek in jagged, disconnected syllables.

"You may have given him a little too much of your libation," Glittervein said gleefully as he weighed the bag judiciously in his palm.

"There'll be lots more of it where I'm taking him." Laughing, Vihata took the torch from the bracket on the wall and strode to the opposite end of the chamber. There he opened a bronze door and fog billowed in. Xemion could hear the sea crashing far below.

"Lethir," Vihata shouted over the sound of Xemion's continued profanities, "Secure him."

Lethir stepped behind the stone chair, wrapped

his massive fists about Xemion's wrists, and, when Glittervein released the restraints, yanked Xemion to his feet with one quick jerk, pinning his arms behind his back.

Xemion saw the Pathan step through the doorway onto the landing of a stairway outside and wave the torch. It was still very foggy and he had to wave it for a while, the billowing fog eerily lit up as though from some conflagration below. Finally the sound of a whistle was heard and the Pathan came back in and beckoned with the brand. Just as Lethir pushed him toward the doorway, Xemion brought his heel down with all his might and weight right onto the arch of Lethir's foot. Lethir bellowed in pain and in that instant Xemion tore free of his grip and tried to bolt away. But the Cyclops was too quick for him and succeeded in grabbing back one wrist. Xemion yanked his arm with all of his might, but when he couldn't pull free he swung round full circle with his other hand bunched into a tight fist and rammed it into Lethir's nose full force. There was only a second while the Cyclops jerked his head back, blinking and stunned, but in that second Xemion tore his wrist free and bolted off into the darkness.

He couldn't see, but he remembered where the stairs were, and sensed from the way the shouts echoed back around him where to turn. Soon he was sprinting back through the banquet room and into the hallway he'd entered by. But there in the doorway at the end stood a guard.

"Stop him!" came the shouts from behind. The guard looked uncertain, and groped at his waist for his sword.

Xemion attempted to shout "Out of my way!" but as he barrelled straight at the man, what came out of his mouth was some kind of hideous bestial shriek. It startled the guard just enough for Xemion to get around him and dash out into the foggy night.

15

Down

The fog had thinned a little but there was still enough to shroud his flight as he tore down the length of Phaer Point. When he got to the High Street the fog was thinner yet and he began to zigzag and take corners randomly in an effort to throw off his pursuers. All the while he kept cursing and spitting and shaking his hands as though these actions might somehow rid him of the horror and taste of that potion he had swallowed. He wanted it out of his cells immediately. He wanted to get down on his knees and stick his fingers down his throat and vomit until he was emptier than he'd ever been. But he had to get away.

His plan was to get to the wall that bisected the city, follow it along to the place where he and Saheli had entered, then cross back over to the other side of Ulde where he could hide among its spell-crossed denizens until the morning. Just as he got to the section of the wall that curved around the Great Kone he heard a shout echo along the wall from somewhere in front of him. And from behind him, the patter and racket of numerous feet was coming closer. And now there was almost nothing left of the fog. Soon he would be exposed. Right out in the open. There was only one place to go.

The wall around the aboveground portion of the Great Kone, whose disrepair Xemion had seen previously from the east side of Ulde, was better-maintained here. There were no gaps in the brickwork where one might see through to the actual surface of the Kone. But there was what must once have been an official point of entry. Recently, the Pathans had tried to seal it with a bronze gate bolted shut on both sides, but something had caused this structure to buckle inward, leaving a jagged opening in the middle. Xemion stepped between the rusted edges of torn bronze and found himself looking up at the topmost rim of the Great Kone itself.

A cloud had drifted in front of the moon, but the ancient reed paper that bore the script of the Great Kone had been invested with its own luminosity, so that even at night, travellers might be able to read its text. When the Pathans first conquered the city they had tried to destroy the Kone. But these efforts proved futile, so they covered it with numerous rude scrawled messages and icons. Frightened as he was, Xemion felt anger as he beheld the desecration. He took a deep breath and let the green glow of the Kone wash through the terrible red luminescence inside him. How it soothed. How it soothed him.

For a time he crouched just inside the opening. Slowly his eyes adjusted to the darkness and he saw the top of an ancient stone stairway that ran around the outside of the

Great Kone, following the spiral of its text deep into the Earth. As the sound of his pursuers' footsteps got closer, Xemion crept over to the top step and crouched on it in the darkness. He heard voices. They were right outside! Very quietly he began to back down the stairs. As he saw a foot finding its way through the ragged hole above him, he turned and bolted down the staircase.

He ran a long time without descending very far. This was because the circumference of the Kone at this level was greater than that of a stadium. The stairs had only the slightest slant. And, he now realized, if he kept going he would be running right back to a place just under where he had entered. If his pursuers were smart they would just leap over the banister and wait there for him. Panting, the air burning in his lungs, he stopped and listened. He looked over the edge to the banister below.

He could descend much quicker if he climbed straight down. He could hear water dripping somewhere, each drop magnified by its echo. His lips started moving. He was mumbling words again and felt like vomiting. He cupped his hand over his mouth and rocked there back and forth, considering his options. Whichever way he ran, he was trapped. But his best chance was to keep heading downward. Perhaps they would give up on him.

Careful to keep enough distance from the surface of the Great Kone, he swung his legs over the railing and lowered himself until his feet touched the banister below. In this manner he began to climb rapidly, straight down the inside of the spiralling stairs, so close to the surface of the Great Kone he was almost touching it. The smell of burnt paper and mould increased the deeper he got. Every once in a while he would pause and listen in the hope that they had stopped pursuing him, but each time, sooner or later, a soft sound would come — it may have just been water dripping, but it could just as likely be the padding of furtive footsteps. And so he continued down, down. Beneath him it seemed as though the Great Kone was narrowing so quickly that he was sure he should soon reach the bottom. But perhaps the tales that claimed there was no actual bottom were true, because no matter how far he descended the bottom never seemed to come into view. How could he have descended so far and yet still have such depths to go? And when he reached the bottom, what then? Would he just be trapped down there until his pursuers caught him and dragged him back up?

He heard a mumbling voice and started with fear, but then he realized that it was he who was making the sound: incomprehensible words, but words he knew he had heard before. They were the very words Musea had bid him to remember before she died. Xemion clamped his mouth shut tight, but soon the words erupted again beyond his control. He tried to clear them from his mind but they overrode his thoughts. Desperate to stop them, he stared directly at the text of the Great Kone and read it. The words were no longer obscured at this depth and even in his terror he was aware of their beauty. Someone had exercised such artistry in the imagining of these runes. Xemion turned and saw the letter X. His eyes fastened on it, and then his foot slipped. He grabbed desperately at the banister below, but he missed and bounced off it with a scream, crashing through the paper of the Kone and into its interior. He screamed as he fell, the inverted letters rising in a smear straight up as he fell straight down. And all the while the Kone grew narrower and narrower, and the text smaller and smaller, and Xemion seemed to be shrinking smaller and smaller too.

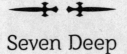

16

Seven Deep

Two days before the equinox, just after the departure of the *Mammuth* on another provisioning journey, Vallaine woke up in the top room of his tower on the west side of Ulde. His hand was white — so white that he could see the blue veins pulsing from within it. Startled, he shook it in the air as though he might somehow fling its pallid hue back into the dream it had escaped from, but to no avail. The hand remained drained of all colour while the dream hung there, dissolving, till all that remained was a feeling of deep dread and one word — one name, the name of the girl from Ilde: *Saheli*.

He stumbled over the heaps of books that had erupted from the locket the night before and reached for the tell-kone on his desk. He had consulted it a lot lately, but had no choice but to do so again now. He grasped the handle and began to turn.

The tell-kone looked like a spell kone but was of a

much more ancient origin. Augurs had spun tell-kones since time immemorial. The mechanism was simple. The crank handle was affixed by various gears to a copper kone mounted on its tip in a frame. This kone contained six smaller concentric kones, each one inscribed with letters and numbers, each surface incised with slits of various sizes set at various angles. When the handle was turned the kones all whirled at their respective speeds until one by one they came to a halt. A practiced augur could then write down the words and numbers revealed by the slits in order to make determinations about the future. Today Vallaine's spin achieved a most unlikely result. The small, vertical slits at the bottom of the outer six kones all lined up as one to reveal the seventh and innermost kone. The augurs had a name for this. They called it *seven deep*. Seven deep meant trouble. Especially when the letter revealed was an *X*, as this was.

The colour drained from Vallaine's face, then he cursed. He scanned the room, seeking something, but when he didn't find it he grew angry and began to use one foot to sweep aside the books that littered the floor. At last, under a particularly large pile, he found what he was looking for: his camouflage cloak and his long hemp rope. Throwing them on as he ran out the door, he stumbled over some books that had spilled out onto the stairs, but the leap he took at the last moment to avoid falling ended fortuitously on the seventh step. He raced down the remaining fourteen stone steps and out into the street, as worried as he'd been in years. Taking great care not be seen, he quickly made his way across the city to the Great Kone. He needed strength, and he needed to see for himself if he was right.

During the two years that had passed since he blasted open the bronze gate, Vallaine had developed an efficient method for descending the Great Kone. He draped the middle of his long rope over the railing and then held on to both halves of it as he lowered himself three or four banisters at a time. Then, by tugging one side of the rope, he pulled the rest of it down, folded it over the next banister, and continued the process. Long before he reached the last spiral of the steps, his sense that something was deeply wrong was confirmed. There had always been a round stone chamber at the bottom of the stairs where successful pilgrims could view the tapering point of the Kone just as it met and went through the focal point of a large lens set in a circular table. The Kone's taper was so narrow here it was said to be "more like light than matter." It was claimed your hand could pass through it and feel nothing. Normally the dim glow filtering back up the Kone from here was Vallaine's first sign that he was reaching the bottom. Today though, only halfway down the Kone, he was already glimpsing a much brighter, much more searing light spilling up from the depths.

For a moment he considered turning back, but even from where he was he could sense the power in the light. He had come here for strength and already his hand was taking on a slight red undertone. He had come here for a clearer foretelling and already he was seeing with new clarity. And if that clarity was only further affirmation of his dread, he had to know it in full. By the time he touched down on the bottom step he had to shield his eyes with his forearm because the light had become painfully bright. He edged his way forward until he got to the table and the lens through which the brilliant spectral light streamed.

He climbed up on top of the table and positioned himself with one foot on either side of the lens as he held his open palm over it. The piercing light at his feet shrieked up at him and he did his best to centre his mind and let it radiate through him, his hand slowly taking on a deeper flush as he did so. This light streamed in at him from infinite worlds. That was his belief. Somewhere just beyond — just a little deeper down, the Great Kone shared its last infinitesimally small and pointless point, with every other Great Kone's final pointless point. This streaming light came not only from the very edge of this world but from the edges of all the worlds created by those other Great Kones, too — all possible worlds. That was why this was the best place to receive intimations of all possible futures. Until now his journeys here had always been encouraging. They strengthened and fortified him with a sure sense of hope. But wherever he gazed now he saw imminent calamity. No matter what future his mind fell upon there was no place for his city and the Phaer way he cherished. No future but one — and survival in that one unlikely future would be dependent on one person. The name he had awoken with sounded for the thousandth time in his mind.

Even as he pictured her face the way it had been that first day he saw her in Ilde, he heard a muffled voice that seemed to vibrate up through the lens. The sound of chanting rose and fell then died away, but after that he continued to sense a presence, an intense agony nearby, saturating every thread of shimmering light. Shielding his eyes with his hands he bent down on one knee and peered more closely into the Nexis below.

The long, tapering ends of infinite kones tilted in from all directions, meeting in a hub at first too bright to look at. But it was from here that the mumbling originated. Gradually as he squinted he began to discern the outlines of a body slowly revolving about that hub. There was a spectral translucent quality to it as though it were more illusion than matter, the lines of light brilliant beneath its skin. As the face came into view Vallaine saw the wrenched features of Xemion, his eyes closed but his lips moving very slightly. Then he heard again that mystical mumbling. Vallaine shook his head, took up his rope, and said, "And now I rescue him a third time."

The ancient mages who made this viewing chamber had constructed one hatch at the back. It was a round black door with two symbols beveled into the top of its frame. One was the symbol for infinity and the other for the void. In all his many visits to the Great Kone, Vallaine had never dared open it before. But today he had to take that chance. The light spilled in even brighter as he inched it open. Before him were seven steps, which led down to a stone platform overlooking the centre of the Nexis.

He made his way through the doorway and down the steps and saw that he was on the inside of a large sphere that looked to be carved out of solid granite. From every point of its surface, barely detectable lines of force zeroed in on that bright light at the centre where Xemion whirled. At first Vallaine's perception of distance was skewed, but as he focused he realized that the luminous hub they all met in was only about twenty feet away. Vallaine took both ends of his rope and leaned way out from the platform so that he could pass the loop at the bottom over the slowly whirling figure. He was sure he was doing the right thing. The light flooding in and radiating through him from everywhere told him so. He needed this boy — this man. He was crucial to the Phaer Purpose.

When Xemion had completed one more slow spin, thereby winding the rope about his midsection, Vallaine tugged at the rope. As he pulled Xemion out of the centre, the light lessened a little, but still remained searingly bright. He dragged him up like a drowned man over the rough granite edge and laid him on the stone floor. Xemion twitched and jerked and continued mumbling and whispering for a short while, but then he suddenly stopped. Vallaine feared he might be dead, for his body was extremely cold and his flesh had taken on a slightly blue colour. But he was breathing shallowly, so slowly it was almost undetectable. Vallaine knew what this was: spell-shock. The boy had been trying to cast a spell — a very powerful spell. Vallaine grew more and more alarmed. He had to do something. His hand was now a deeper scarlet than it had ever been before. Indeed, the intense red had even spread up to his forearm and past his elbow. It felt hot and powerful. He pinched the webbing at the back of Xemion's thumb and forefinger until he began to see a slight grimace appear on the boy's face.

Good, he thought.

He increased the pressure, finally causing Xemion to groan.

"Now stay with me," he shouted. "Stay with me!"

Xemion grunted, his spirit like a moth struggling in thick black tar.

"Wake up," Vallaine shouted, gripping him tight. "If you sink back into it, you will die!"

Xemion clenched his teeth and took another searing breath. In that instant, like someone waking from a nightmare, the memory of his life flooded back in on him. It seemed but seconds ago when he had fallen, less than a minute since the Pathan had poured that concoction down his throat. With great effort he lifted his eyelids and saw Vallaine illuminated by the bright light still radiating from the Nexis. Vallaine's usual projection of mirthful charm had been replaced by an expression of grave concern. He reached out his red hand to take Xemion's, and as it touched him Xemion remembered his suspicion.

"I have to get you out of here or you will die of spell-shock," Vallaine said. "Can you stand?"

Xemion tried to move his arms and legs but couldn't, so Vallaine picked the boy up, cradling him in his arms as he ascended the seven steps back into the viewing chamber. He put him down long enough to close the black hatch, then, scooping him back up into his arms, he carried him to the main stairway and began to climb the Great Kone. It was so narrow here that each step was high while the staircase itself spiralled within a small circumference. Round and round he climbed.

"Are you keeping alert, Xemion?" he asked, seeing the glazed look returning to his eyes. Xemion just barely managed a nod.

"What were you doing down there?" Vallaine asked sharply.

Xemion had a vision of infinite versions of himself drawn from infinite universes: side-selves, under-selves, over-selves, all drawn down as one into the Nexis to chant those strange sounds — and he knew now what those sounds were. They were the words Musea had made him memorize. He felt them spring up again, great echoing helixes of conjury.

"Xemion, are you listening?"

Xemion lifted his eyes again and tried to speak, but he only achieved a muffled groan that hurt his throat.

"Did the old woman plant a spell on you?"

Xemion focused hard. He gave the smallest of nods. The apparent circling of the Great Kone above him was so nauseating he had to close his eyes again. But Vallaine wouldn't allow it. He pinched him hard till he groaned.

"What spell was it?"

Xemion's stomach heaved but it was empty. That larger sense of self he'd experienced in the Nexis was fading away.

"Was it a turn spell, do you think?"

Xemion kept retching and retching. Vallaine answered his own question. "I think it was. I think she planted a spell on you in hopes of somehow getting the Great Kone to turn again. Do you remember any of it?"

Xemion's eyes flickered as he shook his head just a little in answer.

"Well, try," Vallaine said, his voice urgent. "I need to know."

Xemion turned away but he couldn't hide that flicker again and Vallaine saw it.

"What? You mistrust me?" Vallaine asked, startled.

"At the very moment I am saving your life?" Xemion did not meet his eye. "When have I ever done anything to earn such mistrust?"

Xemion managed to get the words out in a dry croak. "Last night."

Vallaine blinked in confusion.

"Glittervein," Xemion added, his voice raw, the anger welling.

Vallaine actually paused in mid-step. A look of understanding entered his eyes. "Are you telling me that Glittervein took you in for examination?"

"And a Pathan."

"And a Pathan?" This latest piece of information seemed to leave him quite shocked. "Inside Ulde?"

Xemion nodded, the lines in his brow deepening accusingly.

"Look, Xemion," Vallaine said angrily. "This is very serious. It wasn't last night you gave the locket to me. It was a fortnight ago. I haven't even seen Glittervein yet. I still have the locket at home in my tower. I thought you had gone on to the camp in the mountains."

Xemion showed no reaction. He was trying to move his legs.

"What would I gain from selling you into Pathar?" Vallaine persisted angrily. The power from the light below was flooding through him now and he was full of that strange strength it gave him. "Do you really believe I could do such a thing?"

Xemion tried to shrug but his shoulders didn't quite obey him.

Vallaine was offended. The pitch of his voice rose

slightly and he spoke quickly as he climbed. "There is something very wrong going on and there's too much at stake here to—" He took a deep breath, and when he exhaled he let the feelings go. "Listen," he continued in a softer voice, not yet breathing heavily from his exertions. "You will recover from your spell-shock before long and regain your strength, and when you do I'm going to need you. Suddenly we have a Pathan trader in the very heart of the Phaer capital trying to steal our young away from us. But it's worse than that. Your friend Saheli is in grave danger."

This information hit Xemion with a jolt. *If she was in danger then she was not dead.* The flame of hope was rekindled in Xemion's heart.

"Yes. But to save her you're going to have to trust me. So I'm going to tell you something you may have figured out for yourself. I was born a middle mage. I told you before what a middle mage is. In the time before the spell kones we were carriers of spells. We had no spellcraft of our own but we could absorb the natural magic from others and transfer it. When the spell kones came, people thought there was no need for us, so we did other things. We were carriers of water. We delivered messages. We carried and exchanged currencies. Wherever some kind of transfer was needed through a middle ground, it was to us they came. Some of us were diplomats and advisers. My great skill is that I have a certain amount of foresight. It comes to me naturally with my middle nature."

Perhaps it was the quickness of the pace he was keeping that caused Vallaine to speak so fast, but the words had now begun to pour out of him at great speed. Farther and farther below them the light from the Nexis was slowly beginning to dim.

"When I first met you and Saheli, I saw a great destiny in you — in both of you — and I knew it was tied up with the destiny of our whole rebellion. But today when I awoke I sensed something terrible was about to happen. And that is why I came to the Great Kone. Not to rescue you. I had no idea that you were even here. I came because it strengthens me and because the foretelling is clearest here."

Vallaine continued quickly striding up the widening loops of the stairway, each step slightly lower than the one before. "But as I descended, many of the possibilities that seemed so imminent just weeks ago were suddenly … gone. And the deeper I descended the narrower and narrower grew the range of possibilities. When I stood directly over the Nexis light at the bottom of the Kone I felt ahead of us only two possible futures, and in only one of them could our Phaer culture survive. And that depended on one thing: Saheli's survival. There was no other way in any world that I could see. And yet in every world but one I saw her pierced through the breast, pinned to the ground by a sword through her chest. I saw her life ended and the Phaer purpose swept away."

"No!" Now that Vallaine had expressed it, Xemion saw it, too, and in that moment he knew that Vallaine wasn't lying. He strained against his immobility as though against a chain, but his arms and legs were still all but paralyzed.

"Yes. And that is why I need you. You and I must stop it from happening. We must guard her and, if necessary, we will fight for her. I have long training with the sword, but you, too, are crucial to this somehow. I warn you, though; there is some spell cross at work on the two of you. I can't read it clearly. It must originate from some ancient spoken spell that my own small magic is not powerful enough to penetrate."

"You said you had no magic," Xemion croaked.

"I said I have no spellcraft, and that is true. But all Freemen have a certain amount of natural magic that wells up in them over time. And when it is ripe, a middler like me can come along, and, by shaking hands repeatedly with, let's say, a whole village of fisher people, bring their common magic together in one hand and then let it go into one place or purpose. But it has to be *their* purpose, not mine. This is a simple and natural thing. It has nothing to do with spellcraft; in fact, it pre-dates spellcraft by thousands of years. This is the way our ancestors did it. Whatever energy I can gather into me will all go to protect her. But I fear the time for that is coming very soon. We have to hurry."

They both looked up and the light filtering down from the top of the Great Kone was still so far above them that it might have been the last thin rim of moonlight before a total eclipse.

"The equinox," Xemion croaked.

"That's right," Vallaine answered.

"Montither," Xemion growled. The very word brought the taste of blood back into his mouth. It was the taste of hatred.

"Yes," Vallaine said. "And we still have a day's climbing left in front of us." It had now grown considerably darker in the Kone, not just because they had travelled some distance from the light at the bottom, but because that light was slowly dimming. And with it, unknown to him, so was the depth of the red in Vallaine's hand. "So now will you tell me what you remember of the words you spoke below?"

Xemion nodded, a look of contrition on his face. "Turnspell," he said, his voice still ragged from its long overuse.

Vallaine said nothing, but the light filtering down from the top of the Kone eerily outlined the dark lines of worry in his face as he picked up the pace. He was beginning to feel the strain of his exertions.

"But I'm not a spellbinder," Xemion added.

Vallaine shrugged. "Who knows what you might be. You have a rich voice. Many people have rich voices and yet they are not spellbinders. So many children have lost their lives so needlessly for the simple sin of having a good voice. That's probably why you were raised in such a remote location. But there's only one way to tell if someone is a spellbinder and that is if they bind a spell and it works."

"So …"

"So it is highly unlikely that without training anyone could manifest even a small spell, let alone bring about the turning of the Great Kone."

"Which is not turning," Xemion rasped, nodding his head toward the monumental curve of reed paper beside them. No trace of revolution was detectable.

"It's too soon to tell," Vallaine said. "But if it does turn, then it will be a different world in a different situation and we will have to find a way to deal with that. But right now in this world it is your skill and your sword and your friendship I will need. And whomever else we can trust to help us keep her safe. I don't know where she is or what she's doing. But this is a most crucial time for her. I believe, however, if you and I can get her through the next few days, the worst will be over."

Xemion nodded uncertainly. His heart had begun to beat rapidly with the thought that she was indeed alive. He was now able to move his toes a little, and the tips of his fingers.

"Why will it be a different world if the Great Kone turns?" he asked.

"It *won't* turn."

After that there was silence between them for a long time while Vallaine climbed. Xemion, with his head hung back over the crook of Vallaine's elbow, watched the slow backward revolution of the words on the Great Kone as he passed them by. Finally, Vallaine said, "There are different beliefs about the Great Kone, Xemion. I believe the Great Kone remakes the world every instant. Since it stopped turning it has been only the forces of nature and our own actions in it that have moved the world. If it should start to turn again, which it won't, I suspect it would just take the world the way it is now and work with it magically from there, transforming it perhaps suddenly, perhaps violently, in accordance with the strictures written down upon it. It might arouse a new golden age for the Phaer people. It might empower us once again to raise a wise and just civilization that will be a light to the ages. Or it might take us and break us again because we are foolish enough to think that we can control it by naming it. In any case, as I've said, we're not likely to find out."

Vallaine was breathing heavier now. He had been climbing all day, and now that night had fallen there was no light at all filtering down from above. He slowed as it grew colder; the only light now the faint green luminescence of the kone itself. Slowly his steps grew more and more laboured until he was gasping for breath. And always there were more steps, wider spirals.

"Xemion, I must put you down and rest awhile." He stopped and lay Xemion gently down on the staircase. "I just need a moment to catch my breath." Vallaine slumped down on a step, his head hung over into his hands, his elbows supported by his knees. Xemion tried to rise from the cold stone, but his limbs were still too numb and unresponsive. He tried again and was able to raise his left hand just a little. And then his arm.

Waving the hand, he showed Vallaine. "Look!"

Vallaine nodded. He waved back, and when he saw his own hand he was shocked. It was bleached white as bone.

"No!" Even in the dim light, Xemion saw the look of pain in Vallaine's features. "Xemion, take my hand. Take my hand before I disappear."

Xemion could barely move his own arm, yet but he managed to do so enough to grab hold of the cold white hand.

"I'm seven deep here," Vallaine said desperately. "I'm not going to make it to the top of the kone and I've left something terrible undone. You will soon be stronger. You must climb. Nothing must stop you. Go to my tower on the eastern side of Ulde. It's the tallest one there. Search for the book. The book from the locket you gave me. It is called *The Thaumatalogical Lexicon*. It is a book of spells. I managed to extract it just before I came here." Vallaine's voice was so quiet now that Xemion had to strain to hear him. "Take the book and hide it, or if there is no other way you must destroy it. But don't let the Pathans get their hands on it. It is *The Grimoire*, the book of spells. Even Saheli's leadership will make no difference if the Pathans, or worse yet, the Necromancer of Arthenow, should get a hold of it. Do you hear me? If you have to — if there is no other way — destroy it." The light in Vallaine's eyes was like a flame in a high wind swept back as he struggled to continue. "This is not dying. This is not death."

Vallaine's face had taken on the same bleached trans-lucence as his hand. "Do whatever will save her." His voice was hardly more than a whisper. He could see the confusion and horror in Xemion's eyes as he released his hand and fell back on the steps, his face wrenched with pain. There was a red incandescent flash that rose up from his feet and into his body. When it was done there was nothing left of Vallaine but his rope and his long camouflage cloak.

17

In the Cloak

For a long time Xemion could do nothing but shake and retch as the cold from the stone steps seeped into his ribs. He could still only move his arms and legs very little and the final sleep was calling him. On his own account he would surely have died right then and there, thirsty and freezing. But there was so much more at stake now than just an end to his own misery. Still he hesitated before inching his hand over to Vallaine's cloak. In some way it repulsed him. He looked up and thought it must be morning because there was a little crescent of light shining again at the top of the kone. It was still so high above him, though, that it might have been the flash of a distant scythe seen across a thousand fields. He felt defeated and betrayed. And poisoned. He felt broken and stupid with the thought that he'd been tricked by Musea into carrying a spell into the Nexis. The thought that he'd been taken over by a potion or that he himself might be a spellbinder terrified him. But all of this was secondary to the thought — or the image that had leapt from Vallaine's mind into his own. Saheli lying dead, pierced through the chest by Montither's sword. However many steps there might be between here and the top of the kone, he would climb them. Nothing would stop him. He dragged the cloak toward him and draped it over one shoulder. With trembling hands he used all the reserves of energy he had within him and reached slowly up to the banister and dragged himself to his feet. Inch by inch he managed to get the cloak over his other shoulder and secure it in front. He slid his left hand farther along the banister until he was leaning forward, and then he dragged one foot up to the step above and straightered up. Hand over hand, step by step, groaning with agony, he began to climb. He had to put everything he had into every step, and each step seemed like it must be the last, but out of sheer will there was always one more. And all the while it grew steadily colder, so that even inside Vallaine's cloak he shivered, his teeth chattering.

Soon thirst began to assail him. Always he heard the sound of water dripping, but as he came around the curve of the ever-widening spiral steps, he never saw even the slightest stain where water might once have been. Parched and brittle and freezing, he somehow drove himself on, that arc of light still so far above him that it seemed like a horizon he would never reach. But he had to reach it! And soon. Tomorrow would be the equinox and he had to be there or Saheli would die.

By early evening he was down on his hands and knees, crawling up the stairs. Just before he lost consciousness, he collapsed. It was still cold but the air was tinged now with a salt scent that told him he must be nearing the top. He tried again and again to rise. But he couldn't. He slumped face down into the steps and stayed there, shivering. He was freezing and afraid, but not afraid for himself, afraid for her. He was the only thing between Saheli and death. For a second he wished he really was a spellbinder, or that there really was some kind of God such as the Thralls worshipped from whom he might now draw some extra strength, for he knew he had reached the very bottom of his own.

But just then a huge bass voice shook the Great Kone: "I beg you do not die."

Immediately, something warm and wet touched his left cheek. Hot breath and a rough tongue slid over him, quick as a flickering flame. Xemion turned. "Bargest," he groaned. Excited to get a response, the huge dog hunched over him and licked all the faster, the heat of his tongue warming Xemion's face. Xemion tried to say "water," but all he could do was croak. And then the dog was gone. Xemion slumped back down, shivering against the steps, the ache of thirst deep in his throat, willing himself not to die. He was hanging on by one word. It was a spell that would not let him give up — her name: *Saheli*.

Finally Bargest returned with a dripping rag in his jaws that he dangled over Xemion's parched mouth. Drinking the liquid was almost as painful to him as the thirst had been. But when the dog returned he drank again. And when the dog came back carrying an apple in his jaws Xemion ate that, too. All the while as he slumped there eating, the dog kept nudging his hip with his massive nose as though he wanted something. Grateful as he was, Xemion chided him. First he said "No." Then, when the dog persisted, he raised his voice a little. "No begging."

By now the air in the Great Kone had begun to grow warmer. Xemion could see by the light above that he must be only seven or eight spirals away from the top. He tried to rise but crumpled to the ground. He kept trying until finally, with one hand on the banister and one gripping the thick fur on Bargest's haunches, he managed to struggle farther up the steps. And all the while he sucked feverishly at the rag like some newborn child desperate to stay in this world.

As the two of them climbed, the wind changed direction, and by the time Xemion emerged from the top of the kone the air had warmed considerably. He stepped through the hole in the bronze gate into a humid, windy evening. The air smelled of salt and seabirds and distant spices as though it had just blown seconds ago right off the distant continent of Aruk. Almost crimson, the sun was going down, slowly dipping its rim into a heap of clouds piled up like a ziggurat on the horizon.

He felt a moment of relief that he had arrived before the equinox, but then the wind gusted strongly against him and he realized how weak he was and how much he had to do. He thought of Montither and wished he had some great weapon — or any weapon at all. He had a vision of himself hurling bolts of fire from his palms, blasting Montither to ash and bone. Almost hopefully he looked back at the Great Kone and studied it intently to see if it moved. But it was utterly still. It had not moved a hair since he'd gazed at these vandalized letters a fortnight ago. He was relieved and disappointed in almost equal measure — relieved because he had great disdain for spellcraft, but disappointed because he had no sword, no food in his belly, and very little remaining strength. The wind was picking up, coming in off the southern sea with a warm tang and sting that whipped Xemion's hair back off of his shoulders. He leaned into it as Bargest pushed his nose against his hip.

"I beg you." Bargest sniffed at Xemion's hip.

"No," Xemion said gruffly. He gestured with his hands to indicate his complete lack of any kind of biscuit at all, but when the dog persisted and said "I beg you, look inside the cloak," he did, and thereby found a small pocket hidden in the waist. At first he thought it was empty, but crammed down in one corner was some kind of wafer. He took it out and it was dark on the two outer layers, but a golden amber colour in the middle. Bargest stared intently, his head cocked to one side. What looked to be a smile appeared on his great black face.

"I beg you. Eat."

Xemion took a cautious bite and immediately a warmth and taste that was somehow familiar entered his mouth. Bargest began to jump around excitedly as he saw Xemion's eyes light up. It was so sweet. It was almost too sweet. He took another small bite and felt the energy stream into him. He didn't know what it was, whether it was the fabled ambrosia talked of in the Phaer Tales, some spellworked honeycomb, or some middle thing between the two, but it was quickly giving him a renewed vigour and strength. His first instinct was to swallow it all at once, but just as he was putting it to his lips he thought better of it. There was already sufficient energy in him with just two bites taken. His exhaustion was evaporating from his cells and each breath he took seemed to go right to that fire burning in his heart, stoking it, making it want to leap up and grow huge. Vallaine had told him to go to his tower and find the book of spells, but there was so little time. And there was something else of greater importance, he decided. Something he had to make sure of first.

"I must find Montither," he growled.

Bargest looked up at the sky and let loose a howl of triumph. Immediately he lay his long nose down on the ground and said, "I beg you, accept me in service as your dog."

Xemion looked at the dog with gratitude. "I will try you out," he said, a little reluctantly, his voice still rough and hoarse, "but there is much at stake and you must obey me."

Like some great burning galleon, sinking under the weight of its own gold, the sun was now deep in the mist-like clouds on the horizon, their dark tentacles looking as if they were trying to pull it down faster. He thought for a second of Vallaine, and there must have still been some shred of suspicion left in him, because he looked at the wafer, still in his hand, and wondered: if such miraculous food was right there in his pocket, why hadn't Vallaine eaten it? But perhaps he hadn't even known it was there. He put the remainder of it in his pocket and drew the cloak tightly about him, pulling up the hood, which was already shifting its colour to match that of the storm clouds overhead. He turned to Bargest and said, "Come!"

Bargest lifted his considerable snout from the ground, took a sniff at the wet spring air, and then he and Xemion headed toward the Panthemium at a run.

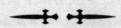

18

A Specially Made Sword

Even though he wore Vallaine's chameleon cloak, Xemion kept out of sight lest Glittervein or one of his confederates should see him as he made his way to the Panthemium. He had no clear plan yet what he'd do if and when he located Montither. It would not be wrong, would it, to cut off his hand as he had once tried to cut off Xemion's? Or to break it? Or to shatter his head?

"Stay here," he ordered Bargest as he entered the Panthemium. Unnoticed, he approached Gnasher, who, along with several other of Montither's thugs and drink Thralls, was loitering in the common area, covertly gulping down great quantities of grain alcohol from a large jug.

"Where is Montither?" he asked from inside the shadow of his dusk-grey hood. The lifelessness in his voice startled him. The words had come out in a dull, almost threatening tone.

"And who is it that asks?" Gnasher inquired with nearly concealed malice.

"The representative of Mr. Glittervein," Xemion growled back, his voice as menacing as he could make it.

One of the others piped up, "Well, you've missed him."

"He's already gone up to the stack," another said.

Xemion had nothing more to say to them — for now. He felt the strength from the biscuit surging within him, but he would not waste it on such as these. With no further comment, he turned and quickly walked away, ignoring Gnasher's repeated calls. The oncoming storm was gathering momentum over the sea as he dashed through the clinging, damp air toward Uldestack. Ready to help if need be, Bargest loped along just close enough to keep Xemion in his sight.

Xemion kept under cover, darting from one shadow to the next at full speed as he made his way up the long, slow, sloping roadway that led to the stack. He got to the top just in time to see Montither knocking on the wooden door of the workshop. Montither turned around and peered back the way he had come before furtively entering. Xemion dashed up the road and took up a place at a window through which he could see a narrow slice of the smithy's interior.

"Well, hello again, O Lord of Nains," he heard Montither say with snide politeness.

"Ah, yes, the young Montither," Glittervein replied with an equally disdainful courtesy. "What brings you to my smithy on this windy night?"

"I wonder, sir, since as always my question requires

some discretion, if your helper there might leave us alone for a moment." Xemion had to lean in a little closer to see that Montither was indicating the large Thrall girl who was quietly eating cheese curds at a table on the other side of the room. Xemion began to salivate at the sight of the cheese curds. He was hungry.

"That is Oime," replied Glittervein. "She neither sees nor hears."

Montither walked over and examined the gentle-faced Thralleen more closely. Suddenly he clapped his hands loudly behind her left ear.

"I see," he said with a smile when there was no reaction. "What possible use is she to you?" he asked with a laugh. "Is she your—?" Montither raised his eyebrows and finished his question with a lewd movement of his hips.

"She is a nocturnal Thrall from deep under Alder," Glittervein explained dryly, his smile stopping far short of his eyes. "She has the strongest arms for hammering I have ever seen, I promise you."

"But, sir, if she's blind, how does she know where or what to hammer?"

"I position her," Glittervein replied with clear disdain. He definitely did not enjoy being interrogated. "Very accurate, I assure you. I tap her shoulder and she knows what to do."

"That is so kind of you," Montither said, giving a sudden loud clap of his hand by her ear again, just to make sure.

"Now, what can I do for you?" Glittervein asked curtly.

"Mr. Glittervein, you know very well what you can do

for me. You can give me my new sword." At these words a chill bit into Xemion's blood and he started shaking, whether with wrath or fear he couldn't quite tell.

"Well, I'm sorry, but it is not quite ready."

"What?" Montither dropped all pretense of courtesy and spoke with anger. "I paid you an enormous amount of money for it. Now I want my sword and I want it tonight!"

"And as I told you on your last inquiry," Glittervein replied with apparent calmness, "it requires only one more firing and then it will be done. I told you that I would have it to you on time for the tournament. That is still my intent. And I might even have had it for you tonight but other things have had to take precedence and my machinery is overheated. Just be patient while it cools and I will have it for you in the morning." Glittervein's pipe, hanging at an angle from the scarred side of his mouth, emitted regular quick bursts of thick smoke as he sucked at it.

"The Phaer Tourney *is* tomorrow," Montither bellowed, his jaw thrust forward in rage. "I need to practice with the sword I intend to use. That is *my precedent.*"

"I really do wish I could help you." The Nain's ability to maintain a calm voice and game face was possibly reaching its limit. "But I possess no north wind to suddenly cool my machinery down and—"

"I want my sword!" Montither bellowed, actually stamping his foot.

Glittervein put his hands on his hips, tilted his head back a little, and grinned. "Well, I want my rest."

"Look, if I don't get that sword, I'll—"

"You'll what, I wonder?" There was a slight glint of

mirth in the Nain's expression now. "Bring in the … family?"

"I don't need my father to get my way," Montither spat back, enraged.

"I'm sure."

"Well, be sure, Nain. I have my own way. It's just not as subtle as my father's."

"I can see that." By now Glittervein's tone had sharpened. He would not be intimidated.

Montither softened. "Just be fair with me," he said, almost sweetly. "You did promise."

After an intense silence, during which the two glared at each other eye-to-eye, Glittervein let out a raspy chuckle and then smiled so broadly it was very difficult to tell if he was being sarcastic.

"All right then, let's not you and I fight. A promise is a promise. Maybe I will have to summon up a bit of extra north wind tonight."

Montither nodded and Xemion could see that he'd become so emotional that there was a threat of tears in his eyes.

"Yes, no need to be upset," Glittervein cooed. "Your family has been good to me, but as I said, my machinery does have to cool off a while. If you come back, let's say just after midnight, I will have it ready for you."

Montither smiled with relief. "And this sword will definitely be hard and sharp enough to do what I told you I needed it to do?"

"Of course," Glittervein confirmed, his pipe accenting his words with three quick jerking billows of smoke. "*If* you have sufficient strength and know where to strike.

But you have to come at it right. If you want to penetrate, you have to strike at the place of least resistance in the breastplate with the point of maximum thrust in the sword."

"Maximum thrust?"

"The point, boy. Surely Lighthammer has taught you that. If you hack or hew with the edge of the sword, that only dissipates the impact all along the length of the blade and thus diminishes it. Look." Glittervein took up a half-finished bronze sword from his worktable and, after whipping it through the air a few times, lunged forward with amazing quickness. "With a thrust forward, all your power is concentrated in one place: the point. You throw the whole weight of your body into it. That's how you penetrate armour."

Montither beheld this with raised eyebrows. "You know the sword well," he said with admiration.

"Of course."

"But you won't be … competing?"

"Of course not. Why would I? What would it prove that Nains haven't always proven but can never get accepted?"

Montither laughed and shrugged. "A shame," he said, but the look of relief on his face was obvious.

"I had you worried, did I?" Glittervein had become very solicitous and avuncular. "Look, the best thing is to show you. Let me give you a lesson in fighting dirty, my boy. I have an iron breastplate all set up in a vice in the workshop. We'll quaff a brew or two while my machinery cools down and I can show you some extremely nasty things, I promise you."

"Well, yes, that is most considerate of you, Mr. Glittervein."

Xemion crouched down in the dark as Glittervein closed and bolted the shutters to the window.

Glittervein chortled as he and Montither exited the smithy. "And so are you. But not too considerate to fight filthy, I hope."

"No, not quite that prissy," Montither joked.

"Well, we shall drink to dirty fighting then."

"Yes, we shall, Mr. Glittervein."

"To secret weapons," Mr. Glittervein chortled.

"To secret weapons and to poison."

"To secret weapons and to friends with secret weapons."

"And to friends with friends."

"To friends with friends," Montither returned. The two of them crossed the yard laughing equally as though each had just one-upped the other.

19

Glittervein's Machinery

As the dark of night edged up over the top of the stack and the storm brooded on the dark green dreams of the sea, Xemion quietly tried the door. He didn't yet know what his plan was, but he had to stop Montither from getting that sword. The door was locked. He tried the shutter, but it, too, was bolted shut. There was only one way to get into the smithy — he would have to climb up the great stack and enter through the hole in the top.

There were plenty of ropes about the smithy grounds. He had seen the Nains use them to lower iron rods over the edge of the promontory as they constructed the small gate at the end of the ridge. Finding one coiled against the smithy wall, Xemion climbed onto the roof of the workshop. Quickly, he wrapped the thick rope around the wide, upwardly slanting base of the stack, kicked off his shoes, put one bare foot up against the smooth stone, and began to walk up the side of the stack. Little by little, edging the rope higher and higher as he leaned back against it, he made his way to the top, and lifted himself over the rim.

The opening of the chimney was even wider than he had expected. The smoke of one hundred fires at once used to stream through here. The thick deposit of soot all around the great rim testified to that. He peered down and beheld, far below in the darkness, the dim glow of a long pit from which hot air and a terrible stink arose: Glittervein's kiln. But where was the sword?

Xemion had planned to loop the rope under the outside lip of the rim, but there was no need. The long-ago builders had allowed for the labours of their massive Cyclopean chimney sweeps by installing wide iron loops on either side of the flue. Quickly tying a firm knot through one of these, he began to lower himself hand-over-hand into the dark. It took longer than he expected. The bottom of the smithy, where the great kiln and Glittervein's other machinery lay, was much below ground level. The stink intensified the lower he got until finally the rope stopped. It was impossible to tell what was immediately below him, nor how far down it might be, but Xemion let go.

He sensed the whoosh of the ground coming at him just in time to roll so that even though he hit hard he was only winded. Standing up and peering into the dying glow coming from the open kiln, Xemion spied a large hill of shadow: *A huge mound of coal to fuel the machinery?* And there, beside it upon a stone table, was the sword. Xemion started to run toward it, but just then there was a great whooshing sound as though someone had stepped on a giant bellows. Xemion stopped in his tracks and gasped. Warm air rushed over his face and with it the hideous smell intensified. Staring into the hill of shadow, Xemion now saw wisps of smoke billowing up from two dark holes, and there, could those other two holes be large reptilian eyes? Surely he didn't see the hill shift a little.

Xemion clasped his hands together with the fiercest grip of his life. He pictured some guardian tiger demon about to spring. He prepared to die. But to his amazement, there followed a sob, a sigh of some kind. Then a small flicker of flame shot out from one of the two holes. It was by the light of that flame that Xemion at last saw the source of Glittervein's intense heat. This was no hill of coal, no heap of tiger; this was a dragon. In fact, Xemion knew beyond a doubt that this was the very same dragon he had encountered months ago in the Valley of Ulde.

As his eyes adjusted to the darkness, Xemion saw that most of the dragon's lower body was contained in a long rectangular pit. A gate made of metal so finely meshed it might have been a net stretched over the exposed upper portions of the dragon's back, its frame fastened into the rock floor by hinges on one side and a short length of chain on the other. This served as a lid, keeping the dragon in the pit and constraining everything but her head.

The dragon sobbed again, exhaling enough fiery breath for Xemion to see the crisscross of cuts and welts on her once scaly back where the beast's attempts at escape had caused the mesh of metal to cut into her flesh. Other cuts, gouges, and bruises were too deep to have been caused by such exertions. Everywhere the flesh was open, stripped of scales. There were white edges to some of these thin cuts as though they might be infected. Xemion felt sick to see such a tortured being.

Just then, from above, came the sound of a key turning in a lock and light suddenly flooded into the chamber, casting a shadow of the stairs that led up to Glittervein's workshop. Xemion ran and hid in the dark at the back of the smithy. Oime, who held aloft a burning brand, slowly descended the stone stairs with Glittervein following behind.

"How are you then, my little darling?" Glittervein called out malevolently to the dragon. "Are we having a nice evening then?"

The dragon shuddered and strained against the latticework as he approached.

Xemion watched, horrified, as Glittervein took Montither's broadsword from its place on the stone table and put it into a dark vice in front of the dragon's snarling mouth. Glittervein darted away and thereby avoided the sudden jet of blue fire, which the poor beast exhaled at him.

"Oh yes, prepare to flame, my dearie," Glittervein mocked with a sinister, angry laugh.

Steering Oime to the edge of the pit, over which the dragon's upper body projected some six or seven feet, he placed a long, black metal rod in her hand. Just as she might have swung the huge hammer in the foundry, poor blind Oime, not knowing what she was doing, swung the heavy metal rod with a great sodden thump that drove the metal mesh deep into the dragon's already raw flank. At first there was no fire, only those screams and roars, which Xemion had heard from outside the smithy that night when he'd gone to Uldestack to practice the sword. The dragon bucked and strained against the harness, but there was no escape, only the lashing, until finally, when the screams stopped, helplessly, the fire began.

Repeated bursts of blue flame exploded incandescent yellow and orange again and again, as the whipping continued. If he'd looked, Glittervein would have seen Xemion lit up by the fire, crouched at the back of the smithy, but Glittervein's eyes were riveted eagerly on the sword, which was beginning to change colour in the terrible heat. Xemion remained utterly still as the increasing heat of the sword shifted it through every colour of the spectrum until all but its extended point was red-hot. And here the fire briefly began to fail.

"Keep it up," Glittervein screamed, smacking Oime on the back. Oime lashed harder and the intensity of the fire increased.

Now Glittervein began to dance and sing that strange chant of his. Xemion had heard it before, but Glittervein's tone had been pure and clear compared to what it was tonight. He was obviously enraged. He was gritting his teeth and stomping about in fury as he sang. Xemion wondered if it was Montither who was the object of his rage.

> Hard is the hand
> And hard is the heel,
> Hard as the soul
> Make this steel.
> Hard as my flesh,

Burned and scarred.
Of my mettle make this metal
Hard, so hard.

Sharp, sharp,
As the lie is sharp.
Sharp as wind
That cleaves the scarp.
Sharp as the cry
In a newborn's heart.
Of my mettle make this metal
Sharp, so sharp.

Flailing and staggering in wider and wider circles around the dragon, the Nain was coming alarmingly close to where Xemion crouched. Just when it seemed he might almost stumble over him, the fire decreased again.

"Every ounce! Every ounce!" Glittervein shouted, running back to tap Oime three times on the back. Incredibly, Oime's energy redoubled and she began to hit the dragon's back with even mightier and more rapid blows. This final assault cost the dragon her silence, for she started to scream with each exhaled fire burst. The whipping continued until at last the long narrow point of the sword turned to steel and the job was done. Glittervein signalled Oime to desist. Using long tongs, he retrieved the glowing sword and quenched it with a great hiss in the water of the font. The dragon, whose whimpers had only just subsided, arched up again in terror at the sound of the hiss.

"Oh, you'd like to, wouldn't you?" Glittervein patted Oime's back. "Give her one more for good measure," he said, poking her, "just to light my pipe." He held out a long piece of kindling before the dragon's mouth and Oime lashed. A long, thin flare of pale blue fire shot out of the dragon's mouth, lighting the kindling. Glittervein lit his pipe with it and exhaled the smoke into the poor beast's eye.

"Good. Good. Now you rest up, my little darling." Glittervein poked the dragon's hide with the heel of his boot, causing the exhausted beast to bare her long, fanged teeth and snarl weakly. "You think you can frighten me, my darling?" he hissed. "You think you can take the other side of my face? I think not," he growled and poked the sword into the beast's side. Xemion's blood turned very cold and he shook with shame. The dragon hissed weakly and steam shot out of her side.

"Oh, you'd like me to cut your heart out right now, wouldn't you, my little pet," Glittervein crooned. "I think not. I need one more steeling from you yet." He tapped Oime on the shoulder and the two started to leave. "You just catch your breath, my darling," Glittervein called over his shoulder, as he ascended the stone stairway that led back to the smithy. "I shall soon return with some more caresses."

As soon as Glittervein and Oime were gone, Xemion did what he had to do. He could not leave the dragon here like this. He crossed the floor and took Montither's still-hot sword in hand. Raising it over his head, he approached the dragon, and when he was close enough, he brought it down with all his might on the chain that bolted the latticework to the stone. The sword rang out in his hand like a battered bell. It sent a severe vibration up into his bones that jangled his teeth and hurt his elbow. But the blow had left a deep nick in the chain. Again he raised the blade and again he struck. Five times he suffered the great reverberation of the sword until finally the chain was severed. At that, he signalled wearily to the startled beast, which had all this time whimpered and cowered at each blow like a frightened puppy.

"Go," he whispered to it. "Fly." Xemion pointed up to where the cloud-muffled moon glowed through the great hole in the top of the stack. He backed away, expecting the beast to break forth immediately, but she remained there, utterly bound. Xemion was scared, but he held on and tiptoed forward so that he could grab the very edge of the framework that kept the dragon down. He lifted its back edge just the tiniest amount and let it clang back down. Xemion repeated his action but the dragon did not get the meaning of his act. She continued to cower in her bleak condition. Xemion had to do something to break the dragon's stupor, so he poked her with the pommel of the sword. With a jolt the dragon came alive. Quickly as a flame might leap with the first great gust of wind over long-smouldering coals, she leaped up. She was much larger than Xemion had thought. She swelled under the mesh so that the whole frame strained on her spiny back and Xemion saw that there was another, smaller chain that still secured the latticework. Constrained, enraged, in panic, so near freedom, the poor dragon glared down at Xemion, and seeing him with the sword held up high to hack at that last piece of chain, she let out a great gust of fiery breath upon him, so that as the sword struck the metal, the flame struck the man. And so Xemion was caught in a fiery wind, which scorched his skin and singed his eyebrows. Lucky this was a weary dragon, a drained dragon, or he would have been dead. As it was, the sword was flung from his grasp and he was knocked against the far wall from where he watched as the dragon breathed in deeply again and swelled herself up. The metal mesh shrieked in protest, the frame strained, the dragon shrieked, and with that, the half-severed chain snapped. Like a Jack-in-a-box, the mesh popped back with a mighty crash and the dragon shot up from her captivity and began to circle around under the wide mouth of the chimney, another long chain hanging from a metal collar about her neck. The hole above was wide but not so wide as the dragon's wingspan. In a panic, she slapped around and around, beneath her the long chain rattling against the conical walls.

Suddenly Glittervein reappeared atop the stairs. "What have you done?" he shrieked, spying Xemion and seeing his dragon flapping about overhead. Lifting his sword, the little man rushed down the stairs with a blood-thirsty shriek. "I will kill you." High above Xemion, the dragon kept circling around under the opening. Seeing Glittervein, she looked as though she might just swoop down on him and bring the final fire upon this place of her torment. Indeed, for a second, she did fold her wings to her sides and dropped toward him, but at the last moment the dragon must have realized her flame was weak and her freedom frail, so she wisely soared straight back up and right through the hole in the top of the stack.

As Glittervein's sword arced toward Xemion's neck with terrifying speed, Xemion grabbed at the last few links of the dragon's chain, just then whirling by him with the momentum of the dragon's swoop. A great tug yanked him up and away from the enraged Nain, whose red, scarred face shrieked "No! No!" over and over again in rage as Xemion disappeared through the hole in the top of the stack — out with the dragon into the wild, raw wind.

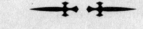

20

Reading by Lightning

The chain that hung from the dragon was quite long, so Xemion was swept along far below the struggling beast as she fled, weak and weary from her wounds. But she was flying very high, as though she thought she might be able to get above the storm clouds. Xemion's only thought was to get back down to the ground as fast as possible. Five of his mightiest blows had barely dented that sword. And now it was back in Glittervein's hands — and soon it would be in Montither's if he did nothing to stop it. He hated doing it but he began to yank on the chain about the dragon's neck. This obviously had some effect because he could hear the poor beast wheezing as she struggled to maintain altitude. But she only climbed higher. Hanging on with his arms and legs he continued to yank on the chain, but to no great avail. The dragon proceeded into the eastern side of Ulde and then turned toward the mountains. This was a part of the city with many towers and Xemion desperately tugged on the chain, trying to pull the poor beast down even as she slapped her wings, trying to gain altitude. Fortunately for Xemion this was a tired and beaten animal or he would have been dragged away to who knows what nest she came from. Slowly he yanked and as the dragon mightily flapped, her altitude lessened until Xemion was in ever-increasing danger of crashing into some of the higher tower tops. He kept preparing to leap off and grab hold of one of them, but there was never one entirely close enough.

The storm was brewing ever-darker clouds from the South Sea, making it difficult to see, even at this height. Suddenly he beheld the looming shadow of the tallest tower yet. If they stayed on their present course, the dragon would fly over it — but he would be slammed right into the middle of it! With strength he never dreamed he had, he began to swing his body back and forth, making the chain a long pendulum in the hope that he might somehow swing up and over the tower. He managed to do this deftly enough, but the effort had pulled the poor dragon down even lower. And that was when the next tower, a building much higher than any of the others, jutted up out of the darkness before he had a chance to even think. He had swung so far over that when the dragon passed on one side of the tower, he passed on the other. The chain caught the tower in the middle and both he and the dragon were wrapped round the ancient building like two balls on the end of the same tether. There was a crumbling sound as the dragon's body crushed the frail roofs of old houses at the tower's foot. Xemion hit the ground with a great thump and blacked out.

Xemion was awakened by the fierce beating of rain on his face. The sky above was dark, but distant streaks of lightning sent waves of flashing light cascading over the city. He stood up and took his bearings. He had let the chain go just before he hit the ground, so he had been flung some distance from the dragon. She lay unconscious, curled about the tower, a small tendril of smoke, made visible by the lightning, curling up from her nostrils.

He had no idea how long he'd been lying there unconscious, but it must now be deep into the night. The Panthemium was a long way off and if he didn't get back there by dawn, Saheli would arrive and sign up for the Tourney. If she drew Montither in the first round then it would all be over. He wanted to risk it all and just dart back the way he had come, trusting that he could somehow find his way through the ghoul-inhabited darkness. But he couldn't. Not yet. This was a very tall tower — the tallest tower in the landscape. He had realized it the moment he had seen it. This was Vallaine's tower.

He staggered toward the building. The dragon's mouth was open and it was aimed right at the doorway. He wasn't eager to feel again the searing wind of her wrath, so he passed by quickly and quietly. The beast didn't move. Silently he opened the old wooden door and stepped inside, finding himself at the foot of a steep, straight staircase. If this was Vallaine's tower, the locket and book were up there. And Vallaine had told him that unless the book was taken or destroyed, it wouldn't matter whether he saved Saheli or not. This had to be done.

If he hurried, he could still get the book and be at the Panthemium by dawn.

It was dark inside the tower, but he left the door open and found his way to the top of the stairs aided by the flashes of lightning. Here a doorway opened into a large many-windowed room half-jammed with books that spilled out onto the stairwell. He recognized some of these books. These were the full-sized copies of the *Phaer Tales*, which Vallaine had released from the locket. But Xemion had no time to marvel. In fact, he didn't even care about these books anymore. There was another book here he needed to find.

Desperately, as the thunder crashed and the lightning lit his way, he searched through the piles, flinging aside like useless rubbish volumes once precious to him. He'd almost gone through all of them when a flash of lightning cast a sudden shadow of a podium. And there it was on top, much bigger than the other books. It must have been a foot thick, its cover completely black. He had never seen this book before, but it was clearly *The Grimoire*. He attempted to remove the massive volume from the podium but couldn't budge it, even though he exerted all his strength in the effort. One foot against the bottom of the podium, he leaned away, gripping and tugging at the book with all his might. But he only succeeded in flipping back its huge black cover. Then the room became utterly dark as the lightning briefly subsided.

Before he could reach to close the book, a streak of lightning so bright it was almost incandescent streaked across the sky, followed immediately by a loud thunder-clap that shook the ground. One small, searing offshoot must have crackled through the window and hit the book with a flash because whatever words were on the page suddenly ignited so bright Xemion had to fling his forearm over his eyes. But it made no difference. The words shone through, burning two spells on opposing pages into his vision, steady and luminous — *Spell to Bind* and *Spell to Free*.

He groped blindly at the book in hopes of closing the cover, but a great wind rushed in and began riffling through the pages. Even as this happened the night erupted with streak after streak of thin-veined, coruscating light, igniting the words on page after page, leaving them suspended and ablaze in the air — *Spell to Send. Spell to Bring Back.*

He edged nearer the book, trying to close the cover, but the force of the wind and the brightness of the letters prevented him. Lightning bolt by lightning bolt the words ignited — *Spell to Make Many from Few. Spell to Bring Light. Spell to Make Silence. Spell to Bring Fertility.* Even though he turned his back and pushed the heels of his hands into both eyes the spells burned into his vision, searing themselves into his mind — *Spell to Awaken Peace. Spell to Awaken Desire.* Finally the wind relented and the pages came to a halt. There the book lay open to its middle, displaying a spell in two verses laid out on opposite pages — *Spell to Make a Sword Which May Never Be Defeated.* Xemion crept toward the podium, coming up on the book from below, hoping to close that cover for good, but a thin fork of light sizzled in and lit up the spell so bright it flung him back into the corner.

After that there was a longer break in the lightning.

In the ensuing darkness the very tower started to shake as though some demon were attempting to topple it. He knew now there was no way for him to take the book. That left only one option: destroying it. But how? The thought of approaching that magical tome again for any purpose scared him. He was terrified he could be blinded forever, but the thought of Montither's blade entering Saheli's breast terrified him even more.

The next flash of lightning revealed a stone fireplace in one wall. He dashed over and held his palm over it, feeling the slight heat still rising from somewhere within its embers. With no hesitation he groped through the ashes until he felt a coal that was still warm. Quickly he rolled it out to the hearth and blew. It began to heat up and glow, but he needed some tinder. Xemion grabbed a book from the floor, rolled the coal into its opened centre and carried it over to *The Grimoire*, where he continued to blow fiercely until a small tendril of smoke arose. The sky exploded again, and a fraction of a second later there was the loudest crack of thunder yet. Like a nest of serpents suspended in one hand, fangs lashing at the ground, the lightning struck again and again. A great gust of wet wind filled the room and Xemion was dimly aware of the illustration of Amphion gazing up at him as he continued to blow. It darkened, curled, and then a small flame ignited. He ripped another page from the book and fed it into the flame, and when it erupted he touched it to the open face of *The Grimoire*. The fire that resulted was so bright that Xemion saw nothing but a searing blue dot that completely consumed his vision as he backed away into a corner, hands pressed over his eyes. There was an unusual smell in the room and Xemion heard a shrill hissing as the fire made its way through page after page, each giving up its writing in an eruption that illuminated the whole room.

The tower shook so much Xemion feared it might crumble any minute. But he waited until all that was left of the book was smouldering ash before fleeing. Still half-blinded by the light, he nearly stumbled over the books at the top of the stairs, but the leap he took at the last moment ended fortuitously on the seventh step. He raced down the remaining fourteen steps.

Outside, he saw it was not supernatural forces that had been shaking the tower; it was the dragon. She had regained consciousness while he'd been inside, and now, terrified for her life, she tugged furiously at the chain, trying to escape. But the chain was wrapped twice around the tower and she did not know enough to walk counter-clockwise to freedom. The wind blew ferociously and a heavy rain hit them sideways, stinging Xemion's cheeks. He was in a hurry to get to the Panthemium, but he had to stop. The dragon caught his eye and he called her by the name he had used for her in the valley.

"Poltorir!" he shouted in a voice he didn't recognize. "Stop!"

The dragon's nostrils widened as she looked at him. Her huge shoulders were hunched and she drew a sharp breath, held it, and stopped. He saw a shiver run through her frame.

"Wait!" he shouted. Xemion tugged with all his strength at the chain until he drew it out from under her bloody scales. Then he walked it counterclockwise until it was no longer wrapped around the tower. And since he couldn't cut it free, he wrapped it round her neck, all the while trusting her not to turn on him. When he finally had the chain secure enough that it wouldn't hang free, he looked into the dragon's eyes again and said "Xemion."

The dragon let the breath she had all this time been holding go and the warmth of it swelled up about him as the rain continued its sideways drive. "I will free you now for a second time," he said, pointing to the sky just as it was shattered by an explosion of lightning that illuminated the whole city. Poltorir reared up on her haunches in the driving rain. The timbers in the crushed houses cracked and groaned beneath her as she lifted her wings and propelled herself into the sky. He watched her disappear into the storm and then turned and surveyed the streaming, ruined landscape about him to see which way was west and what might be the quickest way to get back to the other side of the city by morning.

Suddenly the lightning lit up a great black shadow speeding toward him like an arrow to a target. Xemion gasped and ducked crouching low against the tower wall, prepared to defend himself with his bare hands if need be, but the creature stopped at his feet.

"I beg you, Lord, do not fear this dark dog." It was Bargest, and he had a very familiar-looking stick in his mouth. "I beseech you, sire, take up again this staff."

Xemion slowly stood back up, shaking his head to and fro as he took the stick from Bargest's mouth. He stared down at it, straining to see around the blue dot, which still hung suspended in the middle of his vision. Finally he realized with a shock that it was his old painted sword. The last time Xemion had seen it was when Montither had flung it into the swamp beside the Castle Road. Judging from the wet mud that still clung to it, Bargest must have retrieved it. This connection to younger, more innocent days made Xemion momentarily happy. He felt like throwing his arms around the dog and kissing him. Seeing the joy in his master's face, Bargest lifted his huge paws onto Xemion's shoulders and began to rapidly lick the rain away from his face until Xemion had to stop him. The dog lifted his snout to the rain-riven night and in a deep voice rumbled, "Never let me stop loving this master."

Xemion held the blade firmly in his right hand, still not realizing the true nature of this stick he had found in that riverbed in Ilde. Its silver star paint was now somewhat faded, and here and there the paint had peeled away, revealing the original white surface beneath. "Fine then," he said in a grumbling voice as he slid it into the long narrow pocket of Vallaine's cloak. "Now I need to get back to the other side of the city."

Bargest nudged Xemion's hip with his nose.

"No!" Xemion said, almost automatically, but the dog caught his eye. "Ah … yes," Xemion said, "You're right. I *am* feeling a little … hungry." Bargest watched him intently through the rain as he removed the remainder of the wafer from inside Vallaine's cloak and bit off half of what was left. Panting a little from his exertion, he savoured the taste for a moment as he stowed the last piece absent-mindedly back in the cloak. It was a taste like no other; a taste that could go on forever. He could already feel his strength and confidence picking up. Lightning again struck hard and close. Bargest reared up on his hind legs and barked back at it with a terrible thunder of his own.

"I beg you, sir," he said when he was back on all fours, head contritely hung down, voice soft as milk. "Let me show you the fastest way."

21

The Phaer Queen

An hour later the storm subsided. It was dawn of the spring equinox. The first day of spring, and true to form a bright and fertile sun rose up from the horizon. In celebration of Glittervein's newly completed iron sea gates, a crowd had gathered in the cavern where the tunnel from the top of Phaer Point emerged at sea level. To a ship entering the Bay of Ulde the cliffside into which this cavern was recessed looked much like the head of a recumbent lion with the cavern as its mouth. Two long, stone limbs of land extending out into the bay from each side of the mouth not only gave the added effect of being the lion's front legs, but served to create a smaller harbour within the bay — one whose entrance was just wide enough for a narrow cargo boat to pass.

The first of the gates, which Glittervein's Nains had rebuilt, was placed here, between the Lion's Paws. Most vessels, in the days of old, would have come no farther than that. Here, their goods would be removed and stored in one of the two storage towers at the ends of the Lion's Paws. Only the select few would be granted entrance to the inner harbour. And fewer yet would make it through the Lion's Mouth to the shelter of the cavern and the tunnel, which led to the city above. It was at the mouth of this cavern, the very spot were Tiri Lighthammer had slain a Kagar Prince fifty years earlier, that Glittervein had built the second gate.

If last night's smithying had taken a toll on him, he showed no sign of it. In fact, he looked quite chipper. Dressed in a lime-green robe, pointy-toed red shoes, and a peaked black hat, he had taken extra care this morning to draw his long hair down over one side of his face so that only that pretty left side smiled out at the crowd. Doffing his black hat, he pulled the lever that sent the signal to the gateman high atop the city walls. The gateman began turning his wheel and slowly the vast grill descended over the cavern mouth. Most of the workers, and most members of the staff who were there for the celebratory occasion, began to applaud. The new Lion's Gate, as the construction was called, had been forged from huge metal rods a foot in diameter. Its bottommost bars, when lowered, slid into matching iron sheaths beneath the water so that there might be no digging under it, even at low tide. Its metal had been extracted from pins and needles, pots and pans, and old trophies, anything that might contain a shred of iron, and it had been smelted and refined and hammered and shaped, much of it by giant nocturnal Thralls of Munia such as Oime. She stood there now, with a number of her fellow workers, shielding themselves from the bright sunlight, which found its way over the sea fog and through the bars of the gate, to sparkle on the green waters inside the cavern.

The only other access point to the heights of Ulde, the narrow ridge up which the wounded Tiri Lighthammer had been carried fifty years earlier, was on the far eastern side of the larger bay. It was too narrow, precipitous, and exposed to offer anything but a suicide mission to any invader foolish enough to try and climb it. Even so, Glittervein had taken the precaution of having a third, much smaller gate constructed there.

"In times to come, when you have received the just fruits of all your labours," Glittervein was saying to the crowd as he puffed away on his pipe, "I hope you will think of me and these fine young workers who gave so much of their life and energy to the poetry of digging, I promise you. You cannot tell me that the shovel is not as mighty a sword as a sword itself. Or that the mighty awl is not as serious a dagger as a dagger is. Let us have a cheer for these brave workers."

The great shout that followed was interrupted by an eerie call reverberating out of the mist and over the waters from the centre of the bay.

The crowd hushed and everyone watched in excited silence as Glittervein gave the signal for the far gate to be lifted. Slowly it rose and a magnificent red and gold painted barge with a green-curtained canopy in the middle of the deck and a red velvet banner waving overhead passed between the Lion's Paws and entered the inner harbour. A crew of twenty or so Phaerlanders with barge poles were steering her along the side of the inner harbour toward the cavern. A man with the head of a bird stood at the prow, holding on to a long, coiled rope.

Hardly a heart was not beating wildly as Glittervein gave the signal to raise the larger gate at the Lion's Mouth. Without a squeak, the massive grill of iron rose again, while a single flautist played the ancient anthem, "Phaer Domain." Even as the gate lifted, a majestic carriage rolled down the rails through the tunnel from the city above and came to a halt a few feet from the dock. Slowly, the barge slid through the Lion's Mouth and into the waters of the cavern until it was close enough for the birdman to cast his rope toward the dock and be slowly drawn in.

An elegant hand parted the golden curtains and a magnificently attired figure stepped out onto the deck. She had done her best to resist the invitations of the staff to take on this position. It might send the wrong message, she had said, but they had assured her that it was tradi-tional and that no Equinox Festival could be authentic without it. So there she now stood — quite majestically, just as the position demanded. Veneetha Azucena, Queen of the Equinox! A great murmur went up from the crowd when they beheld her in her high crown. The mist off the sea and the shimmer of rainbows refracting through the many diamonds and amethysts in it gave the whole scene an almost spectral radiance. Gently, the elegant barge nudged against the dock. All of the crew but the birdman alighted and tied it securely to mooring rings, so that the Phaer Queen might step delicately ashore.

Veneetha Azucena motioned regally to all those down upon their knees to arise. The cavern resonated with a mighty cheer that echoed beyond the gate and out across the waters to the wraith-like morning moon, which was just then lifting its head above the horizon. Slowly, as the carriage ascended, taking Veneetha Azucena and her entourage to the city above, Glittervein's newly made black gate lowered once again into place. Even as Glittervein smiled triumphantly, the tiniest sheet of sea-water atop that salty cove began to slowly draw back; for as they have always done, and as they did fifty years ago, the tidal waters obeyed the dictates of the moon.

Glittervein wore an expression of great satisfaction. He reached into the ceremonial robe he wore for this special occasion and from one of the many pockets inside it withdrew a small, cooing pigeon.

22

Two-Spell Well

The number of rumours about the end of the Pathan civil war underearth was matched only by the number of rumours about its expansion. Some swore that Akka Smissm, the former governor of Ulde, was sailing toward Ulde with a massive army of mercenaries, others that the Pathans were bankrupt, their ranks in tatters and their empire in chaos. Cyclop mercenaries and slavers, it was said, once again roamed the seas. A week previously, there were stories of a vast Kagar fleet bearing down on the Phaer Isle, but today there was absolute confirmation from Glittervein that a thousand Kagar ships had been sent to the bottom of the sea by last night's storm.

Whatever the truth, there had not been such a hopeful mood in the Phaer Isle for fifty years. The Phaer people were jubilant, joyous, and in love with life, ready to be courageous. All of the brigades had returned in good health and fitness from the camps in the mountains and the city was as clean and orderly as it had ever been. Its gems sparkled; its surfaces shone. The weather, too, had played its part in showing off Ulde's new look. The sun was a warm balm on the flesh, the air a moist, spring day perfume that made all who breathed it exuberant and glad to be alive. And there were thousands of people. Many more than had been expected, for word of the recent changes in the ancient city had spread rapidly through the Phaer Isle.

Those who had planned for the influx from the well-populated western portion of the Phaer Isle had vastly underestimated. They'd had to double and triple the number of guards and inspectors at the western gate, but these were quickly overwhelmed by the sheer magnitude of those entering the city. Unsearched, unscreened, the Phaer people poured back into Ulde en masse. It was almost as though something elemental had changed, for not only had the normal hordes of Nains, Thralls, and Freemen come, as was predicted, but an unforeseen number of others. Chimerants from the other side of Ulde, who normally kept their spelled-crossed features hidden, strolled about right out in the open. There were strange two-faced people and an alleged fortune-teller who seemed to be half woman and half man. Most delightful to the crowds was a small troop of triplicant jugglers, one of whom also had the hindquarters of a horse.

Chief among the items of gossip and rumour was a story of a new warrior maid by the name of Zero. A tale of how she could disarm and defeat any opponent but had only had her own sword stricken from her once — and that by her master, Tiri Lighthammer. Some said she was

203

an avatar of old Queen Phaeton come back to lead the Phaer people to a new golden age. Others proclaimed she was a forest sylph, a genius with the sword, but a genius even more with the heart.

Zero took her place in the lineup of those who wished to compete in the Tourney and stared out solemnly at the faces of the multitudes. Her iron breastplate had been burnished without adornment. She wore a simple tunic underneath it and her hair was bound and hidden in her helmet, which came down to just above her eyes. Yellow streaks of war paint radiated out from her lips and over her face.

The vast open arena where the tournament would be fought had a strange history. Originally, two hundred years ago, it had been intended as a well. But when two mages fought over its design, it became one of the first casualties of cross-spelling. One mage had conjured it to be as big as possible, while the other conjured it to be as small as possible. In Phaer fashion, the well obeyed the first spell by becoming bigger in one sense — it became much wider, but it obeyed the other in another sense, by interpreting "small" to mean incredibly shallow. The result was something a little like an immense but virtually depthless wading pool. It covered a level area three times the size of the playing field, but not deep enough to hold more than a thimbleful of water. Though this rendered it useless as a well, it still bore the name Two-Spell Well, and for that reason, ignorant people still made double wishes on it, thinking it a wishing well. The Pathan Imperial Council had insisted after the spell fire that this practice be stopped, but to this day Veneetha Azucena had to employ two glitter Thralls to go out every morning and pick up the fresh batch of double-bound coins thrown into its centre.

As Zero made her way forward in the line, there was a massive blowing of trumpets. It was the royal procession. Led by a baton-twirling Phaerlander, a full battalion of Phaer infantrymen marched by, their golden swords flashing in the sun. Behind them, drawn by two white horses, Veneetha Azucena waved at the crowds from a golden carriage. Everyone stood at the edge of the road waving back and marvelling as the carriage rolled by. Some people bowed and some took off their hats and many openly wept. Zero, inspired by the magnificence of the parade, bowed deeply.

At the centre of the arena, Veneetha Azucena dismounted nimbly from her carriage and to everyone's delight gave a speech.

"Blessed be the Phaer people. We have accomplished something wonderful. We have done what we were told we could never do. We have taken back our Phaer city and revitalized our culture. For the first time in fifty years, thanks to your hard work, there are sea gates at the Lion's Paws and the Lion's Mouth. Our young men and women are well-trained and ready. Our fortifications are as strong and well-guarded as any fortifications anywhere. We … you … are magnificent, and I tell you quite honestly I do not think we can be stopped now. So let us not hold back today in our merrymaking, our valour, or our love, for this feast of action, which we gratefully prepare today, is a treat time has long hungered for. Let us not disappoint."

When she finished, a great shout of joy went up. None

of those who cheered so wildly in that moment had ever felt so right about anything. They were in the right place, at the right time; the right mood abounded and the right things were about to happen. Thralls were hugging men, men were kissing Nains, Nains danced with Thralleens, and little children laughed at the antics of triplicant jugglers, most of whom claimed the last name Lighthammer. Among the waving flags and strutting gulls, the cawing kittiwakes and skralling terns, no one noticed the flight of a single pigeon overhead with something affixed to one of its legs.

The Tournament Begins

As in days of old, various weapons and pieces of armour were made available by their owners for the use of the participants. The old Elphaereans had instituted this policy so that these contests would be accessible to anyone, not just the wealthy. This meant that the earlier bouts of the day were filled with a lot of what Tiri Lighthammer called "flailing." By early morning many an unskilled Phaerlander newly arrived at the city with high hopes had been dispatched quickly by one of Lighthammer's more skilled recruits. Zero's desire to win the tournament had grown stronger in the past few months, but her victory, she realized, was by no means assured. Her worthiest opponents, the three Thrall sisters, were still in the running, as was Fargold, the fellow with the long nose who was always trying to meet her eyes.

So far Zero had been living up to the stories that were circulating about her. Her sense of balance, the deftness with which she moved her blade, and the great intricacy and strategy of her footwork that day were immaculate. By noon she had won seven matches, all by disarms. She was one of the frontrunners and the clear crowd favourite, but you would hardly have known it to look at her. She kept what little could be seen of her face expressionless and seemed to fight completely without emotion. All of her focus centred trance-like on her sword.

As word spread of the startling new swordswoman, an even larger crowd began to gather at Two-Spell Well. Barkers and hawkers worked their way amongst packs and hordes and gangs of all kinds of creatures from underearth to oversky. There was a great beauty in their variety that caught in Zero's throat when she first looked out over the crowd. And that first win, when she raised her sword before them in victory — that first great cheer thrilled her. But Zero knew that too much thrill would be bad for her focus, so with great discipline she restricted it as much as she could. Her next salute had very little flourish. In fact, it was a little automatic. Still, the crowd roared.

Not everyone was delighted with Zero, though. Montither, who had won just as often that day, watched her progress through narrowed, envious eyes. He wasn't popular at all with the crowd. It wasn't just that he always managed to win inelegantly, with lots of clubbing, whacking, hacking, and one obviously unnecessary kick to a young northern lad who was already down, it was that he did so by a great advantage in weaponry. While everyone else in the competition used swords and shields, which were at their hardest made of iron, Montither had access to a small armoury of solid steel shields, sabres, dirks, daggers, axes, and rapiers. The collection had arrived the previous night, a surprise gift from his newly reformed and officially forgiven kwisling father, an attempt at reconciliation. The craftsmanship of these weapons — the engraving, for instance, which decorated the hilt of the sword and the crest of the shield — was sumptuous and impressive.

When he had first arrived at Two-Spell Well, adorned in his brilliant new armour, Montither knew for a little while the glory of mass adulation. But when he switched his steel broadsword for a serrated steel sabre halfway through his first fight and used it to hack a jagged wound into a young northerner's shoulder, there were shouts of protest. Several bloody battles later, aided in changing his weapons and armament by his cronies, Gnasher and Ring'o'pins, Montither had won several more victories but lost the approval of the crowd.

His greatest advantage, he discovered to his surprise, was not so much the sword of steel but the shield and breastplate of steel. These were much harder and far superior to the thin, battered iron and leathers worn by his opponents and afforded him the luxury of absorbing many blows that should have defeated him. Fargold, for instance, had become a superb swordsman under Lighthammer's tutelage and several times got in under Montither's guard, close enough to deal him deadly thrusts, but these, to the crowd's loud disappointment, did little more than glance off the hard steel. The third time it happened, Montither followed up with a sudden slash at the back of Fargold's retreating thigh. It must have cut through his leathers and severed a hamstring, for he fell immediately in great agony to the ground and proceeded to bleed and scream. Veneetha Azucena scowled, obviously not pleased. While Fargold was removed groaning to the infirmary, the crowd turned on Montither with boos. But Montither merely bowed in return and wiped the blood lustfully on his leather jerkin.

He would show them ruthless. He knew all about ruthless. He had his dear friend Gnasher out there somewhere. And Gnasher had a little mirror, and if a moment ever called for it, Gnasher was quite prepared to use that mirror in a thoroughly nasty way. But that moment had not come yet. No, in fact all of Montither's successes so far had come from no other advantage but those of wealth, strength, and superior equipment.

After each contest the victors would determine their next match by drawing straws. In the early afternoon, Asnina and Atathu drew each other, but they had agreed ahead of time not to fight if this happened. As a result they both had to withdraw from the Tourney. Despite herself, Zero felt relieved at this. As much as she coveted the prize, she dreaded having to fight any of the Thrall sisters.

In the next round her relief was complete when Montither drew his biggest and brawniest opponent so far — the third and largest Thrall sister, Imalgha. All decked out in bright orange war paint and thrallish leathers, the magnificence of her physique was apparent to all. She didn't have the reach of Montither, but her shoulders were twice as broad. Her forearms were as thick as small trees and she held her bronze blade with the unwavering precision only seen in the eyes of those deep in sword thrall. Close to her, as he'd always been ever since he'd heard the first whisper of her return to Ulde, stood the wiry, intent Lirodello, his eyes as big and round as plums. He was in a thrall of his own.

Zero, too, drew a most challenging opponent: a mighty warrior, heretofore unknown. A chimerant, he had the head of a bull but spoke and acted like a man. Zero took him in dispassionately, immediately noticing the weaknesses in his armour and the slack grip with which he held his sword.

By now, the much-fattened crowd had divided into cheering sections based on their preferred champions. Zero had a very large contingent, including the Nains Belphegor and Tomtenisse Doombeard and all their newly arrived family and friends, who were many.

Montither's match did not at first go well. Imalgha was stronger and clearly a more skillful fighter and it looked as though she would dispatch him early in their bout. Montither relied, as usual, on the hardness of his armour and a lot of sheer, wild whackery. He came at the noble Thrall like a mad slasher, but she had noticed the joining places of his armour and was directing her sword deftly to those spots as Lighthammer had taught her. He responded with ever more errant blows, all of which she skillfully deflected, but every time her bronze sword took a head-on hit, a small chip flew out of it. Montither's plan was to continue absorbing her blows until inevitably his sword would whittle the Thrall blade down to its weakest point and then it would break. But this was not happening. She kept finding ways to turn her blade sideways and deflect his thrusts without damage, while her own darting point grew ever closer to a place in his shoulder where she knew her sword could enter. All the while a thoroughly incensed Lirodello stalked back and forth among a group of his fellow kitchen Thralls. The small flecks of purple foam gathering at the corners of his grim, grey-lipped mouth gave clear evidence of the trouble he was having containing his outrage.

Montither might have lost that bout, but just as Imalgha found him with his guard wide open and swooped in with her hacked sword for the thrust, the sun somehow caught her right in the eyes and she was momentarily blinded. Before she could recover, Montither bashed her brutally over the head with such force she staggered to the ground. Here, another bright sun flash caught her eyes and before she could rise Montither struck her sword out of her hand with a crude double-handed swing.

Lirodello, his eyes two black, steaming tar bubbles, had to be restrained by his fellow Thralls from rushing at Montither with a knife. As it was he shrieked non-stop "Cheat! Cheat! Cheat!" The crowd took up the chant, "Cheat! Cheat! Cheat!" but Montither insisted that his tactics fell easily within the terms of fight "by all means." Veneetha Azucena reluctantly agreed with this and his victory was allowed to stand.

24

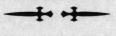

The Crossing

Xemion and Bargest kept the fastest pace possible. As they came to the parklands surrounding the Great Kone, the dog, his great black snout to the ground, made as if to lead them right by it, perhaps with some other crossing point in mind, but Xemion stopped him. "No, I want to cross over here the same way I did before."

Bargest cocked his head, but before he could protest, Xemion had his finger up in the dog's face. "No!" he said, his voice made more intense by the poor condition of his vocal cords.

And so the two hurried toward the Great Kone, each step leading them deeper and deeper into its shadow. They didn't have too far to go before they reached the place where, by Xemion's reckoning, Saheli had kissed him. He felt a despairing rush of desire shoot through him at this memory, but he had not come here for nostalgia. He had come this way for a reason. There were many bricks missing in this part of the wall and he was trying to find the exact gap his eyes had landed on that day. He did his best to stand in the same position he'd been in when she kissed him, but the gaps in the brickwork that he could see from here were still too numerous for him to be sure. He glowered at Bargest, who was gazing at him impatiently, and said, "Look away." When the dog complied he tilted his head as he had that day. He felt a little foolish doing this, but when he did he finally found what he was looking for. Because of the different position of the sun at this time of day, this particular gap was still in shadow, but he was certain he'd found the right one. He walked closer until his eyes adjusted. What he saw, even though he half expected it, still shocked him. The letter on the Kone that the missing brick revealed had changed. It was no longer the letter X — at least not entirely. Only the right half of it, in the shape of an arrowhead, was still visible on the left side of the space. On the other side was half of the letter O. He felt his knees tremble. A wave of terror ran through him and the same pain ignited by the memory of her kiss ignited tenfold. He looked to the sky in agony but there was no relief to be had there. Nor would there ever be relief from this particular pain. The Great Kone had begun to turn! Whatever that meant to the world, it meant one certain thing for him: He was a spellbinder.

"Well, that might be," he proclaimed angrily to Bargest as they hurried off, "but I do not have to abide by it. I may have had a spell forced upon me by that woman but I don't have to ever do a spell of my own." Bargest reared up and barked fiercely in that great muddy voice of his. He barked again and again, causing numerous long-beaked crows and ravens to rise up indignantly from the top of the Kone.

For a second Xemion's sense of strength and purpose had faded and he almost reached for that last morsel of wafer in his cloak, but as he and Bargest raced toward the wall he thought better of it. Better to wait till he got to the Tourney. Who knew when he might need to be at his strongest.

25

The Challenge

A mood of thrilled expectation filled the crowd when Zero, with her usual skill, at last disarmed the Minotaur. At the signal from Veneetha Azucena that the match was now over, the loser bowed his two sharp horns all the way down until they touched the ground at Zero's feet. The crowd cheered this gallant act as he made his way with dignity out of the arena. Finally, Zero would face Montither. In anticipation of this, the spectators started to spill over the rim of the arena and crowd into the bowl area itself. This limited the space the swordfighters had to contest in.

Zero felt the presence of the crowd close around her. She felt the stone of the bowl vibrate with their screams, and when the trumpets blared after her name was called, she almost smiled. Falling back on her training, Zero took a deep breath, slow and long. Easily she exhaled, feeling the excited turmoil in her belly subside. She had done her best to blight whatever beauty some of them thought she had. Her hair had been cut short, she had blackened her cheeks under her eyes to keep out the sun, and, like the Thrall sisters, she had painted orange chevrons on her cheekbones. She was going to win. She could feel it.

It was right around this time that she spotted out of the corner of her eye a cowled man approaching her from the middle of the crowd. When he noticed that she had seen him, he waved and began pushing his way toward her. But the crowd was thick and he was having trouble getting through. "Saheli!" he yelled.

Zero quickly averted her eyes and concentrated. She didn't know who Saheli was, but something about the sound of that name caused a strange distracting pain in her chest.

"Saheli," he yelled again.

Just then Montither, who had finally taken up Glittervein's new sword, was going through a sloweddown version of some of his favourite sword moves before the crowd. In the midst of it there was only one moment when he showed his true speed, making a quick thrust forward at the air in the exact posture Glittervein had taught him. He did this with such great force and with such a murderous look on his face that Xemion's heart began to race. He could see that Glittervein had done a magnificent job finishing the sword. Any dents Xemion had made in it the night before had been hammered right out of existence, the whole blade sharpened to a deadly steel point.

He wanted to barge through the crowd to warn Saheli about the danger she was in, but he felt weak and spiritless.

And now that he had seen her up close, he wasn't even sure that it actually *was* Saheli. This girl seemed bigger than Saheli, and what little of her face wasn't covered by the helmet was covered with paint. But whoever she was, she might die soon if he did nothing. He groped through the pockets of the robe in search of the wafer, but he couldn't find it. Frantically his hand darted into pocket after pocket.

Suddenly there was the sound of fanfare. Three enormous song Thralls marched by, each one blasting a large, curved horn with a wide bell of bronze that, when it tolled, sounded like the bellow of an elephant. The sun caught and flared off first one and then another of these shining bells and the two blinding flashes touched off something in Xemion's mind. Suddenly it was as though he was standing once again before *The Grimoire* as last night's lightning ignited its pages. He reeled back as the bright blue letters of that last spell seemed to burn in the air before him — *Spell to Make a Sword Which May Never Be Defeated.*

"No!" Xemion cursed. He waved his arms as though this might dissipate the letters. But still they hung there, luminous and blindingly bright, tempting him. If he could cast a spell to turn the Great Kone, he could cast this spell, too. And an undefeatable sword could definitely save this girl. But even if he did choose to willfully cast a spell, he still needed something — something like a sword — to cast a spell upon. He didn't actually make the decision, he just did it. He crouched among the milling crowd, and there, with one knee on the ground, he took out the painted sword. He knew if he spoke the spell now it would be by his will and his alone. The bronze bell flashed again and the words re-ignited in his mind brighter than before. But this time he didn't look away. He didn't throw up his arm to protect himself. He looked directly at those shining letters and heard them in his mind. Still, he had a strong urge to go and find something else — anything else but this silver painted stick to cast them upon. But there was no time. He gritted his teeth and began to say the words of the spell. At first he spoke very quickly and in a hoarse whisper.

> *Iron, wood, steel, and stone,*
> *Muscle, gristle, flesh, and bone.*
> *Pierce all metal you may meet.*
> *You may never taste defeat!*
> *Always vict'ry ever sweet!*

After he finished, the glowing letters slowly faded away. He examined the painted sword. Nothing seemed to have changed at all. Those places where its long soak in the castle swamp had worn away the silver still revealed the paper-white surface beneath. In fact, some of the material was so waterlogged it had become swollen and spongy.

Zero and Montither were taking their places before the crowd. Angrily, Xemion spoke the spell again, this time slightly slower, but when he finished the sword still seemed unchanged. Enraged, he banged the hilt on the stone ground so hard the people packed in around him looked down and backed away with some alarm. But now something *was* happening with the sword. It felt more solid and heavier in his hand. He examined it closely, trembling. Yes, it had definitely changed! It was no longer silver. It was a cold grey colour with a strange green tint that only showed at certain angles. Xemion was certain now, and the joy of it almost made him forget the terror he felt knowing he had bound a spell for the second time. But he hardly had a moment to take in the significance of this fact. The match would start any second. And for all he knew Montither might choose to end it with one quick thrust. Xemion stood up with the sword and pushed his way forcefully through the crowd.

Zero kept her eyes closed as Veneetha Azucena approached to initiate the match. When she opened them again, she saw that the man in the hood was now standing almost beside her. A cloak the same shade of blue as the sky overhead hung about his lean, long frame so that most of his face was cast in shadow.

Xemion tried calling the name the crowd knew her by. "Zero! Zero!"

Still she ignored him.

"Zero, I bring you a much better sword." He held the weapon before her. "This is a much better sword for you, Zero."

"Go away!" she hissed.

"Get him out of here," Montither growled.

"Look," he persisted. "Montither plans to kill you. But this sword will save you." Xemion held the sword out to her again. Annoyed, she eyed the thin streak of grey as dispassionately as she could, and then looked away. Any further exchange was cut short by Montither, who, eager to get to the fighting, kicked the strange, cowled figure from behind, sending him crashing into the crowd. This caused many to laugh, despite the crowd's general dislike of Montither.

Enraged, Xemion gripped the hilt of the sword tightly and stood up. At that instant he felt a surge of power slip out of the sword and into his arm. He slumped to the ground, shaking and frightened by what he had felt. For a second he sat stunned and silent among the many legs towering around him.

"And now," shouted Veneetha Azucena, "before our final bout, before I officially close the lists and initiate this ultimate contest, I must ask, as they did in times of old, is there anyone among you who would first beg leave to challenge either of these two?"

At this point in the contest, in days gone by, both remaining combatants would harass and harangue the crowd, hoping to provoke more challenges, for the winner would be judged not only by ultimate victory, but also by the number of challengers who had been subdued along the way.

"Who will fight this woman?" Veneetha gestured toward Zero.

Zero, saying nothing, held her blade straight up and bowed slightly. There were wild cheers from the crowd. Someone shouted, "I love you, Zero," but no one arose to challenge her, for none wished to be beaten and all were anxious for the big fight to begin. Veneetha Azucena turned next to Montither.

"And who will fight Brothlem Montither of Phaeros!"

Montither inflated his chest and began to strut and swagger back and forth before the crowd. The same person who had shouted before now bellowed "I hate you, Montither." There was a great hoot of laughter from the crowd, but Montither seemed not to notice.

"Who denies I am the fear of the Phaer," he shouted, with not a trace of self-mockery. "Who denies that I am dog's bane?" There was some hissing and a lot of rude gesturing of fingers from the crowd, but no champion dared venture forth. Now Montither turned to Zero, who still held her blade straight up in stringent meditation. "Who denies," Montither shrieked, "that I am lightning to dogs." He moved closer to her, bellowing. "Who says I am not the lash to chattel, the prod to cattle."

The crowd gasped at the vulgarity of this insult, but Zero took a deep breath and calmly exhaled. There was no other moment but this. She stepped forward confidently to offer Brothlem Montither his official challenge, but before she could, Xemion jumped up from his place on the ground.

"I do!" he shouted.

The crowd jeered. Montither shook his head and continued to face Zero, his shoulders slightly hunched, a deep eagerness in his eyes.

"I do," Xemion repeated even louder. The crowd now began to try to shush him, but Veneetha Azucena intervened.

"We must suffer all challengers," she shouted. "Bring him here."

Zero felt her concentration wavering. She glared angrily as the young man stepped forward with a sword in his hand. Xemion did not return her glare. He was too intent on Montither.

"I challenge you!" he spat at Montither as he threw back his cowl. A brief flash of fear appeared on Montither's face as he recognized this new, gaunter version of his old opponent. But this was replaced almost immediately with an expression of delight.

"Oh, do you?"

"Can this be stopped?" Zero demanded as she stared angrily at the stranger before her. But Veneetha Azucena, who had also recognized Xemion, shook her head help-lessly. "It is all in the tradition," she said. "And he has suffered hard and long to have this fight."

Xemion gripped the sword tightly at his side. He was certain he could feel that dark current flowing again.

"Do you accept this challenge?" Veneetha Azucena asked Montither in a high, imperial tone.

Montither's answer was little more than a snarl. "By all means."

Xemion chose carefully from among the pieces of armour available. The breastplate he strapped on was much heavier than he would have liked. And when he realized how much the slit in the helmet restricted his vision, he wanted to fight without it. But this was not allowed.

Zero still felt no flare of recognition. The fact that the face of this boy, thin and haggard, tugged at something inside her, registered only slightly. She wished only that she could take a little sip from the brown bottle and make the feeling go away, but the brown bottle was no more. When she noticed the inexperienced way he handled the armour, she wondered what could have possessed this fool to take such a terrible risk. Finally, fully armoured, the young man held up his sword and waved the tip in Montither's face.

Veneetha Azucena turned to Xemion. "Young man, are you ready?"

Xemion swallowed hard and nodded.

"Very well." Veneetha Azucena signalled and for a second the two swords crossed. One of them, newly chosen from Montither's armoury, was broad, sharp and serrated, the other, though it now looked like a good, solid broadsword, was until very recently little more than a painted stick.

Montither and Xemion were finally blade-to-blade, eye-to-eye. Montither leaned forward and, in a voice so quiet only Xemion could hear, said, "Time to get that hand off you."

The crowd booed and Veneetha Azucena said "Let it begin."

26

The Bout with Montither

Standing at last before his old tormentor, Xemion was suddenly afraid. He recalled the description of the spell he had spoken — *Spell to Make a Sword Which May Never Be Defeated*. May? Why hadn't it said *can* never be defeated. There was a definite difference. And Vallaine had said the written magic was so literal. Did it mean *may* as in *maybe*? Why had he been so certain of this sword's powers?

Montither, sensing the sudden fear in Xemion, smiled sadistically. His sword was new, forged of solid steel, and finely honed. He could make quick work of that piece of dull iron but taking it slow would be much more enjoyable. For a time the two circled each other, staring intently into one another's eyes. The crowd occasionally hooted or yelled for some action. The sword felt empty, powerless in Xemion's hand.

"Hold up your sword," Montither commanded.

Trembling despite himself, Xemion did just that. Montither smiled. Then he struck Xemion's blade forcefully, knocking it to one side. Quickly, Xemion brought his blade back into position. There followed a whirlwind of slashes and clangs and hacks rarely seen in a proper sword fight, for these two were both full of mutual hate and would do anything, whether proper or not, so long as it meant they got in another hack.

At first Xemion's sword held up well under the barrage of Montither's much harder and heavier weapon. But he was still weak from the after-effects of his spellwork. Without the help of some supernatural agency he would not last long. Even as he had this thought, Montither caught him with the flat side of his sword against the side of his head. So great was the force of the blow that it knocked Xemion right off his feet and down to the ground. The crowd cheered, glad to have some action. Xemion rose as quickly as he could, but he was disoriented and stumbled a little, prompting some in the crowd to laugh. Nevertheless, Xemion succeeded in raising his sword again just in time to meet Montither's next assault. Somehow he managed to deflect the swing to one side but it shook him to his bones. One more like that and he would surely be shattered. But another came and somehow he still stood. And then another and another and he began to hear a slow rising cry of approval from the crowd.

Xemion dropped to one knee, took the hilt of his sword, and banged it straight down to the ground with a shout. He sprang up anew, reenergized. Once again the two closed face-to-face, and just before he struck,

Montither said, "You were right about one thing. When I finish with you I'm going to skewer that girl right through." After that the two of them hacked and hewed at one another for a long time, but Montither never once succeeded in striking Xemion's body. He kept trying and trying but Xemion was mounting a defence that seemed always to find itself at the right angle with the right power to send Montither's blade skidding away harmlessly.

Montither doubled and redoubled his whacking and slashing but each blow was ever more skillfully returned by the increasingly confident Xemion. Suddenly, Montither stumbled. It was only a small misstep, but in that second when he was off-balance Xemion's blade crashed into Montither's helmet with such force it almost toppled him. There was a hushed moment and then the crowd erupted in ecstasy.

Enraged, Montither charged at Xemion, but it was now Xemion who was on the attack. He hated Montither, and the deeper he felt that hate, the more power he seemed to acquire. Montither continued to parry and block what he could, but Xemion kept cutting inside Montither's defences and poking him hard, leaving little dents in his shiny new armour. Alternately, he unleashed quick sideways whacks against Montither's helmet. These in particular made the crowd rapturous, but one of them was so violent Veneetha Azucena, as was her prerogative, commanded them to pause in their conflict. This time she asked, "Do you wish the fight to continue, Mr. Montither?"

Montither, despite a mounting feeling of panic, gathered his courage. "Yes!"

But Veneetha was obviously worried. She had only recently restored her business relationship with Montither's father. It would not help their future dealings if his son were to be wounded here today. "There is no need for anyone here to be seriously injured," she shouted. "There is no need to take this to the limits. Our greater goal is to have you both in good form for the defence of this—"

"I said *yes!*" he bellowed.

Once again, Veneetha Azucena had no choice but to allow the match to continue.

As their blades met for a third time, Montither leaned in again to speak to Xemion. He was panting from his exertions and his breath stank of blood. His voice was hoarse and strained. "Whatever you do to me, I swear by my ancestors — I will kill her for you."

But Xemion feared him no longer. He had no self-doubt now. He felt only one thing — devout and unwavering hatred. Dancing in and out of Montither's flailing guard he unleashed a flurry of blows on his helmet, occasionally hacking off little bits of metal as he did so. All the while, Montither weakly waved his blade and screamed like a trapped animal. But he wouldn't surrender. "Gnasher!" he yelled, with what little was left of his energy. "Gnasher!" But Gnasher had been violently taken out of action by some disgruntled kitchen Thrall who'd seen what he'd done to Imalgha with his mirror. "Gnasher!" he shrieked.

"Yield!" Xemion demanded, and with that he severed Montither's sword at the hilt.

Montither's scream of outrage could not be heard over the noise of the roaring crowd. But Xemion was still not seeing what he needed to see in Montither's eyes. With a final, contemptuous swipe he knocked the hilt out of Montither's grasp. The crowd roared again, but then drew to a hush as Xemion swept his sword up to Montither's thick neck and inserted the point between his helmet and breastplate. The scared face that had looked at Xemion from the end of the same sword on his very first day in the city again stared back at him. He had never felt such a surge of hatred as he felt gazing into Montither's unsurrendering eyes. It would be so easy, so *perfect*, to slide the sharp point slowly forward and put this disgusting piece of vermin out of everyone's misery. The crowd watched and waited silently.

"Do it!" someone yelled. Xemion gazed into Montither's eyes. Another surge of malice rushed through him and into his sword arm as though from some well of endless hatred deep in the Earth. His hand flexed. Montither closed his eyes.

"Do you yield unto me?" Xemion roared in his highest and mightiest tone.

Montither wished he had something smart to say in return, but all he could do was shake his head. Xemion's vision went dark for a moment. His sword arm drew back quickly in his hand, ready for the necessary blow. Just as he might have brought the blade down, a voice cried out. "All right. It's over. I will not see such blood quarrels here under my command. Both of you stand away."

Xemion sneered, still propelled for a moment by the forward motion of his hate. Finally, though, he nodded in compliance with Veneetha Azucena's command and backed away. A few people jeered, but when Veneetha officially pronounced Xemion the winner, a loud cheer went up from the crowd. Shamed and broken, Montither stalked off into the crowd. "Gnasher! Gnasher!" he kept yelling, enraged. *"Gnash-errr!"*

"And now," Veneetha Azucena announced, turning to face Zero, who had all this time been watching through narrow, angry eyes, "if there are no new challengers, we have come to our final bout."

Somehow, it hadn't occurred to Xemion that when he defeated Montither he would have to fight … *her.*

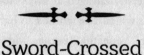

27

Sword-Crossed

Zero was deep in concentration. Xemion, fresh from his first taste of glory, was half-terrified, half-thrilled. What little he could see of Zero's face behind her helmet was brightly painted with streaks of sun-yellow, just like a battle Thrall. He was almost certain it was Saheli, but she was focusing her gaze in a way that slightly frightened him. It was as though she'd found a way to insert the edge of that gaze into whatever was weak or exposed in him. There was a sick feeling in his heart, a cold churning in his belly. His strongest urge was to throw down the blade now and kneel before her in surrender.

Zero saw a faceless opponent. There were only points of potential impact and entry — in particular that thin line at the neck where the helmet met the breastplate. It made her hand twitch almost automatically, and in her head she heard Lighthammer's voice: "Cut! Cut!" But before the match could begin, Xemion lowered his blade and said "I yield to her."

Someone in the crowd yelled out, "I want to yield to her, too." But there was no laughter at this. This was a serious moment.

Zero's voice broke in anger. "You can't do that!"

Even as the murmuring in the crowd rose in support of this, Xemion shook his head. "I can and I must."

Zero was clearly enraged at this. "You think you can cheat me of this which I've worked so hard for?"

"She's right," Veneetha Azucena added sternly. "What kind of victory would it be for her or for any of us if it happens like this?"

Xemion bowed his head, the sword hanging down from his hand at a slight angle. "I'm sorry. I yield. I have to. I believe she is my—"

"Well, I have to do this."

Zero suddenly snapped her blade toward his, hitting it with a quick whipping motion that caused it to vibrate so hard he nearly dropped it. The crowd cheered in approval. Xemion showed no response. Again Zero struck Xemion's sword. "Come on!" she shouted fiercely. But still Xemion resisted.

"I can't fight you. I only fought him to save you. Don't you recognize—"

Until then, Zero had struck Xemion only with the flat of her blade. But this time she thrust it forward quite hard, aiming the metal tip straight at Xemion's chest. Xemion felt his sword move quickly to block the blow. She struck again and once more the magical sword defended him.

"No!"

232

Zero's next strike was lightning fast. A surge of power jolted into Xemion's body with the impact, and without thinking he struck back. In an instant there was a flurry of clashes and clangs that made the crowd cheer ecstatically. But Zero was a far better opponent than Montither had been. Her concentration was immaculate, her footwork supreme. She landed several more whip-like blows against his armour. She blocked, parried, thrust, and returned, and nothing Xemion's blade did seemed able to breech her defences. The next time the crowd cheered it was for Zero not Xemion.

"No pity!" Lighthammer yelled from nearby.

In all of his fight with Montither, Xemion had not been hurt once, but Zero managed to get around his defences and land a solid blow against the armour plate that protected his lower ribs. The force of it sent a sharp pain up into his side. He felt his sword dart toward her neck, but he pulled it back at the last moment. Even so, it came so close to its target that it severed Zero's chinstrap, causing her helmet to hit the ground with a dull ring. There was a unanimous gasp from the crowd.

For the first time in a long time Xemion beheld her un-obscured face. It *was* her! He already knew that she was taller and broader than she'd been before, but he wasn't prepared for the changes the last few months had wrought in her face. Her cheekbones seemed more defined, harder than before. There was a new fullness to her lips and there it was — the diagonal scar over her left eyebrow. But this was not the child he had rescued from the torrent on the mountain. This was a full-grown woman, a woman so beautiful it hurt him. The crowd quieted; all eyes were on the two of them as he swallowed his feelings.

"Are you injured?" Veneetha Azucena asked Zero with concern.

Zero felt her neck where the strap had been. "No." She was not even shaken. She had no fear of this young swordsman. The line between his shoulder plate and his helmet was wide enough for ten blades thicker than hers. She knew she could end this any time she wanted.

"Do you wish to continue?" Veneetha Azucena asked.

Zero stared back at her competitor. He was gazing at her with such a strange, almost imploring look on his face, just like Fargold did. It sickened her. She gritted her teeth and let her blood grow colder. "By all means," was her answer.

The crowd remained quiet as Veneetha Azucena turned to Xemion. "And you?"

Xemion wanted to say, "No, this is my beloved," but the words that came out of his mouth surprised him. His voice was deeper, nastier than he'd ever heard it. "By all means," he replied.

Zero's sword arced through the air quick and hard. Automatically, Xemion's blade rose to block it. With the force of that impact, more of the dark energy erupted into his body. Thrice more she brought her blade down on his, and with each impact the urge of the sword — the urge to win at any cost — flowed into him stronger and colder, silencing the voice of protest within. Still Zero came at him, connecting here with his shoulder, there with his forearm. In the last exchange they came face-to-face and Xemion saw close up the utter, unrelenting coldness in her eyes. It froze something in his spirit that shattered and exploded with her next blow. He suddenly saw her with that vision he'd had in the Nexis. He saw her under-self and her over-self. He saw all of the fanned out, contrary versions of her that there were or ever could be in all the worlds. His hand tightened on the hilt of his sword, on every sword in every world. Spell and spellbinder shifted. The dark energy reversed its polarity and began to flow from him into the blade. He no longer needed to be fooled and subdued by these shallow facets of her face, this wisp of grace that fluttered so falsely before him. She was a dream-thief. She had taken his dream and made it her own. She had betrayed him entirely. And if she had to, she would kill him.

How foul she looked to him now as he closed in. His last shred of reluctance fell away and, as he hacked closer to her, the cheers of the crowd seemed to die down. That larger self, that myriad self he had experienced inside the Great Kone, merged into him now. He drew on that snakelike, hideous part of himself that wanted nothing more than to destroy, and he swung at her with all his might. Zero stared right into Xemion's soul just as his sword cut its terrible arc through the air on course for the narrow of her neck. At the last second a shiver went through him and into his blade and he pulled it off course.

But his blade had not completely avoided its target. Zero hardly felt the wound at first. On the upper left side of her face, just above the brow, there was a small cut — only the very point of the sword had caused it, but it crisscrossed exactly that straight, diagonal scar that was already there. In the very instant that the first trickle of blood ran down her cheek, a vision flashed before her, a scene that seemed to spring from every cell in her body. The thin, sharp edge of a large, wide blade, like that of an axe, coming straight at her, striking her. Someone's eyes looking eagerly on. A pain like she was being cut in half. In that moment all that had been spelled away by the waters of forgetfulness and the touch of Vallaine's red hand outside the Great Kone began to come undone.

Zero touched her fingers to the wound on her brow, looked at the fierce face and upraised sword of her opponent, and let out a kind of screaming sob. Shocked by the pain in that cry, Veneetha Azucena held her open palm out to Xemion to signal him to stop. She then asked Zero, "Do you yield?"

"No!" Zero pressed her palm against her cheek and signalled with the other hand that she wanted to hold. She hunched over, frozen for an instant. When the crowd saw this, many of them began to boo and hiss and urge her sarcastically to fight him.

"Zero, you must answer me. Do you yield?" A visible shudder shook Zero's body as she tried to regain control of herself. But more memories were breaking free from the sea bottom of her amnesia, clear and fresh and raw. A red sky. A red river. Those eyes again, red and even redder at the centre. So many, so quickly, she could barely even see.

Even through the shouts of "Fight! Fight! Fight!" even through the dark energy, which coursed up the sword and into his arm, Xemion could see the agony in her eyes as she finally answered "I do."

The crowd bellowed with disapproval. But Veneetha Azucena wouldn't be swayed. She stepped in quickly, raised Xemion's arm over his head in a signal of triumph, and loudly declared him the winner of the Tourney. The horns blared, the crowd reluctantly accepted the verdict and cheered, and as Xemion sheathed his sword he was lifted by the kitchen Thralls, who began to pass him from hand to hand overhead. As soon as he had taken his hand off the hilt of his sword a great wave of exhaustion hit him. Just as the spell he'd said in the Nexis had drained him, this second spell was taking its toll now. His body went limp in their arms and only for one fading instant did he see her as she fled the arena, a look of shock deepening in her face.

"Xemion! Xemion! Xemion!" they cheered. "He is victor. He is lord. Hail, hail the shining sword."

28

Lighthammer Remembers

As evening fell, Tiri Lighthammer staggered and drank and coughed his way from Two-Spell Well to the beginning of Phaer Point where the tunnel led down to the sea. There was something wrong and he knew it. Zero should not have lost that match and he had begun to suspect foul play. But it was more than just that. He felt a deep dread and knew somehow that there was more at stake here than winning or losing a tournament. At the entrance to the tunnel, he commanded the guard to let him through. The guard, like most of the people of Ulde that evening, had had too much to drink. Lighthammer made his way on foot down the long tunnel and into the cavern. Two other intoxicated guards came to attention as he approached the inside of the newly installed Lion's Gate.

"You are both drunk," he shouted at them.

"So are you, sir," one of them shot back a little cockily.

This enraged Lighthammer. "What's your name?" Despite his drunkenness he said it with such a sense of authority that the man came immediately to attention, if only in a notably unsteady way. "I'm sorry, sir, my name is Ilygadryth."

"Ilygadryth what?"

"Ilygadryth Feyn, sir."

"Do you know, Ilygadryth Feyn, that I lost seven brothers right here fifty years ago because some fool like you did not take his job seriously enough? Now you get yourselves sober right now. You are on guard duty, and if I catch you in this condition again, I will have at you with my blade whatever the rules about it may be."

Neither Ilygadryth Feyn nor the other guard replied. Both of them gulped.

"Now where is Glittervein?" he asked.

The guards looked at each other. "We have not seen him," said the one who had not yet spoken.

"Not at all?" Lighthammer asked, clearly upset.

The man shook his head.

"Well, who is keeping watch over the harbour then?"

Ilygadryth Feyn jerked his thumb up in the direction of the gatehouse mounted high on the sea wall. "We have a man up there," he said in as sober a tone as he could muster.

"And one who watches from the bird's nest by Uldestack," said the other.

"And that's it?" Lighthammer roared.

Ilygadryth Feyn nodded.

The second guard said, "Most of them are out ... celebrating. It is, after all—"

Such was the ferocity of Tiri Lighthammer's glare the man stopped speaking instantly.

"Let me out," Lighthammer ordered. The two looked at each other, puzzled, but the lever was pulled and the signal was given to the gateman. The massive iron grill at the entrance to the cavern slowly rose to let the old man through. In the sky beyond the towers, at the ends of the Lion's Paws, that luminous red planet hung over the harbour, the full moon at its side. This gave the horizon a ruddy glow that seemed to summon Lighthammer forward. Still drinking and coughing so hard he frequently had to stop walking and double over with the effort, he made his way along the east side of the inner harbour, all the while looking suspiciously about. When he reached the end where the east side of the Lion's Paws nearly met the west, he stood on the receiving dock beyond the stone tower and glared out across the water. Then he took out his telescope and scanned the horizon.

For a while the old soldier gulped down mead as he teetered, occasionally reaching out to steady himself on the gate with one hand. He continued scanning the horizon, the telescope moving back and forth. After a while he stopped and lifted his flask, noticing again the strange portent of the heavenly bodies above. The same red planet had hovered by the moon fifty years ago, on that dreaded day when he had lost so much. Lighthammer put away his telescope, took a deep breath, and let the image of his younger brother come to him. He saw the two of them as little boys in their childhood home, playing swords and dreaming of being great heroes some day. Then he saw him again, many years later, on the floor of this very bay.

cut open, gutted, lying in his own blood, a look of horror frozen forever in his eyes. Lighthammer lowered his gaze and let two bright teardrops splash down into the water. The tide, he saw, by the light of the moon and stars, was ebbing away already. Looking down into the dark flow, he coughed and spat and coughed and spat again. But finally the time came for the other thing: the hardest thing. That other face he had to remember.

He closed his eyes and allowed himself for the first time in a long time to look back into the bright eyes of his baby daughter, so full of promise and trust. It was the day he had departed for the war, and the last day he would ever see that little cherub of his, for the Pathans had spared no one, not even children, the most brutal of deaths in their vengeful rampage after the Battle of Phaer Bay. Lighthammer stared into those innocent eyes for as long as he could and let the memory and the pain come. It had not lessened in the last fifty years. If anything, it had grown stronger. When his own time came to die, his family line would end with him. But maybe if those Thrall gods were really up there in their heaven, maybe on that day he would look again into her eyes.

He took out his telescope again and searched the horizon, but it didn't stop more tears from welling up in his eyes. There was a sound like the light tread of someone on the dock behind him, but before he had the chance to react, there was a loud crack and a sudden piercing pain at the back of his skull. Tiri Lighthammer toppled forward into Phaer Bay.

29

Why Don't You Take It

The celebration of the equinox and the first Phaer Tourney in half a century continued in the great ballroom of Castle Phaer overlooking the Bay of Ulde. This was the very castle where Xemion had been taken by Lethir. The same castle from which, fifty years earlier, the Phaer generals had watched the slaughter of their troops on the tidal flats below. But like so much of the devastation of that day, the castle was now being reclaimed and redeemed. A new history for it was being sought. In the past two weeks the finest marble craftsmen, the stone Nains of Ilderhaven, had been employed to shape new slabs to take the place of those shattered by the weight of the mammuths the castle housed in its days as a stable. And last week, when seven cedars in the sacred grove of Thorne had been mysteriously felled, the timbers were salvaged to rebuild the lofts that now surrounded the banquet hall, and gave a small throng of children in attendance a bird's eye view of the proceedings.

The original architects had designed this magnificent chamber to contain and feature the Great Stone of Urgarud, a massive grey meteorite that had jutted up from this spot since long before the last time the glaciers came and went over the world. A platform had been built around the stone. Aligned symmetrically about it were rows and rows of stone tables, each of them at least forty feet long. Lit from above by a galaxy of glittering chandeliers, the tables hosted a vast number of merrymakers, many of whom had been celebrating the Phaer Tourney with repeated toasts.

The lavish banquet had just come to an end and the honour guard was about to present arms. Holding swords of gold over their hearts in the Elphaerean salute, they came to a halt in unison in front of the platform where Veneetha Azucena sat as the Queen of the Equinox, smiling down at them. There was a sharp command from the sergeant-at-arms followed by a stomping of feet and flashing of metal as they withdrew their weapons ceremoniously and came to attention before her.

Xemion, wrapped and trembling inside Vallaine's cloak, struggled to remain alert at the front table. He had finally eaten, but he still felt weak, hungry, and sick. That look of terror and betrayal on Saheli's face kept flashing at him like a distant fire behind dark, rushing clouds. He had saved her from Montither, but had he lost her himself? His muscles jerked with strange, cold spasms and his hand would not stay still. It kept twitching toward the hilt of the sword, which still hung at his side. But he resisted. The immensity of what he had done when he made the sword was becoming clear to him. He dreaded ever touching the weapon again.

Veneetha Azucena was newly attired in her splendid evening regalia. A purple cloak hung from her shoulders, streaming down and about a shining breastplate, which had been custom made for her. On her head a peaked bronze helmet supported a high red feather, once a symbol of Elphaerean leadership. Still seated on her throne, she commanded her honour guard to be at ease. Then, taking a quaff of green ale from a tall cup, she did her best to address the crowd in a manner befitting the celebration at hand.

"We have just passed our first equinox in this ancient capital, my friends. We were told by no less a personage than Prince Akka Smissm that we would not last. We were told we would be routed and slaughtered and enslaved. But look at us; here we are today, safe and thriving in our ancient home. We must not gloat, but those who once enslaved us are now locked in the death throes of their own civil war."

There was a great cheer and much thumping of cups at this news. When the noise had subsided, Veneetha Azucena continued.

"But let us not rejoice in the misfortunes of others, for we all share this same blue planet. The Pathans call it Ov; the Nains call it Arf. We Freemen call it Eph, and I am even told that the Kagars call it Earth. And so, I do not name any of them enemy, for with such a common name for our common home, I am hopeful that one day there might be enough commonality to find peace amongst all of us. That is the Phaer way. To peace amongst all our peoples!"

Once again she lifted a full glass of the green ale that

the absent Glittervein had generously sent in his stead, and drained it. The crowd followed suit. She signalled to have the goblets refilled, and when this was done she toasted again. "Peace to us. Peace to you. Peace to the Pathans and Kagars and Cyclopes alike."

"Peace." Almost everyone but Xemion repeated this and they all chinked their glasses and drained them to the dregs, as was the Elphaerean custom.

"And now it is my delight," Veneetha Azucena announced, "to welcome the winner of our inaugural Phaer Tourney. Please, a courteous welcome for Xemion of Ildewood."

Xemion swallowed hard. He didn't know what to do. He felt like vomiting or fleeing. Instead he rose unsteadily and made his way toward the platform as the crowd cheered. The kitchen Thralls, including Lirodello, who was sitting with his arm wrapped comfortingly about the still-dazed Imalgha, were particularly ecstatic, as were some scruffy unattended Thrall children who had snuck in.

"He is victor. He is lord. Rah, rah, the shining sword," they chanted. "The beast is beaten, gouged, and gored. Rah, rah, the shining sword."

Xemion mounted the steps to the stage and stood with his head half bowed looking around the room for Saheli. He couldn't see her anywhere. He looked up at the lofts where the eager faces of the young children beamed down at him, their eyes full of hope and awe. He began to sway unsteadily and this caused one of the Thralls to yell "Have another drink!"

"There'll be plenty of time for more drinking anon,"

Veneetha Azucena intoned with an indulgent smile, "but first, a more solemn moment is upon us. Here we have the winner of the Phaer Tourney, and for the first time in fifty years the ceremony of the sword is upon us." She turned toward Xemion. "Xemion, please withdraw your blade."

Xemion's hand jerked toward the hilt in obedience, but then he froze. He looked out at the gathering and saw Tomtenisse's madly glinting eyes, his head nodding up and down in reluctant approval. And there beside him was the gruff Belphegor doing his best to maintain a look of disdain. Lirodello was comforting the still-smouldering Imalgha, his arm half-pulled out of its socket by the attempt to get it around her massive shoulders. He, too, nodded approvingly and gave Xemion a thumbs up. But still no Saheli.

"Xemion?" Veneetha Azucena persisted.

Without looking at her, Xemion reached for the buckle that bound his hilt to his side and undid it. Slowly he lowered sword and scabbard to the floor, his head hung over in shame.

"Whatever are you doing?"

"I do not deserve this honour," he began, but one of the little Thralls yelled out "Yes you do!"

There was then a great chorus of "Yes! Yes! Yes!" followed by the loud thumping of goblets upon the stone tables. With some effort, Xemion signalled for them to be quiet, a request, which with some additional gesturing from Veneetha Azucena, they finally obeyed.

"I have won fraudulently," he said, but his voice was so quiet most of the Thralls didn't hear him and, taking it to be some further gallantry, once again set to banging their goblets on the stone tables.

But Veneetha Azucena had heard him quite clearly. "What do you mean?" she asked curtly.

Whatever his reply might have been, it was lost in the crowd's next roar. Something uncanny was happening with the sword at Xemion's feet. It was slowly swivelling around so that the hilt, which had landed on the floor pointing toward Veneetha Azucena, was now slowly reorienting itself toward him.

There were screams of terror. Veneetha Azucena shouted "No!" There was a metallic hiss and the sword pulled itself out of the scabbard. "No," she shouted again but there was no denying what was unfolding before her. Her eyes flashed with rage. "This is spellcraft." She spat out the word as though it were a curse.

Before Xemion could even nod his head in acknowledgement, the weapon jerked across the floor and affixed its hilt to his heel. Instinctively, he kicked it away and it spun halfway across the stage before it stopped suddenly and shot back to his heel. The crowd by this time was almost in a panic. None had seen such spellcraft in all their lives and it was terrifying to them. Veneetha Azucena withdrew her own sword and shouted "Stand away!" to Xemion. But even as he backed away from her, the sword dragged itself along at his heel. Once again he kicked at it, but this time the sword rose in the air in an elegant arc so that its hilt came down, butting against his palm like the nose of an eager dog.

"No!" he shouted again, his voice twisted with rage and fear. In response the sword shoved itself at his hand so hard it hurt his knuckles. But still he refused it. Everyone by now was screaming and many were running for the exits.

"Pick it up," a disembodied voice yelled. This caused the biggest uproar yet from the assembly. There was a clear sense of terror in the room. Some of the little children in the lofts began to whimper and hide their eyes.

"Don't!" Veneetha Azucena shouted at Xemion over the racket. "Don't touch it!"

"Stop!" Xemion shouted at the sword in the loudest voice he had yet mustered. But the sword had a mind of its own. It followed his hand and kept trying to force itself into his palm, and even when he cupped his two hands together it tried to force itself between them.

"No!" Xemion shouted again, tucking his hands into his armpits. But the sword was determined. It suddenly withdrew from him and, revolving about its axis, stopped with its point aimed out at the crowd. There was a quick flash of light, and then it sped toward the front row and swung at the leg of the nearest stone table there, cutting it through. The young men and Thralls who were sitting at it gasped at the weight, which now pressed down upon their knees.

"No," Xemion shrieked. He knew the sword was doing this to force him to take it into his palm and there was rising fear in his voice. But the sword swung anyway, cutting through the opposing table leg, so that the entire end of the table slanted downward, sending a long line of golden goblets tumbling off, clanking upon the floor. The sword flew back to him once more, hitting his hand hard, trying to open it.

"TAKE IT!" the voice commanded. It was so loud it caused the windows to rattle. This was when Veneetha Azucena brought her own sharp sword down upon the spelled blade's back. She struck it to the floor with a slanted swipe that sent it hurtling off, spinning into the empty area behind the stage. It hit the flagstones hard and kept skidding and turning until it came to a halt, its hilt facing directly at her.

"Get out of here!" she screamed to the crowd in a voice that could not be ignored. "Somebody find Tiri Lighthammer and get him here immediately." She had barely gotten this command out of her mouth before the sword launched itself at her so fast it was but a blur. She held up her own broadsword reflexively and managed to deflect it, but she saw that it had left a deep nick in her weapon. Still she held the damaged sword defensively in front of her while the spellcrafted sword hung in the air, swinging to and fro malevolently. It took two more quick hacks at her, both of which she parried excellently, but when the third came the weakened sword gave way and the blade fell to the stone floor, leaving her with nothing in her hand but the shorn hilt. As she swayed it backed away a little before lunging toward her chest with great force. Her breastplate held strong but Veneetha Azucena staggered back three steps, all the air knocked out of her. Before she could even gasp, the magical sword swung sideways and drove its cutting edge into the side of her helmet. It hit so hard that it breached the metal and remained wedged in her helmet as she struck the ground. There was a shriek of metal on metal as it tore itself free and rose once again into the air. Veneetha Azucena remained prone where she had fallen, a rim of deeply red blood already welling up and over the split in her helmet.

By now every able Phaerlander who had a sword

had drawn it and as one they tried to subdue the magical sword. But no matter how they struck, no matter how they fell upon it and drove it to the ground it would always cut free, often leaving a screaming mess of torn metal and streaming blood in its wake. Many a sword was left deeply dented and many were sheared off at the hilt. Xemion, more alert now that the sword was no longer at his side, kept trying to get them to stand away from it. He knew that the more they attacked it the more it would attack them. If they left it alone it would return to him. He almost felt he knew its mind and ways as it wreaked havoc upon the great hall. He knew something else, too. It was not yet fully empowered. It needed him. It needed his commitment in full to the spell he had cast. And that was something he was not going to give it. But what other option was there?

Sensing his continued refusal, the sword shot up out of the melee. Soaring to the great vaulted ceiling, it began to hack away the heads of the stone gargoyles, sending them crashing to the flagstones far below. Then it began to cut down the high chandeliers that lit the hall. They fell, shattering and sputtering and flickering onto the flagstones. It was darker in the hall, for night had long since fallen, but the sword had a light of its own. It radiated with an awesome green emanation, shooting from chandelier to chandelier until the whole place was a mass of scattered, shouting people, screaming, terrified children, and sputtering candles rolling along, still lit, over the flagstones.

By now, those who could had fled the castle, but the children in the highest loft, terrified by the sword, were frozen, screaming for their mothers. Sensing them there, the sword hovered and swayed a moment, as though suspended from a thread, its point aimed straight at the loft, its hilt aligned with Xemion's hand. It was as though it were challenging him, forcing him. In some way it was still part of him, and suddenly with that knowledge he knew what was going to happen next. The sword lowered itself and began to slash at one of the supports that held up the stairway to the loft where the children were. It took only three hacks to cut the new wood right through. Three more hacks and both supports were gone. With that the steps fell away, leaving the children stranded thirty feet in the air. The sword paused and then swooped down and turned its pommel once again very deliberately toward Xemion. "TAKE IT!" the increasingly deeper and more ghoulish voice shouted.

Xemion now knew that taking it was the only way to control it. But if he took it, would the sword also control him?

"Why won't you take it?" one of the mothers screamed.

30

Zero Remembers

Striding toward her room at the Panthemium, Zero recalled the flickering fin of a fish and the fin made her remember a wing. And the wing recalled a leaf and the leaf recalled a hand, and so one memory led to another. But there was no apparent order. The scent of a breeze brought back the sound of a stream and the stream was connected with her own reflection as she stared down at it, scared, the rapidly flowing water summoning a nightmare feeling of running away and never getting anywhere. That feeling echoed back to a place and that place like all places led back to the one place, the one face, the one melody that always seemed to be playing behind all these scenes, lovely and lilting. It called to something deep inside her, but it also inexplicably gripped her with terror. As she walked, the melody grew more refined and there was more of it and then it ran round again and she was shaking her head. "No." But the melody came once more. And a sweet voice sang it now. And she started to hear words: *Open my heart, open the door…*

Without warning the bright image of a wide blade came swinging at her. It was so clear and present she cried out and jerked her head back instinctively. And just as the new cut over her eyebrow stung and welled with blood, the old cut, diagonal to it, opened a deeper cut in her memory. She saw herself from outside herself. Her neck bent down over the butcher's block. A woman clenching her by the hair trying to keep it there long enough to let the ax in her other hand do its work. She was struggling and she pulled away from the veering of the blade. It just nicked her over the eyebrow as it went by but it felt like it cut her in two. She stood up screaming, the blade embedded in the block, the woman screaming, too, yanking her hair and hitting her in the face. Calling her a fool and a dog and a curse. And still the memories dragged one another out of the darkness and pulled themselves before her as she entered the Panthemium and proceeded down the long hallway to her room.

When she opened the door and saw her staff still leaning in the corner she got a brief respite. She remembered the sunflower stalk it once had been. She touched it and smiled for just a moment and envisioned the glade where that sunflower and so many other, lesser sunflowers had grown, and the sunflowers made her think of the sun — of a particular sun on a particular day — and suddenly she remembered a golden swan.

"Chiricoru!" she gasped, immediately clamping her hand over her mouth as though she could somehow push that name back in. For a second there arose the vision of a kindly old woman's face, but it was so quick it was but a glimmer. In the next instant it was replaced by that other woman's face again: the one who looked a little like her. And she knew now that it was her mother. In this memory she was still bleeding from that cut the axe had made, but the blood was shimmering up and away from her and getting thinner and thinner. She gasped and realized she had been holding her breath. She gasped again when she saw, rippling above her as though through the surface of a rapidly running river, her mother's face. And there was such love in her eyes, but her hands … Zero choked and gasped again. She heard herself try to say no, but she was underwater and her mother's firm hands were clenched about her neck. She felt herself blacking out and hardly knew if it was memory or the present. She felt herself going down to the weedy bottom, drowning, but rising again. And then she remembered being swept along down the river.

For a long time Zero sat on the edge of her bed, still dressed in her armour. She rocked back and forth, wincing and shaking her head. And just as Xemion was saying "No! No!" to the sword in the great banquet hall at the castle, she kept saying "No! No!" to the words and images that burst into her consciousness. No to the insanity. No to the violence and the justification of violence. No to the whole long list of abuses, betrayals, and shocks.

The truly shocking thing, though, was something she didn't want to say no to. Whenever she dared to look directly into her mother's eyes the only thing she ever saw in them was love.

Love.

So strong was this impression it made her stop remembering for a moment. How could this possibly be? Before the answer could come to her, another vision spun it out of her mind. A crooked-backed, wrinkled old man with long, wild hair like lichen bent over a handwritten spell kone as high as his waist. *He's going to turn it.* He shushes her and winks. He smiles at her. She is just a little girl and he is very kind looking, but a little confused. As if to remind himself, he speaks the old rhyme:

> *As the eye goes down*
> *The words go around.*
> *All in one turn*
> *The spell is bound.*

Then he starts cranking the handle clockwise and the beautiful kone spins and the words go round and round and the glass eye descends and somewhere she can hear her mother singing that song. And now she begins to hear the rest of the words:

> *Open my heart, open the door*
> *Every day to love her more.*
> *Break O wave upon the shore*
> *Every day I'll love her m—*

At that moment Asnina burst into the room. "It was a spell-wrought sword!" she screamed. She was very distraught. Her hair had come all unbound and there were streaks through the orange chevrons on her cheeks where tears must have run.

"What do you mean?"

"I mean you didn't lose. He's up there right now confessing. He made a sword that couldn't lose. He says he made it with a spell. It's there right now going mad on him."

Zero didn't quite know who or what she was talking about, but she saw the urgency in her eyes and grabbed the sunflower staff from the corner of the room. Together they ran out of the Panthemium and off toward the castle.

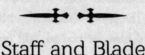

31

Staff and Blade

The sword slowly levitated until it was level with the loft where the children cowered. There it hung like a compass needle, swinging back and forth, back and forth, in a narrower and narrower arc. Screaming, the children kept rushing from one side to the other, trying to get out of its path, but there was not much room and the weakened structure had begun to tilt to and fro with their movements. Children on the sides of the loft were being squeezed up against the railings and some of them looked like they might soon either fall or be squashed. Their mothers had gathered below, screaming their children's names and preparing to catch them if they should fall. But they were quite high up and many of them would likely be injured, or worse, from the fall.

"Take the bloody sword!" a huge, red-faced Thralleen yelled furiously in Xemion's face.

"I can't!" he yelled back. But he had to do something.

Instead of reaching for the sword, he took off down the aisle between the stone tables, heading toward the exit. A new series of outraged screams rose from the mothers and the stranded children, but Xemion had a plan. When he was halfway down the aisle to the doorway, he turned back, opened his palm, and shouted "Here!"

The sword stopped swiveling back and forth in front of the children and turned toward him.

"Come! I command you!" he yelled again, offering his open palm. The sword shot at him hilt first. But just before it reached him, he turned, still holding his hand over his head as if to take it, and ran toward the exit. Once outside, even if he did have to grab it, he would only do so long enough to shove it up to the hilt into the ground and hope it stayed there until the children could be rescued.

Unfortunately, before he got to the doorway Asnina arrived with Zero just behind. Indeed, he almost collided with them. He felt the sword graze by his knuckles as he stopped in front of the mighty Thralleen, but then it was gone again in an arc, upward to the ceiling. "Don't come in here!" he yelled, but Asnina's only response was to tug out her iron blade and come at him with a snarl. Just then the spelled sword, having completed a wide loop in the air, was heading once more for Xemion's palm. Hearing it before she saw it, Asnina struck a mighty blow, but the spell-made sword, full of momentum from its long flight, met her blade full force in the middle and cut it in half. Enraged, she struck at it with the hilt, but it was too quick. It pulled back and with a quick push forward pierced her through the shoulder. For a second she was pinned right up against the stone wall. With a grunt of pain she dropped to the ground as the sword yanked itself out.

Zero had tried to prepare herself for the reality of the spellcrafted sword, but now that it hovered before her, a whole lifetime of fearing spellcraft gathered in the one scream she emitted as she turned and fled in the opposite direction. Halfway across the hall the sword caught up, surpassed, and then turned and confronted her, eager to fight its old opponent.

"Someone get me a sword!" she screamed, holding the sunflower staff out in front of her in trembling hands, awaiting the inevitable attack. She didn't have to wait long. It struck so fast Xemion didn't even have time to shout. The sunflower staff was old by now and though its exterior was hard as wood, its centre was hollow. It should have been cut in two by the impact of the sword, but somehow it took and deflected the blow.

Zero was startled by the force exerted from the sword. She looked around in a panic. She saw Xemion, but didn't remember him yet. "Somebody get me a real sword!" she yelled again, as she readied herself for the next assault. Xemion was exhausted, but he pushed himself now beyond his limits, struggling open-palmed toward her. "Come to me!" he yelled again. But the sword ignored him, and before he could get to her there was an explosion of green light as the sword struck at her again. Once again Zero succeeded in deflecting it with her staff.

Xemion realized what was happening. "It can't cut through your staff," he yelled, "because it's made from a sunflower not a tree. It can only cut through the things in the spell that made it: wood and metal and—" The

rest of his words were lost in the shouts of the crowd as
the sword rushed at Zero with enormous speed. But Zero
had heard enough of what Xemion said. She held the staff
at an angle to absorb the force just as Lighthammer had
trained her to do. She let it spin her a little and came
round, staff up at the ready. The next thrust came faster,
then the next and the next. Soon a flurry of strikes and
feints broke out. This was a fight of maximum motion
that should have overcome even the most skilled swordsman, but Zero had fought this sword before and she was
beginning to know its ways. Nothing it did could get past
her guard. Seeing the sword begin to lag and fade, several
of the terrified children stranded atop the loft made the
mistake of cheering Zero on. Unfortunately this attracted
the sword's attention. If it couldn't get around her guard,
it could certainly get around theirs. Abandoning Zero, it
soared back to the beams that supported the loft. The children now began to shriek in earnest as it slashed mightily
through the first beam, causing one whole side of the loft
to lurch downward.

"Come to me!" Xemion screamed again, but the
sword would never be fooled by this ruse again. If he
wanted it to stop he would have to say it and mean it. It
carefully positioned itself for another swing at the loft, but
by this time Zero had seen its purpose and was standing
in front of the beam, guarding it, her staff held before her
in both hands.

"Make it stop!" she screamed angrily at Xemion as the
sword came at her.

It struck quicker than it ever had, hurtling down
with full force on the staff, but still the sunflower stalk

held. This enraged the sword. As Xemion staggered and swayed in the centre of the hall, he called out in his most spellbinding voice, trying to stop the sword. But this only seemed to make the weapon more frantic. It hacked and hacked, but Zero followed, warding it away from the groaning beam.

Meanwhile, Belphegor the Nain, his brother Tomtenisse Doombeard, and several others were struggling to stand one of the long stone tables on end so they could lean it up against the wall and rescue the children.

To make matters worse, the wood from the severed staircase had been ignited by one of the fallen chandeliers and it was burning fiercely a few feet away from the lone beam that was supporting the loft. Zero tried to keep herself clear of it. Her fight was accurate, valiant, and brave, but slowly the spell-made sword came at her and began to drive her toward it. And every time it succeeded in getting inside her defences it would hack away a little piece of her breastplate so that after a time, the clasps that kept the two sides together were cut through and began to come undone. Jagged images of her mother ripping her clothes off in a crying, screaming rage burned through Zero's mind and her terror all but overcame her, but she willed it away as best she could.

"Make it stop!" she screamed even more desperately at Xemion. She was tiring, but the sword was tireless. Grey with exhaustion, Xemion stood near her now, trying to get close enough to grab the sword's hilt. "Stop. I command you!" he screamed.

Zero was near enough to the fire now that she could feel its intense heat. With the next hack of the sword, the last link in the clasp of her armour was cut through. The breastplate spun open. Another hack and it fell in two pieces. She was fighting now in her tunic. Terrified, she picked up the largest piece of her breastplate and used it as a shield.

Xemion kept trying to grab the sword, but he was slow and weary and it easily dodged, avoiding his grasp as it closed in on Zero. Soon she would be overcome. The children screamed. The terrible moment was upon them. The sword had finally stricken the last fragment of the shield from Zero's hand. There she stood, backed up against the fire as the loft teetered above her. With one quick, sharp blow the sword steered the sunflower staff into the flames.

"No!" Zero bellowed as her staff began to burn. She held it as long as she could, but it was dry and hollow and the flames began to lick up its length from the inside, climbing to her hand. She swung the staff back and forth, trying to put the flames out. She spun it, leaving a brief wheel of fire rolling through the air, but within seconds her knuckles were scorched and she had to throw it down. There, finally, she stood defenceless and terrified before the dreaded spellcraft. And now Xemion knew the sword would end it just as Vallaine had feared it would end. The sword drew back, its shining point aimed surely at her wildly beating heart. It seemed to notch itself into place in the shadows like an arrow in a crossbow. The children on the loft wailed with terror. The Nains hollered with rage. The Thralls shrieked. But nothing could prevent the flight of that sword to Zero's chest.

There was a sickening thud when it struck, and an

eye-burning burst of sparks. For several seconds, everyone was blinded, but then, as the darkening sparks fell to the flagstone floor, all could see what had come to pass. There lay Xemion, flat on his back with the hilt of the spell-made sword protruding from his chest. At the last moment he had summoned all his remaining strength and flung himself in its path.

By now the Nains had succeeded in getting one of the stone tables up against the wall. They began climbing up and rescuing the children. Barrels of Glittervein's beer were overturned to put out the fires. Furious, desperate mothers began to secure and soothe their terrified children. And there stood Zero, her breast heaving with the effort of each breath as she looked down over the fallen Xemion, her hand covering her mouth, almost remembering him. At that moment there was a terrible howl. It was Bargest. He had finally disobeyed his master's order to stay put outside the Panthemium. Those who had not fled the castle watched the giant dog as he approached his master's body. Sniffing and whining his way forward, he leaned his long snout over Xemion's chest and emitted a grievous, long whimper. "Please. Please, O moon. O stars, I beg you," the dog whispered as he began to lick Xemion's wounded brow urgently. "O Earth, I entreat thee." In the midst of this, with an errant nudge of his nose, Bargest knocked the sword hilt over and onto the floor.

But where was the rest of the blade if it wasn't stuck through Xemion's heart and into the floor? Zero bent over him, gently opened the hole in Xemion's chain mail and tunic, and saw the darkening bruise where the full force of the blade had struck him. There was no incision, nothing imbedded. She looked around, and for the first time saw the sparkling, golden particles that were falling all around them like stardust. And then she realized — all but the hilt of the sword had shattered and burst into a million pieces when it hit his chest. A second longer and Zero might have also noticed that, after landing softly on the grey flagstones, the particles began to move slowly toward one another, little particles forming bigger particles. But just then there was a rattling gasp as the fallen Xemion, whose own sword had been unable to pierce him, attempted to take in air. Someone cried out "He lives! He lives!"

There was a gurgling sound and Xemion suddenly coughed and his eyes fluttered open. He tried to focus. Seeing Zero, he tried to speak, but no words would come, just croaks and coughs. Zero stared down at him, frightened and confused, still breathing so heavily from her own exertions that her lungs felt as if they were burning. A streak of blood-matted hair hung down the side of her face where the wound still brimmed and dripped. The arm of one side of her tunic had been scorched by fire and still smouldered. His eyes closed and a name came to her lips. She said the name — "Xemion" — and a tiny welcome morsel of peace entered her heart. Then she turned and ran down the aisle to help Asnina the Thrall, who, having fainted from the pain of the sword thrust through her shoulder, was just now regaining consciousness.

The next time he opened his eyes, Xemion became aware of another face peering at him. Much of it was covered in blood and his vision was blurry. It was hard to focus. "Do you realize what you've done?" Veneetha Azucena shouted. As she bent in closer he could see that the blood had run like a cloak all down one shoulder and was slowly dripping off her fingers. "You have betrayed us. You've betrayed us!" she shrieked.

Xemion was only dimly aware of what happened next. He couldn't remain conscious. Hands grabbed his body and lifted him. The one they called Zero, the one he knew as Saheli, shouted something. He heard Bargest's growled supplications, and then, just as everything was slipping away, a voice that might have been Vallaine's said, "Get him out of here. We can't have him anywhere in this city."

Xemion felt himself being lifted and carried along. His last thought as he lost consciousness completely was of the sword. *What had happened to it?*

Slowly, almost imperceptibly, the scattered particles of the sword were gravitating toward one another. First the blade reassembled — all but one small particle — its point. For a while it slowly revolved, seeking this one infinitesimally small missing piece, but when it came full circle and still hadn't located it, it began to jerk and tug its way across the stone floor in search of the hilt. This it found easily, close to the place where it had fallen from Xemion's chest. Then, just as these two pieces joined with a click that emitted a sudden, brief light, Veneetha Azucena reached down and grabbed it, her hand and wrist likewise lit by that sudden brightness, which lingered for several seconds.

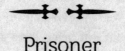

32

Prisoner

Xemion's arms and legs felt as cold and brittle as twigs. He could just barely move the tips of his fingers and breathing took great effort, but he summoned the strength to swivel his eyes around and see where he was. Something tore inside him and he winced. He had a sense of some impending catastrophe, but he didn't know what it was. Outside, seabirds called to one another and, far off, he could hear the slow retreating pulse of the tide. His sense of dread deepened as the images of the day came back to him: his sword arcing toward Saheli's neck, him down on his knees in the crowd speaking that accursed spell.

"No!" His freezing fingers twitched into fists. "No!" he cried again. How could he have been such a fool? And Saheli — the way she looked when the helmet was stricken from her face and everyone in the crowd gasped at her beauty. Her lips, which had touched his lips. All this time he had just been living until the next time that would happen, but now how could there ever be a next time? He had saved her from Montither, and he would never regret that, but at what terrible cost?

It was dark and cold in this place, and for a long time Xemion just lay there with an intense, bereaved sense of loneliness that almost made him want to die. Someone had wrapped Vallaine's cloak about him, but he was still so cold he might have already been a cadaver on a block of ice. Nor did he move when vibrations suddenly came up through the bare stone floor. Someone had entered the building. Upstairs. He both heard and felt the closing of what sounded like a heavy gate and he knew where he was: one of the old towers at the end of the Lion's Paws. Without moving his head he could see a horizontal, slit-like window, which would have given him a panoramic view of the bay if he were standing, but from this prone position only revealed a dark ribbon of night sky — mostly the curve of the bone-white moon and that red planet, larger than he had ever seen it.

He rolled his head over to the right. The dim light from the window reflected off the iron bars of a door, locked and bolted against his escape. He must be in the storage room. This room, which had originally been the receiving area for any cargo from those ships not granted entrance to the inner harbour, was one floor below the part of the tower looking back along the docks and toward the city. Xemion could hear a shuffling sound on the stairs. But was it one or two pairs of footsteps?

He turned a little more so he could just see past the barred door and into the stairwell beyond. He wrapped the cloak around himself and ducked his head into it. First a yellow glow and then a figure carrying a lamp emerged from the stairwell. It was Veneetha Azucena and there was someone else behind her but he couldn't quite make out who it was. When she got to the bars she shone her lamp right in on him.

"Ah, there you are," she said in a voice much softened from earlier that night.

Xemion couldn't even grunt in reply. He could see just the edge of what must have been a bandage wrapped about her head, but she had covered most of it with a green copper helmet. He detected a slight swelling at the left side of her face, but other than that there were no signs of the injury the sword had inflicted.

"I've brought you some blankets," she said gently. "I'm sorry we didn't think of it earlier. You must've spent a chilly few hours in here." She passed two thick blankets through the bars and, using her staff, pushed them across the floor to where he lay. Still peeking out from under Vallaine's cloak, Xemion tried to get a glimpse of the other figure that was lurking in the stairwell. "I'm sorry to have accused you of betraying us," she said with that slight edge of sand in the honey of her voice. "Now that I know the full story, I realize you were only doing your best for all of us. You'll be happy to know I have sent word out to apprehend Mr. Glittervein, and if he's anywhere in Ulde, I assure you we will find him."

"Greetings, Xemion." Vallaine now stepped out of the darkness of the stairwell and stood beside her, his gaunt face lit on one side by the flickering lamp. Somehow Xemion wasn't surprised.

"Yes," Vallaine said, smiling, "I survived." He held up his hand to show Xemion that it was once again dark red, but Xemion could also see the hollow cheeks and look of strain on his face. "It took me much less time to recover than I thought it would."

Xemion again gave the most minimal of responses.

"We owe you a great debt of gratitude," Vallaine said. "I don't know where you got the strength to accomplish all that you did in so short a t—"

Veneetha Azucena interrupted. "Xemion, you must wrap those blankets around you. You look so terribly cold."

Xemion eyed them helplessly. "I can't."

"It's that second spell he bound," Vallaine told her. "I would think it's really taking a toll on him right now."

"Well, I for one cannot bear to see him suffer like this."

Veneetha Azucena took out a set of keys and opened the storage room door. Xemion felt the warmth of her hand in his own and then the two of them wrapped him all round in the blankets. "Here, drink this," Vallaine said, tilting a flask of some warm, sweet liquid between Xemion's cold, blue lips. "It will help with the spell-shock."

Xemion recognized the taste.

"It is ambrosia," Vallaine said. "It will give you strength."

"I know."

"You've had some before?"

"From your cloak."

"In truth?"

Xemion nodded and once again a look of suspicion crossed his brow, but Vallaine gave a little laugh.

"Why, I searched all over for that wafer," he said. "So that was what gave you such strength!"

"You see," Veneetha Azucena said cheerily. "You never know when you lose something who might find it and what good it might do them."

"Do you feel that warming you up?" Vallaine asked in his most empathetic voice. Xemion nodded. The drink was not as powerful as the wafer, but slowly its effects made their way through his system. For a while there was silence as Vallaine continued rubbing Xemion's hands and Veneetha Azucena took his frozen feet into her lap and did her best to warm them with her hands and body heat.

"I'm afraid we have something quite difficult to tell you," she said at last, looking sideways at Vallaine.

"Xemion," Vallaine began, "it is miraculous that you managed to save Saheli and destroy the book of spells. But I didn't know when I told you about the spell book that you would use it to cast a spell of your own."

Somewhat energized by the ambrosia now, Xemion replied, "I didn't want to bind a spell. It was the only way to save Saheli." His voice came back to him, brittle and angry. He hardly recognized it as his own.

"Yes, but do you realize what you cast your spell upon?"

"A stick."

"No, Xemion. That was so much more than just a stick."

Veneetha Azucena cut in almost curtly. "Vallaine has examined your sword and he claims it was not originally a sword at all. It was — *is* the staff of a mage."

Xemion looked back in disbelief.

"I'm afraid it's true," Vallaine said, shaking his head and nervously twirling one side of his moustache. "I did advise you to rid yourself of that stick, did I not? But I had no idea it was a spell staff or I would have taken it from you myself. I told you how a spell staff is made. Do you remember? It is a long scroll of spells handwritten by the mage who makes it. When you cast your spell upon that so-called sword of yours, you cast it upon a thousand other spells at once — all of them the work of a master mage."

Xemion was too stunned to say anything.

"His name was Shalaminsar," Veneetha Azucena said. "The last of the Nain mages. Vallaine says he was slain in Ilde by the Pathans, but before he died he must have cast his last spell upon his staff to draw someone like you to it, so that it might bind to you and work through you."

"But he would never have dreamed that you would turn it into a play sword and then cast your own spell upon it." Vallaine spoke with soft regret. "Do you see what has happened? You have cast a spell upon a thousand spells. Can you imagine a thousand cross-spells all manifesting at once?" Vallaine's voice rose in a way that revealed his anguish at this thought. "And now, yes, the Great Kone is turning and the magic is rising again — but to what new chaos and confliction? I ... I sought to end this era of cross-spells that's been upon us, make the world anew, pure and simple, but this, if we let it go forward, will only make matters infinitely worse."

"None of this was known to me until last night." Veneetha Azucena's tone verged on anger. Indeed she couldn't help shooting an accusatory glance at Vallaine.

"I would've stopped it somehow if I'd known. Please be assured of that. But now the damage is done and all our efforts are in great jeopardy because of it."

"We do understand that it's in no way your fault," Vallaine added with a slight frown. "But unfortunately this spell sword of yours is very dangerous, and now that it has been made you cannot destroy it any more than it was able to destroy you. Even now, as the Great Kone slowly takes up its revolution, the spell you cast on it must be working on the spells written on the staff. All those spell-crossed creatures whose pain you witnessed in Ulde will be nothing to what these thousand crossed spells may inflict on us. We can't take the chance. There is an isle across the eastern sea known as Wizard's Isle. On the entire great globe there is no other place farther from the Great Kone. Its power is so weak there it has almost no effect."

"It will be so much safer for everyone if you should just go and stay there a … a while," Veneetha Azucena said.

"For how long?" Xemion asked. In the ensuing silence Vallaine and Veneetha Azucena briefly caught each other's eye before looking away.

"Aside from the dangers of the innumerable cross-spells you have likely instigated, there is also, according to Mr. Vallaine here, the danger of you and what your power may turn *you* into," Veneetha Azucena said, a slight quaver in her voice.

"What she means is," Vallaine continued, "in the previous era we had seven great mages on the Phaer Isle, each one balancing out the others. But as of now, in this era, Xemion, there is only one. You. You, who though wise and compassionate, have not even one equal, let alone six to balance you out."

"And?"

"And when there is only one mage and that mage has as much power as you do — there is nothing to prevent the possibility of him becoming a war mage."

At this Xemion saw an image from his childhood. A vision of himself upon a great horse in full gallop, his sword held high, an army at his back. But he shook his head adamantly. "No!" The warmth of the ambrosia radiated into his core, and as it melted the ice within, certain wild emotions were beginning to be freed.

"I'm afraid so," Veneetha Azucena countered with a sad but determined look on her face.

"I've spun my tell-kone on this seven times, Xemion," Vallaine said, "and seven times it has come up deep seven with an *X*."

"Did you not feel an unseemly rage when you fought with that sword?" Veneetha Azucena asked. "Were you not ready to slay a young woman whom you held as your own beloved?"

Xemion winced. "But I stopped it!" he said. "I turned it away at the last second."

"Just barely," Vallaine countered. "What will happen next time?"

Xemion hung his head and the great grief of his life flowed into him. Vallaine nodded toward Veneetha Azucena, his face also drawn in sadness.

"I'm so sorry, Xemion." Veneetha Azucena spoke gently and sincerely. "None of this is your fault. You have given us so much and done your utmost for us and it is

273

grievous to have to send one with such a great heart away from our gathering, quite likely forever."

The inevitability of what they were telling him began to sink in, gripping Xemion's heart. He thought of Saheli. He pictured her again in that moment when she kissed him outside the Great Kone. The scent of her hair. The heat of her skin.

"It is a long journey across the sea," Vallaine said, clearing his throat. "Tomorrow, soon after dawn, I have had word that the *Mammuth* is returning. It will sail in to this harbour and you and I must travel to Wizard's Isle, off the northern coast of Arthenow, where the blood magic runs strongest. Who knows, you and I may perhaps go travelling in those realms and do a great deal of good there someday."

Xemion flinched, remembering the taste of his own blood when the Pathan had forced him to drink.

"This is what they did in the days of the Elphaereans when there was trouble with mages," Vallaine said. "It is exile. But it is honourable and it is at least not—"

"I don't want to go. I want to stay here and be part of this."

Veneetha Azucena let go of the heavy sigh she'd been holding back.

"I did everything I could."

"I know," Vallaine agreed, giving the side of his moustache a series of good solid tugs.

"I've been true to you. And true to Saheli." Xemion wanted to say more but he could feel the tears rising in his throat.

"Yes, you have," Veneetha Azucena acknowledged

"And if what Vallaine saw of the future in the Nexis was correct, you truly saved Saheli's life yesterday. And that will continue on in goodness for all of us here and I thank you for that and for the literature you've saved for us also, but …"

"I just wish I had foreseen *this* in the Nexis," Vallaine said regretfully. "But there is some spell bound about you greater than any I have ever known. This future that sends you into exile, I tell you I did not see it anywhere. Though I did at least warn you of the difficulty between you and the maid."

Xemion took another long drink from the flask and felt the heat move deep into his bones. The realization of what lay before him was becoming more real by the moment, but he had one last hope.

"I want to see Saheli before I go."

Xemion did not miss the quick look of concern that passed between Vallaine and Veneetha Azucena.

"She is not doing well," Vallaine said gravely. "She has had almost as many tribulations as you have today."

"I have to see her one more time," he insisted.

Again Veneetha Azucena and Vallaine exchanged a glance. Then Vallaine shrugged. "Very well," he said, "but she is still very disturbed — both in body and mind. The effects of ancient spells, when they wear off suddenly, as it did with her, are unpredictable and sometimes dangerous. So you must be very gentle with her."

Xemion wanted to shout "I have always been very gentle with her." But before he could wrench these words out of his heart he remembered his sword speeding toward her neck and instead said "of course I will be."

"Xemion, you have done something great," Vallaine said as he and Veneetha Azucena stood to leave. "You have saved Saheli and given new life to the Phaer purpose. In time, I hope you will be proud of that." He put the cork in the flask and placed it on the floor beside Xemion. "Drink this if the coldness comes into you again." With that, the two stepped back out of the storage room.

"I am sorry to do this," said Veneetha Azucena as she re-locked the door.

"We have to take every possible precaution," Vallaine added.

"And now I had better go and get a few hours sleep," Veneetha Azucena said. She turned to leave, but hesitated, then wheeled back around to face Xemion.

"Xemion, this must seem very dreadful to you at this moment, but I want you to know that some people think there have always been crossed spells. My mother taught me to consider the whole world as one big stretched mesh of such stuff. There are billions of contesting wishes and wills and underwills and overwills and spells and vows in every move we make. The trick is to be bound by neither one nor the other entirely. It has been my experience that there is a way to ride the line between the two or the three or the four, to centre yourself among them and ride the nexus of your own will to your own avail. Do you understand? That is what choice is. And everyone — even you — can still find a way to choose. Do you see?"

"I don't see what choice I have in this moment," he protested. "I have no choice at all."

"I'm afraid he's right," Vallaine said, shaking his head. "This is something he just has to do."

"Very well, then. I just wanted to make sure I had said that." She, too, shook her head sadly. "Xemion, we will see you just before dawn tomorrow."

Xemion listened as they ascended the stairs and continued across the floor above and exited the building.

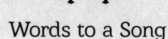

33

Words to a Song

*Z*ero had pulled herself together enough to visit Asnina in the infirmary, where her shoulder wound was being treated by Stilpkin, a rotund, red-faced man with a green hand. Asnina's sister Atathu sat on the bed beside her, stoically stroking her hair, her jaw thrust forward angrily. The one they called Fargold was there, too, but he was only semi-conscious, having obviously been administered some strong herbs to help with the pain in the back of his thigh where Montither had cut him. Even through his daze, though, his eyes kept fastening on Zero as though he needed something from her or had something urgent to say. Just as she had always done at the camp in the mountains, she did her best never to meet his gaze. There had been little feeling then, but now something stirred in her memory whenever she felt his eyes upon her. And more than just her memory, it was as though part of her was part of him, and…. She shuddered and turned away.

It was then that Imalgha, the third and largest of the Thrall sisters, arrived, announcing she couldn't stay long. Veneetha Azucena had asked her to join her personal bodyguard to replace Ormuntia, the huge battle Thrall who had also been wounded by the sword and now lay unconscious on a cot beside Asnina. For a brief time the three sisters, who were clearly almost as shaken by the day's events as Zero, joined hands and prepared to say a prayer to their Thrall goddess, Loceklis. Zero had often witnessed them doing this but she had never before consented to join in when they invited her. So great was her need for comfort tonight, she reconsidered. Placing one of her palms over Imalgha's broad knuckles, she silently took part in their communion. Afterward, she waited hopefully, but if the Thrall sisters received any solace from their prayer, none of it reached Zero.

She was leaving when she found the doorway blocked by a striking young woman with long, curly red hair. She was of average height and very slender, wearing a ground-length yellow dress bound about the waist with a red sash. There was something about the woman's eyes that troubled Saheli. Something about that very slightly freckled face that seemed familiar.

"Saheli," the young woman said, a little surprised and slightly offended by the blank stare she was receiving.

Again that name reverberated down the long dark hallways of Zero's memory. She struggled to remember. Perhaps if the young woman had been as short as she was three months ago, before her growth spurt, Saheli would have recognized her. Or maybe a headband would have jogged her memory, but there was no headband.

"It's Tharfen," the young woman said impatiently.

"Tharfen," Zero repeated. And then she said the other name "Saheli."

"Where is he?" Tharfen asked.

"Where is who?"

"Torgee, of course." At that moment she noticed her brother lying on the bed nearby and she brushed past and rushed over to the boy Zero only knew as Fargold.

"Tharfen," Torgee mumbled. Tharfen frowned, examining the wound in his thigh. "I guess you must've sat on a knife or something, eh?"

"Zero," Torgee called. And then he called "Saheli." But she was already gone.

As soon as she left the infirmary and headed back toward the Panthemium, a terrible sense of shame came over Zero. She felt as though she had done something deeply wrong and would soon be caught. She felt like a sneak and a coward. Even the fact that she had held off the sword earlier that evening meant nothing to her. It was as though the tiny gears she had once imagined operating in the locket library were at work in her own mind, unlocking deeper and deeper codes, smaller and smaller tumblers falling into place, moving the mechanism toward some awesome final opening whose revelation might well destroy her. And all of this was happening in triple time so that one thing could no longer be just one thing. The way her heart was beating arrhythmically, hot and cold. The way she could be Zero and … Saheli.

When she got back to the room she removed the last few shreds of her battered armour and lay down in her smock on the cot. She kept trying to sleep but every time she began the long, slow slide into unconsciousness some small sound, some twitch or spasm, would yank her up and keep her awake and remembering. Saheli. Her name was Saheli.

All night sad and shocking memories tore through her consciousness. But just before Vallaine came there was a change in her. Perhaps she had finally remembered something different, or even beautiful, for in amongst the other expressions that crossed her face there was an occasional smile. It came and went, but the more the sorrows seemed to gather at her centre and weigh her down, the deeper the arc of that smile grew, until eventually there were moments when she was smiling full out and nodding her head as though in affirmation. Eventually, she felt a calmness overtake her. She started rocking back and forth, gripping her hands together palm to palm, and whispering "Thank you. Thank you" as she wept. In the middle of this reverie, there came a knock at the door.

Zero did not instantly recognize the man at the door. She stared at him blankly, and it wasn't until he raised his red-tinted hand that the memory returned. But when it did, it flooded in and she recalled the last time she'd seen him outside the Great Kone, when he'd told her to forget her pain. He was not, however, the figure of health he had been then. He looked ragged and worn and weak. When he told her of Xemion's request, she acknowledged him with only the slightest of nods before rising from her cot.

Seeing her in the light, Vallaine closely examined the cut over her brow. "Does it hurt?" he asked.

She backed away, self-conscious about being in her smock and slightly affronted by his nearness. "It's nothing," she answered, her voice a little hoarse and still quaking from the turmoil of her recent emotions.

"Yet you look as though you're suffering extreme pain."

"I'm just very tired."

"You must be after your day of battles."

She nodded noncommittally.

"Especially your battle with the spell-made sword."

Her glance was suddenly fierce and angry. "I don't want to talk or even think about that!"

"I'm sure you don't, Saheli, but there are things I must tell you."

Fortunately, Veneetha Azucena had sent Vallaine in her carriage. Otherwise Saheli didn't know how she would have made her weary way from the Panthemium to the mouth of the tunnel. As Vallaine guided the horse over the cobbled streets, he began to tell her all that had happened to Xemion. Whatever it was that had made her smile earlier was soon gone with all his talk of spellcraft. The sea wind blew cold on her skin and it felt like every ounce of her was trembling. Vallaine could see that his account was disturbing her. He spoke as gently as he possibly could, but he didn't have long and she needed to know the truth before they arrived.

By the time the two descended through the tunnel and reached the narrow walkway that ran along the top of the eastern side of the Lion's Arms, the full story had been told and a tense silence hung between them. Saheli could hear the crying of gulls riding the sea wind. The blank-faced moon had laid a golden pathway across the dark, withdrawing waters. For a second, before Vallaine opened the door to the tower, she wished she could run out onto that pathway and disappear forever into the night rather than face what she knew lay ahead of her.

"Saheli!" Xemion said when she came down from the stairwell.

She nodded and said his name in return, "Xemion," but she kept her eyes averted, the lantern hanging low at her side.

"You remember me now," he said.

"Yes, I remember myself. And Vallaine has told me everything else," she answered. "I'm sorry ... I'm sorry for what you've been through."

"And I'm sorry for what *you've* been through," Xemion responded, wishing she would look at him. But she hadn't yet. Not directly into his eyes.

"Don't worry. That is past." She said it so jubilantly he frowned. "Now I have hope. And you, too, have suffered."

"What do you mean, you have hope?" he asked, half-wishing that her answer might somehow include his own secret hope — that they would flee this place this very night and never return.

"When your sword struck me ... I suddenly saw my mother," she said at last. Xemion looked with a slight shudder at the raw cut that had crisscrossed the scar. "Not as she was at the place with the wells. I saw her as she really was ... is, and now I know something. You remember how I used to hear that melody? I sang it to you once."

Xemion nodded.

"Well, after your sword cut me the words started coming back to me." She recited them hurriedly and in a casual voice, trying to deaden the effect they were having on her. "*Open my heart; open the door, every day to love her more.*" Here her voice broke with a quickly quashed sob. "*Break O wave upon the shore. Every day I'll love her more.*"

She looked at him as though what she would say next was entirely obvious. "And now I know what happened to her. This is something I had forgotten even before I drank that accursed water. Someone — I think it might have been my uncle or maybe my grandfather — he had some kind of spell kone. I think it was handwritten by him. I think he was trying to revive the spellcraft or something, I don't know, but he turned this big waist-high spell kone just as she was singing me that song and … and I think he turned the kone backward. I think … well, I know … I remember it so clearly: he cranked the handle clockwise instead of counterclockwise and somehow, I don't know how, her song must have been pulled into the spell and … and I think it ran it in reverse."

She was speaking quickly yet the sound of her heartbeat was always there in her voice, pushing through it like some trapped creature trying to break free. "Every day after that, instead of loving me more and more, she loved me less and less. And at first it was just so gradual I hardly noticed, but slowly she got nastier and nastier with me and then it deepened and hardened and she began to get enraged with me and … she took to hitting me really, really hard … and when at the end, just before you found me, Xemion, that was the day she gave me this."

She pointed to her eyebrow where the newly opened scar was. "She meant to … kill me, I think, but I moved. Then she tried to … to drown me. She said she was doing it because she hated the sight of me."

Saheli glanced quickly at Xemion as she said this, her nostrils flaring with emotion. "Well, now I know she didn't really hate me. She was hexed. In fact, every hateful thing she did to me originated from one thing — love. Don't you see? I know from every slap to my face, every horrible curse she spat at me, that she loved me deeply. And so all my pain is a blessing. All my wounds are gifts of love, do you see?"

Her jaw was trembling, her expression a mixture of horror and wild, manic faith. "And that's why I have hope. Because I can undo all that. I can go back to those wells and find her and ... and I'll find a way to undo that spell, I swear I will, and then I'll know at last what the truth of her love is."

Xemion shook his head. "Saheli, that's so horrible."

"That's spellcraft, Xemion," she came back accusingly. "That is what spellcraft does to human love. It turns a mother against her own child." Her eyes fleetingly met his for the first time, but it was enough for him to see the intensity of her anger.

"I made the sword for you," he protested. "To save you."

"But that's the last thing I would have wanted. I would rather have died than ..." With an effort she managed to reel her anger in. "But don't worry. Vallaine has told me all about it. I know he put it to you in a way that made you think you had no choice. I accept that. Not because he said so. I just know that when I looked down on you lying there and thought you were dead that I felt a terrible pain in my heart as though I had just lost a great friend ... or more than just a friend, a great ..." She bit her bottom lip and Xemion waited full of hope for her to finish, but she didn't finish. She just shook her head and shrugged her shoulders as though there were no words for whatever this final concept might have been.

"Now they tell me that you must leave and go away across the sea and never return. They say it is because you've become a spellbinder and that you may be dangerous. And I hate that. I hate spellcraft. I hate it for what it did to my mother and me." She dared to look up now, directly into his eyes for the first time, and just as he saw the change in her she saw the change in him and both were afraid. "And for what it has done to you," she said, her nostrils flaring. "You … you seem so utterly different."

Her eyes, as they held his, were deep and raw and layered with pain, but there was something else in them, too. Something was lurking at the bottom that she was still doing her best to hide.

"We are both different," Xemion said, his heart sinking. "We've had to grow up."

"But you are so different." Saheli blurted this out and seemed to immediately regret it.

"Look, I love you, Saheli," he said desperately. "I always have and that will never ch—"

She cut him off with a curt wave of her hand. "Well, there's no sense in that now," she said very quietly. There followed a long silence in which even Saheli stopped her agitated movements and became still. Whatever else happened, Xemion knew she would not be leaving Ulde with him tonight.

"I have one request before you go, Saheli." He hung his head and gripped the bars tightly, but he could barely say it. In fact, the words came out in a whisper. "Kiss me

… just one more time."

Saheli's heart thumped like a great battle drum on a very cold day. Her chill and shaking redoubled. Yes, she had kissed him. And he'd suffered for her. And she had loved him then. And if he was now who he had been then, she would kiss him again and again. But he was no longer that young boy. He was now—

"I can't."

This hit Xemion hard. The word was out of his mouth before he could even think about it. "Please."

"Xemion, I can't. I can't even make myself do it."

"I beg you. Just hold me for a moment then. I'm going away forever and may never see you again in all of this life." She looked straight at him now and could no longer hide the truth of it from him or herself. She had felt it the moment she'd walked in. There was a strange, haunted shadow that clung to him and hid from him. The horror she had been trying to deny swept over her, a horror at what he'd become.

Xemion felt it, too, and he wanted to rip the bars open and take her in his arms and scream that it wasn't true. He wanted to reach and pull her to him the way the knights in the *Phaer Tales* had pulled their true loves to them and overcome all obstacles with a kiss. But even through his own pain he could see the awful struggle she was having with herself and he felt a deep mercy rise in him and strengthen him. She turned away and he let her.

"You have given me so much and none of this is your fault and I can see how much you want this and I wish I could give it to you, but—" Her voice dropped to a whisper, "I can't."

He said nothing as she pushed away from him for the last time and stood in the shadow of the door to the stairwell. She had her fists up to her eyes trying to stop her tears. She stepped deeper into the shadow so that he couldn't see her, but he heard a sob.

"You see what spellcraft has done?" she shouted in a wretched half-enraged, half-anguished voice. "It has ruined *this* love for me, too." And then, without a good-bye, she turned and ran up the stairs.

"Goodbye, Saheli!" he yelled after her in a voice torn with emotion. "I will never stop loving you."

Not until he heard the slamming of the door above did he allow his own sobs to burst out of him. And when they did, it felt like it would tear him in half. It was as though two kones, two stories were turning against each other, ripping themselves apart in his chest. He felt like he could weep for the rest of his life if only tears would come. For a long time he sat and felt the presence of magic welling up inside him, and he cursed it. What good would it be even if he could burst open these walls with a word? What use was power if it couldn't get him what he wanted? There was no spell … there had never been a spell in all of time to make someone come to you of her own free will.

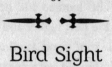

34

Bird Sight

The clouds were stalled overhead like a herd of botched sky creatures, frozen in mid-stampede. Random horns, misplaced hooves, inexplicable extra heads strained over detached beast bodies, unrecognizable but strangely familiar. Xemion flew low over the waves, the mist rising up off the sea. At the horizon was his ghost ship; its prow a skull, its oars bones. It lay at anchor, rising and falling on the surface of the sea. Xemion wished he could avoid the grim vessel, but he soared onward ever closer. On its deck, a huge Cyclops, nine feet tall, peered with his one eye through a telescope. When he saw the bird approaching, he held out the back of his hand and Xemion swept down and alighted on it. The Cyclops removed the roll of paper that had been affixed to Xemion's leg and gazed at the picture on it. Whatever it was, it caused him to let out a great whoop of joy and raise his fist in the air. He turned and spoke to someone in a black Pathan visor standing beside him and then drew something on the paper. Xemion tried to see it, but the image kept shuffling around and dissolving away from his understanding. The one-eyed giant affixed the message to Xemion's leg and again sent him soaring up over the waves. The wind was with him but there was even more unwillingness now. As he approached the dark cliffs of Ulde, he tried his utmost to resist the forward motion. Still Xemion sped on. It was his fate. The dark cliff loomed and he saw the smoking mountain atop it. He flew higher and closer. And there, awaiting him at the top, stood a solitary figure. Xemion wanted to reel back. He did not want to see this face. But the eye in the middle of Xemion's forehead could not look away. Everything was at risk. He tried to cry out but his voice only yielded a strange bird sound. Xemion gasped in his dream as he drew closer to the smithy. The more he felt repelled by that short, scar-faced figure who awaited him, the faster he flew toward him.

Xemion awoke with the figure of Glittervein still shimmering before him. In all the calamity of yesterday, he had barely thought of the man. Now, as he looked up through the small horizontal slit in the wall, fear flooded through him. It was not quite dawn yet but the entire seascape before him was eerily lit by a strange alignment of celestial bodies. The full moon was still suspended low over the horizon and that blood-red planet beside it had swelled to twice its normal size. The effect of this upon the ebbing tide was extraordinary. The sea had drawn back from the shore, far beyond the inner harbour. Almost the entire bottom of the bay beyond it now was exposed, its mud glistening, small puddles and pools reflecting the moonlight here and there where water had gathered in the deeper depressions. The beach, which was normally a narrow curve of jagged rocks against the cliffs, had become a wide expanse of mud and sand, interrupted here and there by clumps of seaweed, numerous boulders, and the debris of long-ago sunken ships.

Just below the red planet and the moon, far off in the distance, Xemion spied a square sail just coming over the horizon. At first he thought it must be the *Mammuth* come to take him and Vallaine to the Wizard's Isle, but as it drew closer he saw the size of the sail and knew it could not be the *Mammuth*. This was the huge, skull-prowed warship from Xemion's dream, and as the dawn mist rose from the waves it sped ever closer to the shore.

Xemion reacted quickly. He sensed he was alone in the tower, but he called out anyway. "Is anyone there?" He gulped down some ambrosia in the hope that it might give him strength to break free. He had hardly begun his futile rattling of the bars before a deep canine call reverberated back. "I beg you hear me, O master." It was Bargest. He was waiting faithfully outside the tower.

"Bargest! Bargest! You must alert the city.

"O master, do not bid me leave thee. I beg you."

In his deepest spellbinding voice, Xemion shouted back, "This is your final test, Bargest. You must run now as you have never run, up to the city, and awaken everyone. You must roar like you've never roared before. Go, Bargest. Now!"

Bargest looked out to sea and saw the bone galleon floating in. It had a long prow that rode high out of the water and was now being propelled at high speed by massive warriors who rowed in quick, joyous unison. Bargest bounded down from the foot of the tower to the drained bottom of the harbour floor. Like a black bolt of lightning his massive paws launched him across the muddy flats of the bay to the foot of the Uldestack promontory on the opposite side. This was the promontory with the narrow footpath along its top, which Glittervein had blocked with the third of his gates. Bargest leapt now from the foot of the harbour, aiming to land immediately behind the gate. He almost didn't make it. His front paws caught the top ledge and he clung there for a while close to falling. But when his front paws began to slip, his back legs started to rip and scurry up the rock until finally he pushed himself up and over the edge. Now he tore up the track and shot past the huge smokestack and down the hill.

"Awake, I beg you! Awake!" he roared as he turned onto the High Street. Something had come unsprung in him now so that when he stood up to his full size he was much more massive than even Xemion would have expected. "I beg you, awake! Awake, I implore you." he roared. As he arrived at the Castle Road, his voice was so loud it could be heard two blocks away at the Panthemium. There, Ewin Gilder, one of the few teetotalers unaffected by Glittervein's drugged wine, was getting an early start to his day. A new high house had fallen in the night and he was just wheeling his first wheelbarrow load full of broken bits of stone along the road beside the sea wall when, seeing the giant dog barrelling toward him, he ran off, leaving his wheelbarrow where it was. "Behold the beach. I beg," the dog howled as he bolted by. When he reached the square, Bargest came upon many people passed out from Glittervein's drugged wine. He set about grabbing them by their clothing and shaking them so that soon, due to his efforts, the awakened were awakening others.

By now the first bright rim of the sun was rising from the horizon, its long, low beams shimmering through the grey, wraithlike mist. Those awakened by the dog looked over the sea wall that ran along the edge of Phaer Point and saw the warship drawing ever closer to the shore. All heads turned to the gate tower high up on the sea wall, and there, to everyone's relief, was Glittervein, scurrying up the ladder and into the gatehouse.

"No! Don't open it! Don't open it," someone screamed as he put his hand on the wheel.

"Pardon me?" the Nain yelled back, holding his hand to his ear. "Did you say open it?'" He shrugged as if in assent to this suggestion and began to turn the wheel.

Two citizens frantically scrambled up the ladder in an effort to stop Glittervein, but he had planned for this. He waited until they were nearly at the top, then bent down to release a single catch and the ladder fell away from the platform and clanged to the ground, leaving his would-be captors groaning and broken-limbed on the ground, the first of many casualties that day.

35

The Only Sword There Is

Veneetha Azucena had awakened just before dawn in preparation for the arrival of the *Mammuth*. But it wasn't until she heard the baying of Bargest that she opened the third-floor window of her tower and gazed out of the sea below and then up at the gate tower where Glittervein was gleefully opening the gate into the cavern that she realized what was going on. She took action instantly. "Shoot the Nain," she yelled. "Shoot him now!"

"We have no bowmen." The voice of her sergeant-at-arms arose from the foot of her tower, where he was roughly shaking an unconscious archer. "They have all been drugged." He picked up the man's bow and waved it at her. "And their bowstrings have been cut."

"Oh, my world. What have I done, what have I done?" she cried, holding her hands over her mouth. She had that feeling that she'd seen this coming a thousand times and still hadn't managed to avoid it. She looked around her room desperately. Drathis with his eye patch and the other two young spellbinders whose lives she had worked so hard to reclaim from the Pathans were holding hands quietly on the divan. Their nurse, Magga Goochelar, hovered around in front of them, gnawing on her nails, her eyes wide with fear.

"Imalgha!" Veneetha Azucena shrieked. The burly Thralleen emerged from the room she had slept in, wide-eyed and ready. Never far away, Lirodello, his eyes slightly smaller than plums now, peered possessively over her shoulder.

"Imalgha. We are being invaded," she shouted as she pointed out the window at Glittervein. "He's raised the gate at the Lion's Paws. We have to stop them before they get to the Lion's Mouth and the tunnel. Gather up whoever you can find. Get your swords. Get anything. Shovels, knives, anything that will serve as a weapon. And don't delay. Where is Lighthammer?" she screamed to her maid. "Somebody find Vallaine!"

As Imalgha and Lirodello hurried out, Veneetha Azucena reached to retrieve her own sword. Then, with a cold jolt of fear, she remembered. It had been ruined by that spellworked monstrosity the previous night. But she had to have a weapon!

She looked out of the window desperately and saw that the warship had reached the shallows. The attackers were jumping over its prow, wading toward the shore. There were Cyclopes, and Thralls, and Kagars, but all were clearly in the hire of the black-helmeted Pathans spread among them in positions of command. At their head she spied the coat-of-arms of the black-clad figure from her most recent nightmare: Akka Smissm. She scanned the city's fortifications. Most of her soldiers were still passed out, and even those who weren't were largely unarmed, their swords ruined in last night's rampage. Something had to stop these invaders or the city and all its inhabitants were doomed.

Hesitating only a moment before she made her decision, she opened the golden trunk where she had locked Xemion's sword. It didn't look like the staff of a mage. It looked like a good, solid sword. Maybe it had de-spelled in the night. Delicately she touched it now and almost thought she sensed a cold shiver flicker either in or out of it, she couldn't be sure. She had doubted Vallaine's theory about cross-spells from the beginning. Certainly she felt nothing like that in it now. Anyway, she did not have the luxury of moral qualms in this moment, she told herself. It was the only sword there was. She grabbed it out of the trunk and flinched. Yes, she definitely felt a charge in it. In fact, so much so she almost put it down again. But she didn't. She clutched it tighter. And then, having gone so far, something else occurred to her. Perhaps if there was magic in it, it was time, as Vallaine had hinted last night, to take back the magic. She hesitated a moment, but then, shaking her head woefully, held the sword out the window and aimed it directly at the distant Glittervein.

"By whatever power there is in this sword," she intoned with terrible urgency, "let him be stopped." If any of the sword's supernatural powers still inhabited it, they seemed to have no effect on the Nain. He just kept turning his traitor's wheel.

"Drathis, come here, please." She beckoned to the

largest of the spellbinders, the one who had touched Xemion. Jerkily, Drathis arose from the divan and walked toward her with the other two trailing along behind, still holding hands. Veneetha Azucena took the spellbinder's palm in her left hand, and with her right hand, as the three spellbinders broke into uncanny shrieks, she aimed the sword out the window and again uttered her curse. But again there was no apparent effect.

Despairingly, she looked at the nurse, and the spellbinders grew very quiet. "This is the time we talked about," she said in a trembling voice. "You know where you have to take them, don't you?"

"Yes, ma'am." The nurse nodded, quaking with fear. "But—"

"Then don't delay."

"I won't, ma'am."

Before she left, Veneetha Azucena bent down and gave Drathis a bitter kiss on the mouth. "Goodbye, sweet Drathis," she sighed. And with that she ran out the door, sword in hand.

Down on the tidal flats, the attackers raced in the direction of the Lion's Paws. The sea gate between these two massive limbs of stone would normally have protected the city even on a day like today when the waters were at their lowest possible ebb, but Glittervein had taken care of that. The entrance to the inner harbour was wide open and he was now cheerily raising the great iron gate at the Lion's Mouth.

The mercenaries had almost reached the narrow entrance to the inner harbour known as the Lion's Paws. They had been ordered to maintain silence, but felt like whooping and laughing as they ran, their cutlasses drawn, eager for the riches and slaves to be had in the soft city above. Just before they reached the opening, though, something, which appeared at first to be a muddy kelp-strewn sea monster, arose in front of them and blocked their way. It was Tiri Lighthammer. And he was standing right between the Lion's Paws, his shoulders so broad there was little more than an inch to spare on either side of them. The gate might be fully raised, but now he was the gate. Perhaps it was the drunkenness that had allowed him to fall so limberly last night, for he had landed unconscious but face up in the already withdrawing tide. Awakened from his slumber in the mud by the cries of Bargest, he swayed now, blinked at the mercenaries who rushed toward him, and, in an instant, had his sword of steel up, out, and ready to fight.

The attackers paused for a moment when he first rose in front of them, but seeing that he was just an old man, they charged, finally allowing themselves to scream with glee as they raised their swords. They thought they could quickly hack him down, but Lighthammer had been wait-ing fifty years for this moment. Holding his ground, he fended off their blows expertly, his own solid steel blade quick and accurate. He stabbed ruthlessly, right through armour. He hacked at exposed fingers and necks, slashed through leather jerkins, and all the while warded off a hundred blows, till a heap of men twenty-thick lay in front of him, groaning and bleeding.

Then there was a loud horn blast, causing the rest of the attackers to stand back. At once a large black-armoured Pathan with the emblem of the royal household emblazoned on his breastplate rode forward, nearly crushing the back of the poor gorehorse he sat upon. It was well into the morning now and the sun shone brightly on the Royal Pathan headdress. Lighthammer stepped forward out of the gateway he'd been so successfully blocking and, raising his sword over his head, yelled "Come on then!"

The Pathan yelled in a voice like shattering glass.

"What's that? You want to surrender?" Lighthammer screamed back.

With that the Pathan rode over to his squire at the rim of the crowd and took up his new meteor hammer, a weapon consisting of a large black spiked ball on the end of a long chain that was fitted to a swivelling haft. Sitting astride the gorehorse, he held the haft out parallel to the ground so that the chain and the ball hung down straight. He spurred the horse on. As he neared Tiri Lighthammer, he lifted his arm high and swung the great black ball in a full circle at Lighthammer's head. Tiri Lighthammer stood there bleeding profusely from his wounds, staggering slightly as though he might soon fall, but when the ball came at him he stepped nimbly back into the opening as rider and ball rode by. He laughed out loud and stepped back out in front of the gateway. "Come on!"

Incredibly, the Pathan rode around the muddy perimeter and came at him again. Again Lighthammer ducked in and again he laughed as his assailant rode by. The Pathan Prince must have been young and untaught in the ways of warfare, because he then angrily rode his horse straight at Tiri Lighthammer and swung his ball forward at the last moment thinking to have it connect with its target vertically. This succeeded to some degree, but when it hit his right shoulder, Lighthammer held on to the chain and tugged it forward with him as he fell. The Pathan was jerked forward off of his horse head over heels so that he landed on his back not far from Tiri Lighthammer. Lighthammer, although weakened by the loss of blood, was first to his feet, but instead of allowing his opponent to regain his own feet before resuming the battle he breached the warrior code and brought his boot down upon the Pathan's neck. The glassy voice shrieked in outrage. Lighthammer bent down and grabbed the upper half of the beaked helmet and yanked it off the crystal head of its wearer. Akka Smissm's only son, Angathon, unleashed screams such as that battlefield had never known as the bright sun poured down upon the delicate crystal of his brow. Even as the others now rushed at the fainting Tiri Lighthammer, those crystal facets with their deeply recessed lozenge-shaped eyes turned a charry black. Quickly, their edges curled like ashes as they withered and whitened, and the Pathan died, the second prince to do so at Lighthammer's hand. He didn't have long left to live now himself, but he could hear the sound of Veneetha Azucena and the others running up behind him and he was almost certain, even as he let his own life go and fell, that he'd held off the enemy long enough.

36

Azucena, Saheli, and Tharfen

The invaders charged through the gateway and the Phaerlanders met them halfway down the inner harbour where it widened out enough for a full-pitched battle. They formed a wedge across the muddy floor, with Veneetha Azucena at its tip, trying to drive the invaders back through the gateway. She slew many of them in that melee but she didn't know if it was by virtue of the spell-craft in the sword or merely her own skills, which were considerable, for she was a well-trained warrior. She used not only the sword but her feet to great effect, kicking out in all directions, straight-legged to break a knee here, bent-legged to catch a chin there. But last night's wound had reopened in her brow and she had already been wounded somewhere else, too. She hardly knew where. She only knew she was bleeding.

Imalgha the Thrall was close by, right in the thick of it, grunting and shrieking as her sword decreased the number of mercenaries with each lightning lunge into their ranks. And as always, wherever Imalgha went, Lirodello was close by. Indeed he was at her other side and proving remarkably effective with a long, hooked kitchen skewer and carving knife. The two Nains, Belphegor and his non-violent brother Tomtenisse Doombeard, were also there. Tomtenisse stood cross-armed, impassive, apparently there merely to be an observer, but Belphegor had finally found what he had been seeking for a long time — a fight he could not avoid. He wielded his pick joyously and with a ruthlessness that would have made Tiri Lighthammer blush. Indeed, he had to rush into the melee in pursuit of prey, for the mercenaries quickly learned to fear his wild, whirling pick and kept as much at a distance from him as they could.

By now, more than a hundred attackers had made their way from the ship, but Veneetha Azucena and the Phaerlanders who had joined her were fighting valiantly, holding them off. Akka Smissm fumed atop his dark horse. He had been relying on the advantage of surprise and the superiority of numbers, but most of his small fleet had been dispersed or destroyed in the previous night's storm and those who remained should have arrived earlier. They should have been through the cavern, up the tunnel, and into the heart of the city by now, just as the fool Phaerlanders were waking from their drugged slumbers. Lighthammer, though, had thwarted all that, and now the Pathan commander was in danger of failing altogether in his mission.

Fortunately though, Glittervein had been keeping a watchful eye. Quickly he let the wheel that controlled the gate at the Lion's Mouth go. It spun rapidly backward and the massive gate shuddered down into its sheath, almost killing several Thralls who were just then attempting to pass through. In this way, Azucena and seventy-five or so others were cut off in front of it, stranded on the floor of the inner harbour without the possibility of reinforcements to fight the ever-growing horde of invaders.

Inside the cavern, a long line of Phaerlanders were pressed against the gate and in great danger of being crushed to death by the weight of those behind them who were still pushing forward. Saheli, who was among them, had brought her whistle, and with it succeeded in establishing order. There was no room for despair in her now. She felt like she had lived a thousand lives last night, but was firmly in this life now. The need for action had chased all those old wisps of shame away. With the aid of some of her comrades from the camp, she quickly established enough order to send word back up the line, thus relieving the pressure on those trapped against the gate. When she had succeeded in turning her fellows around and getting them out of the tunnel and back atop Phaer Point, she quickly ascertained that the situation in the harbour had taken a turn for the worse.

The heroic actions of Veneetha Azucena and the others, including Bargest, who was wreaking havoc, was succeeding in pushing the invaders back, but a second warship was now making its way to the edge of the water and a whole horde of new mercenaries were gathered on its prow, preparing to leap out the moment it reached the shallows. Soon they would be replenishing the ranks of their fallen fellows.

But there would be no replenishment of the Phaerlander ranks stranded in front of the gate. They could continue to hold off the attackers for a while yet, but they were vastly outnumbered.

Saheli's first thought was that she had to acquire a ladder somehow, get up to the gatehouse, and slay the traitorous Glittervein so that the gate might be reopened and her comrades rescued. But looking up, she saw that someone was already climbing up toward him. The climber had wedged himself into a corner of the sea wall and was somehow, apparently by exerting extreme pressure outward against the two ramparts with his hands and feet, inching himself slowly up. He still had a distance to go, and the climbing was slow, but even from here she knew it was someone very capable of doing the job required — Vallaine. Saheli let loose another blast of the whistle and pointed toward the great chimney on the end of Uldestack promontory.

"We can get to the harbour floor if we jump down from the footpath along there," she shouted to them. "Then we can cut in from the flank." With that she pushed through and set off at a run.

Tharfen, having left her brother sleeping at the infirmary, arrived at the road along Phaer Point too late to join Saheli. The group Saheli was leading was already halfway down the Uldestack promontory and would soon be entering the fray. Tharfen ran to the rail along the sea wall and scanned the carnage below searching for Xemion. Seeing a stone, she reached automatically for the leather headband she had always worn about her brow and used as a sling. Then, remembering it was no longer there, she ran her fingers nervously through her red curls. She wished her pirate father would come sailing in here with his crew and his catapults full of boiling pitch and burn these barbarians to ashes. But that wasn't going to happen. And yes, she could sense that Xemion was down there somewhere, farther along the point. And that he was suffering. She ran along the point until she noticed the wheelbarrow that had been left against the sea wall earlier that morning by Ewin Gilder. When she got to it and saw that it was full of broken chunks of statuary and masonry, she smiled and quickly took off the red sash she wore around her narrow waist.

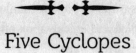

Five Cyclopes

Xemion had been drinking from the bottle of ambrosia and a strange energy vibrated in him like thunder waiting in the air to break. But there was nothing he could do to harness it. He shook the bars and screamed with rage. He hollered and tugged at them. He pried and beat them but they would not be so easily overcome. Like a madman, he strode back and forth, bellowing for Bargest, but Bargest was in the clang and the clamour and the shrieking of the battle, deaf to Xemion's cries. It was at this time that Xemion, gazing desperately out of his window, saw the contingent of Phaerlanders across the bay, making their way down the steep slope that led from the end of the Uldestack promontory to the sea. They were too far off for him to distinguish any particular set of features, but he knew by the rhythm and sway of her body as she hurried down the narrow footpath that the figure at the front was Saheli. And he could see her plan. Once they reached the gate where the dog had made his leap earlier that morning they would jump down to the harbour floor and deploy across the bay so that they could fight a flank action against that second ship full of invaders. But when Xemion looked out to sea he saw what they could not. Beyond the mouth of the bay, coming up out of the rising sun, their masts shimmering in it like frail stick shadows, three, four, maybe more warships were approaching.

It was taking enormous effort for Vallaine to climb the walls. He was not used to such fatigue. Hundreds of years of lives had not yet made him used to it. And once he made it to the top, *if* he made it to the top, he would still have a long way to crawl along the top of the wall right out in the open before he got to the gatehouse and Glittervein. And all the while there was this deep spinning in his abdomen that he had not felt for fifty years. Something slow and ponderous was turning. Something more than just the Great Kone.

Panting, exhausted, he at last reached the top of the wall. Here, in the tiny crook where it curved up to the gatehouse, he rested a moment. He could sense the magic rising incrementally in the air and hoped it was making him stronger, but when he had awoken this morning the red of his hand had faded to a rust-like tint and it had not yet grown one jot redder. Slowly but deftly, keeping low, he began to creep along the long, slanted wall toward the gatehouse. His new robe cascaded over his back, long and black like the wings of a raven. But as it settled down over both sides of the wall it matched perfectly the sleek grey of the stone. He began to crawl along the top of the wall. Once he got Glittervein out of the way he would raise the gate to the cavern just enough to let the defenders get in and then lower it again, shutting most of the invaders out.

He was soon so close he could see Glittervein's shadow cast over the two wheels behind him by the rising sun. Billowing smoke drifted over his head as the cruel Nain had a celebratory puff. He was leaning on the edge of the parapet, watching the battle below. Vallaine wished he could draw him more toward the centre of the gatehouse. His own strength was weakest at the edges of things. But there was no time for that now. As carefully as he had inched up the wall, he now crept a step closer. But Glittervein had not survived this long in the world because he was a man insensitive to danger. As soon as Vallaine moved, he felt it, and he turned. In an instant the two were at each other, their swords clanging with incredible ferocity.

Glittervein was clearly in no need of ruthlessness training. Unlike most Nains, he had made his own sword long ago, and with it he had slain the very dragon that had scarred his face for life. Since then, he had slain many more dragons, as well as men, Thralls, women, and even children. With all the strength of fifty years of hammering he drove Vallaine back against the waist-high balustrade that rimmed the seawall. On a good day Vallaine would surely have beaten him, but today he was weak and his senses kept spinning away from him. The last thing he saw before the Nain's sword came in under his ribs toward his heart was the tower on the end of the Lion's Arms where he knew Xemion awaited him. He had been in and out of a million middle worlds. He had been a midwife, a medium, a carrier, a lighter of fuses, a book reader. He'd been a messenger. He'd been a crosser of seas, a spell-taker. He had carried the charge many times. Many times he had been wounded and sickened even unto death, but he had never died before. Today, which was not a good day, would change all that. Today he would die.

Veneetha Azucena saw Vallaine's body plummet and land motionless on the pile of slain and wounded in front of the Lion's Mouth. She was also now bleeding profusely. Directed by Lord Akka Smissm, who sat in full black-mask regalia astride a black gorehorse, the attackers were following Rule One in the Pathan's battle plan — cut off the head. Taking many casualties, they pincered through the sides of the wedge formation she had been the point of. And there she was now, cut off, with only the ferocious Bargest beside her, backed up against the east side of the embankment of the Lion's Arms. Blood had run over one shoulder and was pooling in the mud at her feet as she held the spelled blade in her one good hand, waiting. If ever she wished there was the power of victory in Xemion's sword, she wished it now as she panted away, her lungs burning, blood streaming down her left side. The invaders closed in on her, but for a long time none could breach her defences, and those that were not slain by her sword were brought down screaming by Bargest.

Then a trumpet sounded, and, with Veneetha Azucena and the dog at its centre, a semi-circle slowly expanded away from them. Soon she would know why. Five Cyclopean archers had finally arrived on the most recent ship. Stepping through the outer perimeter of the circle, they notched their arrows against their strings and aimed. In the second before they let their arrows fly, there was a whizzing sound and a small jagged projectile struck the largest of them hard in his one big eye. The Cyclops bent over screaming, clutching his face, his arrow careening off at an angle into the sky. Bargest ran and leapt. He sank his teeth into the throat of the Cyclops and brought him down screaming on the muddy harbour floor.

Undeterred, the others unleashed their arrows in a flurry, striking both Veneetha Azucena and Bargest, the long black shafts sinking in deep. As they were reloading, a second Cyclops was struck in the temple by a rather larger piece of broken masonry and fell, knocked out cold, at the feet of the others. One of the three remaining, spying a small figure atop the cliffs whirling what looked to be a long red sash, shouted to warn the others, but the words were hardly out of his mouth before the next piece of stone found its target in his eye. Down he went screaming like his brethren before him. The remaining two were more wary now and took care to duck any further missiles that came their way as they continued their attack, unleashing volley after volley until the fallen Veneetha Azucena and Bargest bristled with arrows. Akka Smissm instructed the remaining Cyclopes to desist. With that he signalled the battle trumpets to sound the charge and he and his men trampled over the body of Veneetha Azucena and her spell-made sword, over the still-trembling body of the dog, over the prone bodies of the fallen and wounded, and deeper into the muddy inner harbour. With blood-thirsty yells they joined their fellows, falling upon the small group of Phaerlanders pinned against the gate at the cavern's mouth.

When Akka Smissm saw the toll these few Phaerlanders were taking on his troops, he ordered the front ranks to draw back as he summoned the archers forward. The Phaerlanders interlocked whatever shields they had amongst them and those with the longest swords stood at the forefront, prepared for the onslaught. Once again the Cyclopes notched their arrows and took careful aim. Two Thrall fighters, Molga Smarayha and Ingrisina Daturtia, who were from the same village as Imalgha and her sisters, went down almost at the same time, pierced through their necks by the first volley of arrows because they had not had time to secure their helmets. An untrained Nain lad named Yastgeng Lennkin, who had come only yesterday to Ulde against the wishes of his mother, had taken three mercenary lives with nothing but a jackhammer, but now a long, black-shafted arrow pierced his heart so violently it came out the other side and continued on through the bars of the gate. By now, Tharfen, who had been unable to see the Cyclopes, had rolled the wheelbarrow with its few remaining missiles farther along Phaer Point to where she once again had good sightlines. The distance was farther now, but she had not been practicing all summer for nothing. Yastgeng Lennkin's killer jerked forward, stricken in the back of the skull by a large fragment of marble once part of a sculpture of a fawn.

The remaining two Cyclopes, urged on by Akka Smissm, continued to shoot. One by one, as the arrows flew, more of the stranded Phaerlanders fell until there was only a small group left, including the Nain brothers,

Belphegor and Tomtenisse Doombeard, and Imalgha and Lirodello. And all the while vexed seabirds flew about, shrieking at the clanging and the screaming, some of them with breasts all red where they had set down in the carnage.

From inside the tower, Xemion had been desperately watching Saheli's progress. She and about a hundred others had made it halfway across the harbour, just in time to meet the new horde of thugs and blood Thralls streaming off the ships with swords, axes and spears in hand. He watched helplessly as the valiant fight ensued. Ushyia Asaycha the Thrall, Suanen Booldia, a worker in stone, and Inniada Holom were slain almost immediately. The group gathered closer together and fought back-to-back as the attackers streamed about them, but they were vastly outnumbered and soon three more of the defenders fell. Saheli and the group that remained were good, skilled fighters, and she particularly exacted a heavy toll upon the invaders, but one by one her fellow warriors fell around her until they were whittled down to a small core of some two-dozen fighters.

There they stood, encircled, back-to-back, fighting heroically on all sides, but surely doomed to die — or worse, doomed to a life of slavery. This thought had barely burst into Xemion's consciousness before he saw the flag of Arthenow rippling atop the mast of one particularly large ship that had just arrived. Debarking from it and approaching the shore, several ghoulish-looking blood Thralls shepherded wheeled cages, which they obviously intended to fill. Xemion screamed. He tried to envision again the burning letters of the spell book in his mind

Surely there was a spell to burst open doors! Nothing. Magic had nothing for him! He cursed and kicked at the bars savagely. At least, he thought, he still had the natural power of his body. He would sooner spend his last energies crashing himself again and again into the cell door in an attempt to break it open than waiting here helplessly while she was captured and dragged away. But even as he gathered himself for this, the whole tower shook as though some giant had beaten it with a great stone hammer. There came another mighty blow, and another, and then a loud crash followed by an explosion of bright, yellow sunshine into the stairwell. Someone, something had battered that door open. He didn't have to wait too long to find out what manner of creature it was. There was some hoarse panting, a click-clack of something like claws slowly coming down the stone steps. Xemion backed into the corner of his cell and waited. A large black shadow crawled out of the stairwell.

"Bargest!" The collisions with the door had left a deep split in the dog's brow and his thick hide still bristled with arrows that caught at the sides of the doorway as he entered. Panting heavily, the huge dog dragged himself across the floor. He had retrieved something from the battle but Xemion couldn't quite make it out as he squinted in the sudden brightness. Bargest crawled forward and lay the item on the stone floor beside the bars, as close to Xemion's feet as he could get it. Wide-eyed, Xemion's hand shot out from under the cage and grabbed it. His sword! His spell-made sword. "Good boy! Good boy!" he shouted. There was no hesitation in him now. No worries about cross-spells that might or might not lie in it. He didn't care now if he was a warrior, a mage, or both because another powerful force was flowing. It was the most powerful force in the universe, he thought. It couldn't be bound by oaths or stopped by a trillion cross-spells at once. Love. He loved her and he wasn't going to let her die or be dragged off to be some blood Thrall in Arthenow.

With complete faith, Xemion swung the sword at the metal bars. Two mighty hacks cut them through and he was free. Bargest panted heavily, pressed flat to the ground, his eyelids nearly closed. Xemion bent down, gently stroked the massive head, and whispered, "You will always be my dog, Bargest."

Bargest roared, "Go!"

"Thank you, Bargest," he called as he flew up the steps and out the door of the tower.

"Go!" the dog commanded for the second time. There was no begging left in him.

Xemion burst into the sunlight, sure of the sword's power in his hand. And with a great scream he ran down the embankment, headlong into the streaming throng. Immediately, he fell upon one huge Kagan with such strength he cut him diagonally in half from his shoulders to his hips. And with his next stroke another died at a different angle. Criss and cross, just as he had played as a child. But when next he thrust the sword point-first at the breast of a battle Thrall in full armour and the blade did not pierce it, he knew something was wrong. The sword was not quite whole. A piece was missing. Xemion gasped and ducked and stood back up, warding off a blow that would have killed him if it had connected. He could feel the Great Kone turning. Spells tugging at spells. Everything entangled and at odds with everything else, as though the whole world was caught up in some mass cross-spell. But he was not crooked or crossed. Nor was his love for her.

Having turned the battle Thrall's thrust away he slashed the blade crosswise into the well-armoured waist. He put all he had into that swing, trying to make himself the sword's missing piece, and the blade slid through the battle Thrall's armour like cloth, cutting him in half. And so it was he advanced onward through that river of men, cutting them down with sideways swings to and fro. And there were some as young as him, some who looked like they might have been his brothers or sisters, but he cut through them like he cut through the rest, every step bringing him closer to Saheli.

Glittervein was too busy watching the battle in front of the Lion's Mouth to notice Xemion's entrance into the fray. One hand cupped his pipe, the other rested on the gate wheel, ready to lift the massive iron grill when the time was right. For a while he'd feared that the storm had indeed ruined his plan. He hated improvising, but now that he had and everything was back under control, he could begin to enjoy it a little. Soon the rest of the ships would be here and he would make his killing and his fortune, too. A triumph! A masterpiece of revenge! As intricate as any machine. He looked down scornfully as Lirodello and Imalgha and the small, dwindling group of battle Thralls and kitchen Nains who still stood before the gate struggled against the inevitable. He could lift the gate now if he wanted and let those last flailing Thralls be flushed through and up the tunnel. It wouldn't matter. But he liked the poetry of them dying up against the gate — his gate — so he waited. That would be his gift to them: one more second of futile bravery before they and all their foolish purposes were swept away forever. But a second can sometimes make an enormous difference. In the next instant a dark shadow fell over him and there was a bestial scream that seemed to shake the Earth to the horizon and back again. He looked up in horror as something shot down from the sun. It was Poltorir the dragon. With a great swoop she caught him up in her claws. Kicking and scratching, Glittervein shrieked with fury, rage, and then terror as the dragon arced up over the city and disappeared from view beyond the walls.

Still backed up against the Lion's Gate, which would not now be opened, the small group of fighters, which included Imalgha, severely wounded in one leg, and Lirodello, in full battle thrall, were unyielding. The Cyclops, having exhausted his arrows, had been sent to replenish his supply from his ship while the regular troops returned to the assault. The defenders continued to slay so many, however, that the invaders kept having to drag away the bodies heaped in front of them just to give access to the next group charging in to take their place. But more and more of the defenders were falling. And now as the Cyclops returned, they knew they couldn't last much longer. But just as the arrows began to fly again, there came a great downward push of wind and a huge shadow descended upon the horde. With her leathery wings wide-spread, the dragon swooped in ominously, Glittervein still screaming in her claws. She let out a white-hot jet of pure dragon fire over their heads, so bright it wrought havoc upon the battle, reflecting off shields and swords. So bright, in fact, that the Cyclops, having looked up, was struck all but sightless. Before the dragon fire faded, Tharfen imbedded her final chunk of masonry in the Cyclopean eye and the Titan went down with a terrible scream.

For an instant, Xemion, at the opposite end of the harbour, flinched in mid-swing as the searing brilliance ignited a cascade of burning letters in his eyes. *Spell to Awaken Desire. Spell to Untie a Knot.* In that moment, a mercenary sword came so close to him it nearly slashed through his neck. *Spell to Sing from the Heart.* For the first time Xemion staggered back and felt again that strange charge he'd experienced when the chain lightning had illuminated the book of spells. Indeed, now that he no longer wanted them, the glowing letters burned before him, so brightly they were obstructing his vision and the mercenaries, sensing his weakness, came at him with renewed hope.

38

$$\text{---} \rlap{+} \text{+---}$$

Second Kiss

Poltorir the dragon touched down on the sand at the far side of the bay, about half a league from where the newly arrived ships bobbed in the rhythms of the tide. There, she opened her claws and allowed Glittervein to hurtle out of them like panic itself. He was heading for the sea. Perhaps he thought hiding beneath those red, silk waters could shield him from the terrible punishment coming his way. And indeed the dragon did let him get almost to the shallows before the long billow of her fire exploded forth, encompassing the Nain in a fireball and continuing on across the waters to where it scorched the hulls of two warships. The flames then climbed over their bows and incinerated the red head-feather of the large Kagan warrior crouched at the prow, where he had been waiting, ready to hit the water at a run. He fell screaming into the sea as his comrades backed away and the pilot gave panicked orders to turn the ship about.

With that bright blast, more letters exploded in Xemion's mind — *Spell to Stay Hunger, Spell to Stay Thirst* — but he did his best to see through them and kept swinging, trusting the sword to land where it may. The attackers were falling like straw before a scythe, but no matter how many of them he killed, more and more streamed off the ships: blood-crazed berserkers, huge, red Thralls, cruel Pathans on gorehorses, all of them screaming and hacking while distant trumpets blared and an orange flame crept up the mast of one of the ships. And all the time those letters kept shining in Xemion's mind — *Spell to Send*. Send? Xemion sent an unfortunate blood Thrall screaming to the ground. Every death brought him closer to her. Every slash and laceration narrowed the distance. But there was still so far to go.

Poltorir still stood where she had landed on the far side of the bay. Glittervein, who had at first been driven to the ground by the force of her fireball, had risen up and now ran screaming and burning as he plunged into the blood-reddened sea. Hiding there, detectable only by those curls of smoke and steam rising above him, he clutched at the sea bottom mud, trying to hold himself beneath the surface. But the dragon had not lost track of him for a second. Walking at a waddle, the great lizard made her way over the sand and into the shallows until she stood over him. Then, lifting her head in a great, saurian scream, she brought down the full, baleful fury of her fire upon the submerged Nain. So great was the dragon's flame that the gargling of Glittervein's screams was almost drowned out by the hissing of the waters as they boiled and bubbled about him, rising in a great cloud of steam.

Again and again she brought her fire down until the sand was melted to glass all about her and her torturer was no more.

These last incandescent blasts reflected so brightly off the invaders' shields that the battle ceased altogether for several seconds as all but the sun-shielded Pathans flung their arms protectively over their eyes.

The Spell to Bind. The Spell for Stillness. Xemion squinted through the burning letters as he hacked. He had slain so many of them he was completely soaked in blood. But now a ring had formed around him, no one daring to come close, all of them tall and lanky with long-shafted spears. He charged at them, slashing their spears aside like long grass in a field, slaying their bearers. But they were slowing him down and he had lost his bearings. Where was Saheli now?

Having finished with Glittervein, the dragon opened her great greyish-green wings and, with a few running steps, took off once again into the sky. Xemion caught one more fleeting glimpse of Saheli through the gusting fog and smoke. She was still far across the bay, back-to-back with one last fighter whose face he couldn't quite see. The two of them were working formidably together, but the enemy was still many against them and they couldn't last forever. Just before the smoke billowed in again, the other fighter turned and Xemion finally saw his face. It was Montither!

Desperately, as the spearmen grew ever bolder in their attempts to hem him in, Xemion exploded with pure fury. Screaming with rage, he hacked his way forward a few more yards before he heard again that high, shrieking hiss of the dragon's rapid descent. Neither he nor those who fought him were able to keep their eyes away from the mighty beast's fall. For a second she looked like she might bring her flame down upon Saheli and Montither, but she lifted her head at the last moment and directed the white-hot heat accurately at the attackers in front of them. Screaming, burning, and writhing, they were flung back as the dragon soared up and turned for another assault. Those mercenaries who still remained saw that their fight was futile and began fleeing over the steaming sands back to their ships. Atop the narrow track on the Uldestack promontory a slender red-haired woman ran toward Xemion, but he didn't see her. He was tearing across the wide expanse of sand, still half-blinded by the burning, ever-shifting letters in his mind. He saw only Saheli and Montither, still standing on the opposite side of the bay as the invaders fled.

Finally Saheli spotted Xemion. "Watch out!" he screamed as he ran toward her, but he was too far away and it was too late. Montither, now that he knew he was safe, gripped his sword and, with a little salute Xemion's way, took the hilt in both hands and shoved the blade straight through Saheli's chest. Xemion's shriek of fury could not stop him as she fell to the ground, the sword still protruding. Montither put one foot on her chest, yanked the blade out, and then shoved it in again. Pulling it out a second time, he turned and fled into the mist and smoke. She was nearly dead by the time Xemion got to her.

High above them the dragon screamed and emitted her most furious fire — a flame so bright it seemed for an instant to detonate the very sky. There was an explosion of searing light as Xemion cradled Saheli in his arms, and in that blinding moment, even as the bright letters ignited again in his mind, he saw through them to the fear and love in her eyes. And just then two arrows met point-to-point in the air, each splitting the other. Birds were flying through birds and it seemed for a moment there was a second sun crossing back through the sun above them. "No! No!" He saw death in her coming fast, but life, too, lots of it, fighting to continue.

He took her hand and she gripped back with ebbing strength, biting her bottom lip at the pain it caused her. Holding his gaze, she nodded, saying nothing with words, for words were crashing into words just as swords were crashing into swords, just as the whole Earth seemed to be clanging into and through itself as the two looked at one another. Another blinding flash. *Spell for Leaving.* "No!" he cried again, staring through it into her eyes. "No!" He tried to hold the vision of her dying face clear in his mind, but the wave of light and heat rolling over him ignited one last set of letters too bright to be avoided: *Spell for Bringing Back.*

In her last moments, as she dimly heard the words he intoned over her, she saw him for who he truly was: a great mage. And somehow her wounds had bled the fear of his magic out of her and she realized, fading away, that he was beautiful and true. A numinous, blue light was cycling around him and she could see his wider aspect. She beckoned him. Her eyes drew him closer, and even in her last dying moment, as she kissed him, he finished speaking that spell.

Lexicon of the Phaer Isle

Arthenow: the continent across the western sea from the Phaer Isle ruled by the blood magic of the Necromancer of Arthenow. Original home of the Thralls.

Chimerant: living creatures who are blends of more than one species, usually as a result of spellcraft.

Common magic: magic that can be initiated by the turning of a spell kone rather than by the vocalizations of a trained mage.

Cross-spell: contrary or contradictory or paradoxical spells invoked upon the same person or object or locality. Often the magic will compromise, pleasing one part of one spell and another part of the other.

Elphaereans: the ancient people now departed from the Phaer Isle, who are thought to have created and written the Great Kone.

Era of Common Magic: also known as The Phaer Era, this is the fifty-year period after the invention of spell kones and before the Battle of Phaer Bay. It was a period of increasingly ludicrous magical achievements.

Examiner: an official of the Pathan government empowered to examine Phaer youth in order to detect spellbinders.

Great Kone at Ulde: a huge, mostly subterranean cone-shaped structure. The downward spirals of text written upon it are reputed to be the ancient foundational spell-riddle of existence.

Ilde: the isolated western portion of the Phaer Isle dominated by Mount Ilde.

Kagars: a piratical sea people who defeated the Phaerland forces at the Battle of Phaer Bay at the end of the Era of Common Magic. Surrogates of the Pathans.

Kone: a conically shaped structure upon which a spell or riddle is written.

Kone craft: spells invoked by the turning of a spell kone; textual magic other than that written on the Great Kone.

Kwislings: traitors who have collaborated with the Pathans.

Mage: a learned master of the spoken magic. Applied to both ancient Elphaerean mages and Phaerland mages. All known mages have been executed by the Pathans at the time of this tale.

Middle mage: a mage with no powers, but who is capable of transmitting the power of another mage's spell, usually by hand contact.

Nains: a people of short stature renowned for their earth-working skills and their ferocity when forced to fight.

Natural magic: the inherent biological magic present in small amounts in most Phaerlanders.

Necromancy: blood-based magic most powerful in the continent of Arthenow.

Nexis: the area around the bottommost point of the Great Kone. This point is shared by an infinite number of other Great Kones whose spells create infinite other universes.

Panthemium: the stadium where athletic events such as the racing of gorehorses took place during the time of the Elphaereans.

Pathans: an underearth people whose armies have taken to conquering the surface world. They have a crystal-based biology.

Pathar: city at the heart of the Pathan Empire located deep underearth, beneath the ocean.

Phaer Isle: the mountainous, mid-ocean island, once the home of the Elphaereans and later home to the Phaer people. Lately conquered by the Pathan Empire.

Phaer people: any non-Pathan residents of the Phaer Isle; also known as Phaerlanders.

Shissillil: a former suburb of the city of Ulde. Due to the earliest known case of spell-crossing a place reputed to be without friction.

Spell fire: refers to the fire that occurred in the Great Kone when it stopped turning during the Battle of Phaer Bay.

Spellbinders: Phaerlanders, usually children, with the innate vocal quality necessary to become a mage.

Spell kone: a crank-driven cone upon which a spell is written in one long spiral from the rim to the point. Turning the crank causes the cone to revolve while the eye or "witness stone" descends — thus "reading" and invoking the text of the spell.

Thralls: beings who escaped their enslavement to the blood magic of the Necromancer of Arthenow and migrated to the Phaer Isle five hundred years before the events of this tale.

Ulde: the capital city of the Phaer Isle. The ancient village was formed around the Great Kone.

SPELL CROSSED

BOOK 1

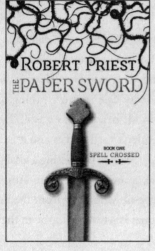

After shaking hands with a man with a red hand, Xemion and Saheli must flee their forest home and cross dangerous lands haunted by creatures caught in the forces of conflicting spells, while being pursued by a traitorous Examiner. They head for the city of Ulde, where a rebellion is brewing against the ruthless rulers of Phaer Isle, the Pathans.

BOOK 2

Young Xemion is at a crossroads. War looms on the horizon, and his dream of becoming a swordfighter is finally a reality, but without his warrior beloved, Saheli, by his side, he's incomplete. He must break the spell that separates them and find his way back to her.

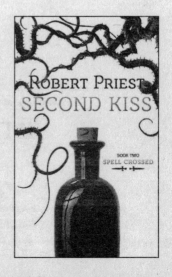

Look for *Missing Piece*, Book 3 in the Spell Crossed series, in 2016

In Book 3 of the Spell Crossed series, Tharfen, now eighteen, and Xemion are still playing unwilling hosts to shattered pieces of each other. This is proving distracting and dangerous for Tharfen in her new role as leader of the Phaer Academy. She tries everything to rid herself of the piece of Xemion stuck inside her, but to no avail. Even if magic could rectify the situation, Xemion's spell staff is also missing a piece. In fact, everyone and everything seems to be missing a vital piece of some kind or another. Meanwhile, a revitalized Pathan armada is approaching from the south, the vengeful Montither from the north, and a plague of badly written spell kones is wreaking havoc in the love lives of the Phaer people.